The Chocolate Box Girls Find Love

GRACIE HART

PENGUIN BOOKS

PENGUIN BOOKS

UK | USA | Canada | Ireland | Australia
India | New Zealand | South Africa

Penguin Books is part of the Penguin Random House group of companies whose addresses can be found at global.penguinrandomhouse.com

Penguin Books, Penguin Random House UK,
One Embassy Gardens, 8 Viaduct Gardens, London SW11 7BW

penguin.co.uk

First published 2026
001

Set in 12.5/14.75pt Garamond MT Std
Typeset by Six Red Marbles UK, Thetford, Norfolk
Printed and bound in Great Britain by Clays Ltd, Elcograf S.p.A.

The authorized representative in the EEA is Penguin Random House Ireland, Morrison Chambers, 32 Nassau Street, Dublin D02 YH68

A CIP catalogue record for this book is available from the British Library

ISBN: 978-1-405-96334-3

Penguin Random House is committed to a sustainable future for our business, our readers and our planet. This book is made from Forest Stewardship Council® certified paper.

MIX
Paper | Supporting responsible forestry
FSC® C018179

To the lovely readers of my books.
Without you, I would be nothing.

PENGUIN BOOKS

The Chocolate Box Girls Find Love

Gracie Hart was born in Leeds and raised on the family farm in the Yorkshire Dales. She writes sagas with a focus on the wars and her native Yorkshire.

She began her career as a glass engraver before raising her family. Gracie has now written several family sagas.

Gracie Hart also writes as Diane Allen and averages a 4.5 star review rating across her titles.

1. York, January 1945

Rose looked in the window of Beautiful Brides on Coney Street and sighed. The last time she'd been looking in the window with her mind on marriage was when she'd been about to marry Larry Battersby, but that seemed a lifetime ago, so much water had passed under the bridge. Back then the war was just looming on the horizon and life had been so much simpler, even though she hadn't realized it at the time. Now the world was tipped on its head as war raged. Everything around her family and life had changed to keep England free of tyranny, but hopefully now with the Allies beating the Nazis and Japs, order would soon be restored.

Not soon enough, she thought, looking at the drab dresses that were for sale in Beautiful Brides, none of which grabbed her heart or her eye as she gazed at the price and considered how many clothing coupons would be needed for a decent dress. She longed to be married to her beloved Ned. It might make more sense to postpone the wedding until later in the year, but Ned had set his heart on an early wedding – this month, if possible – and to be honest, she couldn't wait to get his ring on her finger. Four years of courting had been long enough, and now with an end to the war in sight, it was time to tie the knot. Although danger was never far away every time Ned took to the skies, the Nazis were running out of planes and pilots, and Ned had assured her that the worst was nearly over. Rose sighed and shook her head. There was nothing in the window that took her fancy. Perhaps she would go by train to Leeds and see if she had more luck there. After all, you only got married once and you deserved to look good, no matter if there was a war on or not.

'What's up, Rose?' Winnie Freeman asked. 'You look right perplexed.'

Rose entered her old home, sat down heavily in the chair next to the Yorkshire Range and kicked her shoes off.

'Just make yourself at home, take your shoes off and read my magazine, why don't you?' Winnie said sarcastically. She could tell Rose was in a stew as she picked up the copy of *My Weekly* and leafed through it, barely acknowledging her mother.

'Oh Mam, I was really wanting a special dress for my wedding, but I can't find anything. I'd always set my heart on looking like the perfect bride, but with the war on, there's nothing in the shops. I want it to be perfect – after all, we have waited this long, and Ned deserves to have the bride of his dreams on his arm.' Rose sighed.

'It isn't about the dress, love, it's about your commitment to one another. A frock doesn't make you happy. Besides, Ned would be happy if you walked down that aisle in a sack, of that I'm sure, just as long as he was marrying you.' Winnie thought for a moment. 'Why don't you ask Molly to sew you one? She's getting to be a dab hand at alterations, and I know that she has a length of white parachute silk still hidden in a cupboard upstairs – I'm sure there's enough for a wedding dress. I've still got my hair slide from my wedding – it's nothing fancy but it's bonny – I'll find it out from up in the loft. We'll have you looking pretty, don't you worry.' Winnie patted her daughter's shoulder. 'Anyway, you don't need anything fancy – you're bonny enough without any fine trappings.'

'Thanks, Mam. I just want to look special. It's my big day!' Rose sighed and put the magazine down. 'I'll have to get back to Ivy, she'll be wondering where I'm at. Ned is over at the airbase and she's on her own.' Rose stood up and looked around her old home. It was different from the one she lived in with Ned and his mother – homelier, and she loved the smell that reminded her of her childhood, and the fact that her mother's door was always open to her no matter what.

'Is Ivy all right? I haven't seen her for a while. I'll have to come around and visit. Winnie knew that Rose sometimes found it hard looking after her mother-in-law.

'She's fine, you'll have to come around for tea with her. She gets fed up of being on her own when I'm at work, but I can't leave Rowntree's, not yet anyway.'

Rose considered. 'Do you really think Molly would make me a wedding dress? She has been looking pretty good in the clothes that she's been making lately. She turns heads at work if she did but know it.'

'I tell you what, she's off this Saturday. Molly and I will come around to yours and you can tell her exactly what you're wanting. I can have a natter with Ivy while you two put your heads together.' Winnie followed her daughter to the front door.

'Thanks, Mam, that would be lovely. I hardly see Ned at the moment, he's always on a mission, but at least they've got the Jerries on the run now, even though they're sending those terrible doodlebugs to bomb London with. Ned says they're hard to intercept, but the lads down south are doing their best. I'm glad we live up here and that they can't reach us with them.' Rose hugged her mother. 'I'll see you both on Saturday. Have you heard any news from Annie?' she asked as an afterthought.

'No, not of late, she's too busy with farming and her fella as well. She'll be the next to marry, I bet you anything. I'm losing all my girls.' Winnie sighed.

'No, you're not, Mam, this will always be home to all of us.' Rose kissed her mother on the cheek. 'See you both Saturday.'

Rose hoped she'd been right in thinking that Molly might be able to make the dress of her dreams.

It was Friday evening, the end of another long week of making munitions on the factory floor, and Winnie sat with Molly and Connie around the kitchen table as they talked about their day.

'Production fell last week, I heard, Connie. Nobody is as determined as they used to be – either that or we're all war weary.' Molly looked up from her supper of chicken broth and saw Connie scowl.

'All you think about is work, Molly. Do you never give it a rest? It's Friday night, for heaven's sake. Sit back and listen to the wireless or do something other than thinking about work.' Connie sat back and stared at her best friend. 'You need a man, that's what you need.'

'I'm quite happy as I am. I know Matt doesn't write to me a lot, but I know he's there, fighting for our freedom. It's for the lads like him that I want to keep going. I'm just concerned that if we don't work hard, our lads can never win the war. I'm surprised at you. You loved your job once, but lately you don't seem bothered.'

'It's dragged on so long, this war, and I'm tired. Everyone is tired and everything is so drab.' Connie sighed.

'It was like this in the First World War,' Winnie butted in, 'we all got worn down. But we never weakened and there were a lot more men killed back then. Anyway, we have our Rose's wedding to look forward to. That will be the talk of the street. Our Rose marrying a handsome RAF officer, her father would have been so proud. She's done well for herself, has that one. You know, you could do with setting your cap at that William Allen, Molly, he's always asking after you.'

'Mam, stop it, I went to school with William, we were friends, nothing more. He only asks after me because we used to sit next to one another. And I'm with Mathew anyway. As for Rose's wedding, I really don't know if I'm up to making her wedding dress for her. It's just another worry. I'd do anything to get out of it.' Molly sighed.

'Now who's not showing commitment? Rose is counting on you, don't you go and let her down. She wants to look perfect.' Winnie hoped that her youngest wouldn't let her sister down. 'It's like Connie says, everything is so drab and she can't afford an expensive dress.'

'Yes, come on, Molly, show some commitment, that's what you were telling me a minute ago. Besides, everyone knows that you're a wizard with that old sewing machine and parachute silk.' Connie grinned at the sight of Molly's dejected face.

'All right, if I have to,' Molly conceded. 'I suppose I can't let her down.'

The next day Molly was still doubting her skills. 'Oh, Mam, I wish you'd never said I'd sew our Rose's wedding dress. I don't know if I'm good enough. Altering things and making a dress for myself is fine, but a wedding dress for our Rose, that's a different matter.'

They stood on the doorstep of the Evans home and waited for someone to answer the doorbell.

'You'll be all right, Molly. You can turn your hand to anything, you just don't have confidence in yourself, and besides, anything's better than what's in the shops at the moment from what our Rose says.' Winnie was wondering whether she should nudge the door open and call that they were there, when at last it opened.

'Sorry, Mam, Molly, I was just washing up and Ivy had fallen asleep after her lunch. She's woken now but insisted that I brush her hair before I answered the door to you.' Rose stood back and welcomed in her family.

'I'm not receiving guests looking like a trollop, you should know that by now,' Ivy shouted through to the hall as Winnie and Molly made their way to the front room where she was sitting.

'Now, that's an exaggeration, Ivy, you never look a trollop. A bit of hair out of place isn't a sin. You should see me when I'm scrubbing my front step and doing the washing on a Monday morning – I look like a fishwife.' Winnie grinned and sat down across from Ivy, who was getting more and more demanding with old age.

'I like to look right, you know I do, no matter who it is that's calling. I'll have to get my hair done for this wedding, that's for sure. The lass down the street will come and give me a home perm if I ask her in good time. It doesn't want to look too tight, so I need to book her as soon as I can.' Ivy looked worried.

'I'll book her shortly, Ivy, don't worry, you'll look just perfect.' Rose patted her mother-in-law's hand. 'I'm glad that you've come, Mol. Are you up to making me a dress, do you think?'

'I can, but only if you really want me to. I don't want to let you down. I'll try my best with what I've got, but it won't be anything like what you'd get from a fancy shop, you know. Wouldn't you prefer to take the parachute silk to a proper seamstress?'

'No, don't be silly. I can't think of anything more fitting than walking down the aisle in a dress my sister made for me out of parachute silk, if you really don't mind. And with my Mam's sprig of artificial flowers in my hair, you'll make me the bonniest bride in York.' Rose squeezed her sister's hand. 'Ivy has given me the most beautiful necklace, so all I need is something blue and then I'll have everything that I'm supposed to have as I get married, thanks to everyone in my family.'

'All right then,' Molly said, flattered by the faith shown in her sewing abilities. 'Let's take your measurements and you tell me what you want.' She fished a tape measure out of her cardigan pocket and glanced at her sister with a bright smile. 'I'll do my best.'

'I know you will, Mol, thank you. I'm always amazed at what you can make out of nothing. It's a pity you're still making munitions at Rowntree's, but I'm hoping it won't be long before they go back to chocolate manufacturing, from what I hear on the grapevine.'

'They might be, but I don't know if I want to stay working for them,' Molly said thoughtfully. 'Things have changed since I started there, and so have I. I'm not the shy slip of a lass any more, and besides, I may have something else in mind.' She put her arms around her sister's waist and took her measurement, writing it down on a piece of paper, then noticed the quick sketch Rose had done of how she wanted her dress to look. 'Oh, Lord, that's a bit ambitious, Rose. I was thinking of something a bit more simple but fetching. Here, I'll show you. Something along these lines, straight but flattering with a lovely neckline – you have such a lovely neck.' Molly quickly drew a sketch of what she thought her sister would look good in and passed it to her. 'Sometimes the plainer the pattern the more fetching it is, and I think a nice long length, to show your height off.'

'You do whatever you think I'll look good in, Mol, I was just playing. Now, what have you got going on in that head of yours when it comes to Rowntree's?'

'Do you think I'd tell you? You're one of those upstairs, our Rose. I'm just one of the humble workers, and I'm no snitch. We tell none of you bosses anything, no matter how well you look after us. I'll do whatever it takes to make sure we win this war, but when it's over I reckon I'll have had enough of working for them. I'm going to start putting some ideas together to make a different way in life. Now, keep quiet and stand still, or I'll get your measurements wrong,' Molly teased.

'You know, it's not that long ago that you wouldn't say boo to a goose. Now you're Miss Bossy, you and Connie are a right pair,' Rose laughed. 'I'm so glad that you've found your own voice, Molly. It's good to hear you speak up for yourself.' Rose smiled as Molly blushed.

'It's taken me a long time to accept that I'm more

able than I thought I was at school. Looking back, I realize I just had no confidence.' Molly grinned as she continued to note her sister's measurements down. Rose would be the most glamorous bride in York if she had her way. After all, it wasn't so different from decorating a box of chocolates, and she was good at that. You had to have an eye for style and follow the instructions of the pattern, just like you did when folding a chocolate box.

'I know that my dress will look wonderful, no matter what you do with it. And I will be so proud to wear it, Molly.' Rose looked down at her younger sister and thought how much she had changed since she left school. The workplace had been good for her, and Rowntree's had been part of her development, even though she didn't realize it.

'Do you know, Mam, I'm going to make Rose the best dress she could ever possibly dream of. She's always been there for me, it's the least I can do for her. I can just picture it.' Molly linked her arm through her mother's, feeling contented.

'I'm sure it will be the bonniest dress that she could wish for. I'm proud of my lasses. You're always there for one another, even though you don't always see eye to eye. Now, as for our cuckoo in the nest, Connie, she's a grand lass but she sometimes shows her true colours. You can't change how you've been brought up.' Winnie sighed. 'I do think a lot of her, but she's just not quite family.'

Molly thought about Connie, her best friend, who came from a dysfunctional home and had been living with them since she had first started work at Rowntree's. She had adopted her like a sister, but her mam was right, she would never fully be one of them, no matter how hard she tried. But she did love her.

2

Connie looked down at Molly as she knelt on the floor, her tongue sticking out in concentration as she got on with the job in hand. 'I hope you'll agree to make mine when I get married – that is if I ever get married. Chuck hasn't been to see me for a while. Now he's at Elvington airbase, thank goodness not back in America, he doesn't write either, and he's always busy servicing the planes.' Connie watched in admiration as Molly cut around the pinned pattern that she had laid out on the living room floor. 'Before that, he kept asking me to marry him and go out to America when all this is over. But I'm beginning to think that won't ever happen.' Connie sighed.

Molly looked up from the pattern and sat back on her haunches.

'It will happen, but you're rushing things. You've not known him that long. And if you do end up going with him to live in America, you'll need every penny, so it's just as well you're living here with Mam and me, paying the minimum of rent.' Molly stuck a handful of pins between her lips, hoping that Connie would stop going on about her worries and that she wouldn't have to reply as she pinned the pattern down, but there was no such luck as Connie continued to moan about her lot in life.

'I dream of going to live in Montana and perhaps finding my brother Billy, but now I'm not so sure. I can't understand Chuck sometimes. One minute he's all over me and the next he's distant. He's always blowing hot and cold.' Connie looked out of the window. 'I've got my eye on a flat that's up for rent. Chuck says he would see more of me if I had my own place. It isn't as if I've not got good money in the bank, now I'm in charge of our production line. I hate having to clamp down on the women who do things wrong on the line and account for mistakes made, but them in management should know nobody is perfect. Surely they'll put me in a similar position when they stop making munitions. I just don't know what to do for the best. The more I think about it the more disillusioned I become. I just need a good life, and I would love to live in Montana, but if that isn't going to happen I need a plan B.'

Luckily Molly had used up the supply of pins jammed between her lips, so she was able to reply. 'You shouldn't give up on Chuck so quickly. He's busy at his base, and they're all too busy to write. Matt hasn't written to me for a while, either. His regiment's on the move all the time, now the Allies are making their way into Europe. You just have to have patience. We're not top of their priorities, no matter how much we love them. He was over the moon in his last letter a few weeks ago, saying the French, especially the women, were throwing flowers and kisses at his battalion as they walked through Paris after they'd helped free it from being occupied. Imagine walking down the Champs-Élysées and looking up at the Eiffel Tower, with everybody cheering you on. It must have felt so wonderful to think that you helped liberate so many people. No wonder he hasn't time to write to me. I'm not that important in the scheme of things, even though I do think he loves me.' Molly sighed. She missed her good-looking boyfriend Matt.

'Anyway,' she resumed, 'I thought you were head over heels in love with Chuck? And where has this talk of moving out come from?' She sat back again on her heels, pursing her lips as she picked up a few more pins from her tin and continued her careful work.

'I don't know,' Connie said. 'I just feel it's time I moved out. Your mother's been so kind to me over the last few years, but now I've more sense and can stand on my own two feet. And as for Chuck, he might never return, and I'm not going to be left an old maid waiting for him.' Connie opened her compact and pouted her lips as she applied bright-red lipstick and admired herself. 'Fred Milburn who owns the shoe shop has been showing me a bit of interest.'

'Fred Milburn? He's a bit old, isn't he? He might have money, but that's about it. But you'll do whatever you feel like doing, you always do. Now! I've got to get on. Our Rose has left this to the last minute, I'm sure just to stress me out, although I know she has struggled trying to find something she really likes. I'm going to meet myself coming back, what with the hours put in at the munitions and then sewing for hours on end.'

Molly shook her head, noting that both her and Connie's hair was tinged ginger and their skin was still a light hue of yellow from the toxins in their work. It had been their signature look ever since they'd started working in munitions, and everyone called them canaries. The gunpowder had a lot to answer for. No matter what they were dressed in, nor what they tried, they couldn't get rid of their hair colour and yellow skin. Connie always applied her lipstick thick and bright when not at work and carried her toxin-given hues with pride. Unlike Molly, who tried to keep as low a profile as she could, Connie would always sparkle, no matter what she looked like. She would also flirt with any man that caught her eye, although she always said she kept true to her Chuck.

'Another morning at the madhouse,' Connie moaned as both she and Molly got checked down and changed into their work wear after entering the munitions factory the next day. 'I don't know why they go to such lengths to make everything secure. It's not as if any of us are going to pinch a shell – what would we do with it anyway? And there's definitely no need to check us when we enter work.' Connie pulled a face at the young guard who stood at the doorway of the production line and then made sure that all her hair was tucked underneath her turban.

'You don't half moan. I have no idea how you've been put in charge of quality on our line – you don't really give a damn what goes on in here any more,' Molly scolded Connie as they walked over to their working spaces.

'It's because I get myself noticed. I might be rubbish at my job, but you can't miss me. The bosses like that; they do here, anyway, when we're making munitions. They know that I'll make a lot of noise if something goes wrong, so nobody dares to make too many mistakes. It didn't work like that when we were making chocolates, especially with Rowntree's being Quaker-owned. You had to be quiet and know your place.'

'Connie Whitehead, sometimes you are too big for your boots. Do you know that? Just mind you don't come a cropper. It doesn't pay to get too big-headed.' Molly opened the door to the compartment she'd been working in since she had started in munitions and looked around. Her colleagues were rolling up to their positions, all looking tired and fed up with their lot. None of them had thought that they would still be making munitions five years on from the start of the war. The days of chocolate box-making and chocolate decorating were just a pleasant dream to some of them now.

'I wish I could change my life, I think we all do,' Molly sighed, watching as the first shells of the day came down the production line and the Tannoy wished everybody a good morning and then went on to give out the usual public information news before starting to play the same old playlist that everyone knew by heart from years of listening to it. It was going to be another long day, another long week, and on top of that she had Rose's wedding dress to finish.

'Hey up, Molly, what have you been up to this weekend? I hear that you're making your sister's wedding dress,' Janet, a plump woman who worked directly across from her, asked to break up the monotony of the job that most of them could do with their eyes closed.

'Yes, I've cut out the pieces and put the darts where they should be, I hope. The silk is so slippery it's hard to line up properly, and I don't want any tucks where there shouldn't be.' Molly had to yell over the noise of the moving belt.

'Rather you than me. Is it going to be kept white or shouldn't I ask? What with Ned being respectable and old management.'

'It most certainly is white, Janet, and if I've enough silk left over, I might dye it and make Connie, Annie and myself a bridesmaid's dress each, but that's a big if.' Molly glanced over at Connie.

'What colour dress would you want, Mrs?'

'I'd like a pale blue one, if Rose agrees. You'll not have time to make that many dresses, and besides, she hasn't asked me to be a bridesmaid yet. I'm not family, she'll not want me . . .' Connie stopped short, gasping and shouting down the line at a worker who had knocked over a thankfully empty shell case.

'I think she will. She's not mentioned bridesmaids, but I'd have thought the three of us would be, although I don't know how I'm going to take Annie's measurements with her being in Lancashire on her pig farm. I'll ask Rose next time I take her fitting. She's got to have bridesmaids; I bet she won't have liked mentioning it as she knows I take one step at a time. A nice A-line dress for us three won't take any time. I thought, seeing that it's still going to be cold at this time of year, I'd have a go at crocheting small jackets for us as well. A wedding in freezing January, they must be mad.' At that, Molly returned to concentrating on her job.

'That's why I asked if she was, you know . . . Lord, this dressmaking has gone to your head; it will be Paris Fashion Week next year,' Janet joked, and then thought that she had better keep an eye on the job in hand when Connie shot her a quelling glance.

Back at home that night, Molly looked at the clock. It was nearly one a.m.; she wasn't going to get much sleep before she was up again for work, but at least the main part of Rose's dress had now been sewn together and was starting to look like a wedding dress. She had hand-sewn the inside of the neckline with bias binding, making it strong enough to hold a row of pearl buttons around the neckline without the parachute silk folding with the weight, and she had run the same pearls down the front of the dress, and now it was starting to look the part. A tuck here and a tuck there and Rose would have to come and have a fitting, but for tonight she could do no more as her eyes were heavy with sleep; another five hours and work would be needing her.

*

The following evening, Rose walked around to her mother's home for another fitting. She felt like a princess as Molly walked around her and surveyed her handiwork. 'A tuck here and I need to shorten it by two inches; it won't hang right if it has a big thick hem.' Molly stood back and looked at her craftsmanship. The dress would look perfect by the time she had finished it, she thought.

Rose carefully walked across her bedroom floor to the full-length mirror and looked at herself. She beamed and held the skirt out by her side. 'Oh, Molly, it's perfect, absolutely perfect, I could not have bought anything better. The shape suits me so well and there's just enough finery upon it – not gaudy, just beautiful.' Rose couldn't believe that she was looking at herself in the mirror and seeing a fairy princess. She hugged Molly and stood with her by her side and looked at their reflections.

'I'm glad you like it and I'm glad it fits. Just another night and I should have it finished. Mam says to keep it at ours, though, else it will bring bad luck if Ned sees it.' Molly was relieved that the fit had gone well; she'd been dreading finding out that she'd taken the measurements all wrong and having to start all over again. Now she would have enough silk left over for bridesmaids if Rose had come to a decision about that. 'Have you thought about bridesmaids? You've never mentioned them, but now I've nearly finished your dress, I could make simple dresses for one or two, or even three at a pinch.' Molly hoped that Rose would get the hint that Connie would like to be included as a bridesmaid.

'I hadn't mentioned it, because I thought that you would have enough to do with sewing my dress and I thought to keep my wedding as simple as possible, what with the war still raging.' Rose hesitated. 'Would you be able to make two bridesmaid's dresses for you and Annie? Only if you have enough time. I don't know about Connie; it's not as if she's our sister, although maybe she will expect to be asked.'

'Yes, I can make dresses for Annie and me – something simple, but they will match yours. What colour would you like? I will have to dye the silk so it's just you in white.' Molly hesitated. She had hoped that Connie would have been included, but it was Rose's wedding, not hers.

'Blue, I think, a nice bright blue, for the skies that Ned flies in. That would be wonderful. I feel bad about not including Connie, but do you think she will be upset?' Rose started to step out of her bridal dress.

'It's your wedding, Rose. As you say, Connie is not related, but she sometimes forgets that. Don't worry, I'll make it right with her, and if I have time, make her something for the day.'

Molly wished that she'd never mentioned that Rose might ask Connie to be her bridesmaid. It was going to be awkward to tell her that she wasn't wanted.

Connie looked at the length of cloth that Molly was soaking in the dolly tub in a bright blue dye. 'Oh, is that the colour that we are going to be dressed in? I thought it would be lighter than that.'

'That's the colour Rose chose. Sorry, Connie, I've bad news as well. I've only enough material for two bridesmaid's dresses left. I'm afraid it's only going to be me and Annie. But I promise to make you a dress for the day if I can find more fabric.' Molly tried not to look at Connie as she told her white lie. There would be enough material left, just, but she didn't want to hurt Connie's feelings by saying that Rose had not wanted her as a bridesmaid.

'Oh, I was so looking forward to being part of the wedding. I've never been a bridesmaid before.' Connie sighed. 'Don't worry about making me a dress. I've got that one that you made me for the last dance we went to, that will do just fine. We have to make do and mend anyway.' Connie smiled wanly at Molly. She had so much wanted to be part of the family wedding.

Molly rushed home from work every day the following week. She had written to Annie asking for her measurements, but so far she hadn't heard from her. Time was running out if she wanted a perfect fit. Rose's dress was finished and hanging up in her old bedroom, and the dress for herself just needed the hem finishing and then it would be ready to wear. Annie was holding up the production, and the wedding was the following weekend. Why Rose and Ned had chosen a January wedding was beyond her; it was usually a cold and dreary month. Molly was under pressure and she was tired; she had been stopping up until the early hours crocheting little jackets to match the delicate bridesmaid's dresses, to keep the cold at bay.

Now it was Thursday evening, and she and Connie hurried into the warmth of home. Molly was hoping she might have an hour to herself.

'Come on, you two, there's some corned beef hash on the table and you'll be glad to hear that there's a letter from Annie waiting for you, Molly,' Winnie said as soon as the girls walked into the kitchen.

'Oh, thank heavens for that. I thought she was never going to write and give me her measurements. I haven't got long to make it, anyway.' Molly reached for the letter sitting on the mantelpiece before she had even taken her coat off and tore it open as she stood next to the warmth of the kitchen fire.

Connie looked up from her plate of steaming corned beef hash and noticed the look of dismay on Molly's face. 'What's she saying, Molly, is she all right?'

'Oh, bugger, that's a pity. She can't make it to the wedding, she doesn't think. Here, Mam, you read it, while I get my supper.' Molly sighed.

'What do you mean, she can't make it? It's her sister's wedding!' Winnie took hold of the letter and read it out as both girls tucked into their first decent meal of the day.

Pendle Hill Farm
Clitheroe

21st January

Dear Molly,

Thanks for your letter asking for my measurements. I was really chuffed that Rose wants me as a bridesmaid and was so looking forward to her big day.

However, I don't think unless a miracle happens that I'm going to make it back home. Bloody Jerry bombed our railway line last night, with bombs left over from bombing Blackburn. They have taken out at least three miles of track, making a real mess. There is no urgency to repair it as we are not on a main line, according to the station master, so I can't get to you. Nobody here has transport to get me back home and it would take an age for me to get home by bus. I'm also writing to Rose to say how sorry I am but that I can't get home. It's best that you don't waste your time on making me a dress. Although I will try and make it if I can.

Hope you are all well at home, Mam will be getting excited, the first of us to get married, a big day.

It's wet and mucky here and I can't wait for better weather and to be warm again.

All my love
Annie xxx
PS Just a thought, but maybe Connie could take my place as a bridesmaid.

‘Well, isn’t that just typical! Bloody Jerry, has to go and spoil our big day.’ Winnie sat down in her chair next to the fire and watched the girls take in the news.

‘Well, that gives me a bit of time to myself,’ Molly said, forgetting that she had not told the truth to Connie.

‘No, it means that you can now make me a dress and I can still be a bridesmaid. I can put up with that shade of blue now the material has dried and I’ve seen yours.’ Connie sat back and grinned.

‘Yes, I suppose so. I’ll try and see Rose at work in the morning before we start work and tell her,’ Molly said, wondering how she was going to explain the situation to Rose.

‘I’ll come with you and then I can thank her. I’m so looking forward to the wedding now. I’ll see if Chuck fancies showing his face at the wedding too.’

Winnie and Molly glanced at one another and knew that Connie had got her way by default and that Rose would not have the heart to say no.

Later that evening, Connie and Chuck sat on the bench outside the Roxy. He had finally been given some leave and they had planned to go in and watch *Gone with the Wind*, but Chuck had arrived late.

‘You’re always late or can’t find time to see me. Sometimes, Chuck, I don’t think you care two hoots about me.’ Connie was annoyed as he put his arm around her and attempted to kiss her.

'Oh, come on, doll. You know why I'm sometimes late. I can't control when Hitler and our boys are going to decide I can get time off. I've brought you some stockings and gum to make up for it. Honest, hon, I can't do anything about it.' Chuck sighed and gave up on his attempt to get anywhere with Connie.

Connie had put the stockings and chewing gum in her handbag; it had been a small consolation for the let-down of not seeing Rhett Butler romance Scarlett O'Hara. 'I just feel you don't love me, Chuck. I hardly ever see you.'

'Well, if you had a place of your own, it would be different. You know I don't like showing my face at the Freemans'; it isn't even your proper home and there's no privacy. I want a bit more than sitting politely in their front room drinking tea and being typical English.' Chuck sighed. 'Come on, doll, give me a kiss and forgive me. It's too cold sitting here without sitting next to an ice maiden. You know I love you, give a guy a chance.'

'I will if you promise to go to Rose's wedding with me. It's next weekend and I would love you to be with me.' Connie couldn't stay mad with Chuck too long and this was her opportunity to get him to be on her arm at Rose's wedding. All eyes would be on her, with her Yank in his uniform.

'Sure, if that's what makes you happy, then that's what I'll do assuming I can get the time off. I'll do my best. Now put your arms around me before I bloody freeze and stop moaning.' Chuck held Connie tight. He did love her, but she was always wanting her own way, and oh boy, if she didn't get it he knew he would pay.

'Thanks, my love.' Connie smiled and felt Chuck's arms around her body. She knew she couldn't stop with Molly and her mother much longer if she was to keep Chuck. A place of her own was what she needed, and fast.

'I don't think I could be better dressed for my wedding,' Rose said over the top of the steady rhythm of the sewing machine as Molly put her foot down on the treadle. 'I just wish Annie could be with us. I don't mind Connie being my bridesmaid, but it should be Annie.'

Molly picked up Connie's dress and bit a piece of cotton off with her teeth as it hung straggling down from the shoulder.

'Well, it's too late to tell her you don't want her now, and I'm just hoping this fits. She's never let me take a fitting. She's too busy, doing what, I don't know.' Molly turned the dress the right way out and gave it a shake. 'There, that's finished apart from a bit of lace to be added tomorrow night.'

'She will look lovely in that, Molly, you will both shine. I can't believe I'll be married this time next week.' Rose stood up and hugged Molly tightly. 'Thank you, my lovely sister, for making it all possible. What would this family do without you?'

Molly closed her eyes and hugged Rose close. The family was going to change now her big sister was getting married; she was going to miss her.

3

'Well, just look at you! Aren't you a picture? It might be made out of parachute silk, but Molly has worked a miracle with this dress.' Winnie stood back and admired her eldest daughter as she looked at herself in the long wardrobe mirror in her mother's bedroom. 'I don't think I've ever seen a bonnier bride. I hope Ned knows how lucky he is.' Winnie reached for her handkerchief from up her sleeve and wiped a tear away.

'And I'm lucky to have him, Mam, don't you forget that. At one time I thought that this day would never come, especially when he was lost and hiding in France, in danger of losing his life. I thought that he would never come back, that the Resistance wouldn't be able to smuggle him home after his aeroplane crashed and he went missing.'

Rose regarded herself in the mirror, not quite able to believe that the day had come when she was going to marry the dashing RAF pilot who she had loved for so long. 'Just look at this lovely bracelet that the girls at work gave me.' She held her arm out to show her mother the lovely crystal bracelet that her co-workers had given her the day before. 'They all gathered around me as I left my last shift and wished me well for today. It was so lovely. And then Seebohm came into the office and gave me a cheque for five pounds to spend on what we wanted. Everyone has been so kind and thoughtful.'

Rose played with her bracelet on her arm and thought how lucky she was to work at Rowntree's. 'I've had to be patient and wait until Ned felt that there was hope that we could win the war.' Ned had sworn that he would not marry her just to leave her a widow. Now it was time to be optimistic and for them to tie the knot.

'He certainly has kept you hanging on a while – five years of being engaged and you looking after his mother, I think that has proved your love to him. I'm just glad that he has kept safe. I couldn't quite believe that he went straight back to flying after all that he'd been through.'

Winnie shook her head, thinking back to the last five years of worry and austerity that the war with Germany and Japan had caused. The girls had of course secured jobs with Rowntree's, but it had changed in so many ways, and no matter how they tried to make a life for themselves it was always tarnished with the possibility of losing a loved one. Winnie missed Annie so much and worried about her most days, even though the letters from the farm were always telling her how she was enjoying herself.

'Well, you'll have no need to worry once the war is won,' Rose said. 'Ned is confident that we will. Once the war is over, he's going to go back to working for Rowntree's and then I'll take a back seat and look after Ivy and the house. I can't say I'm happy with the thought of having to give up my job, but we both want to have children and it's only right that I put my time into looking after them.'

Rose did have mixed feelings about this. She had thought of herself as a pioneer for the women in Rowntree's, working her way up through the firm to join the management team, the rest of whom were all male. She couldn't help but feel slightly as if she was letting herself down if she forsook her career for a family. But at the same time she would love to become a home-loving mother, just like her own. The choice would be a hard one to make, but there was time yet to consider that path.

'Yes, family should be brought up properly and children need their mother, but you could work part-time if you didn't have Ivy to look after as well. Talking about Ivy, I'm a little concerned. She doesn't look as well as she used to do, I hope the wedding won't be too much for her.'

'She'll be fine. Ned has got one of his friends from the airbase to look after her, a nice lass from the operations room. She'll be enthralled with a woman in uniform and will be asking her just about everything, if I know Ivy. Now, where are my bridesmaids? I can hear them giggling, so they must be ready. I just wish Annie could have been with us today, then we would have been all together as usual.' Rose sighed and made her way to the bedroom door. She had so wanted Annie to be with her on her special day, but it couldn't be helped. This blasted war. 'I know Annie can't help not being here, what with the line being bombed, but it doesn't seem right without her. Still, she's sent us a lovely wedding card wishing us luck and saying how sorry she is.'

'Careful, don't catch your dress, silk is so delicate,' Winnie said sharply as Rose caught the door handle. 'I still can't believe how beautiful you look, Rose.'

Winnie gasped as Rose stood elegant and beautiful in her wedding dress of parachute silk; it flowed smoothly over her hips and fanned out slightly at the back. On the front was a row of delicate pearls that Molly had sewn on from a broken necklace; it was plain but perfect. 'I have no doubt I'm going to cry when you walk down the aisle. If only your father were still alive, he would have been so proud to see his eldest happily married.' Winnie pulled the back of Rose's wedding dress straight as Molly and Connie appeared from out of their bedroom. 'Just look at my girls, you are all so beautiful.' Winnie wiped away a tear as she took in Molly and Connie in their matching blue dresses made from what was left of the parachute silk, with lace around the collars and sleeves to match Rose's. 'Aye, your father would have been so proud. And I wish Annie was here.'

'Stop blubbing, Mam,' Molly said bracingly. 'Father looks down upon us every day. We all know he does, he's always in our thoughts anyway. As for Annie, of course we'll miss her, but we'll send her some photographs. A bloody bomb on the line from Jerry won't stop today. Bloody Jerry!' Molly put her arms around her mam and kissed her on her cheek. 'We do look posh, and look, I've been keeping these as a surprise, but I've crocheted each of us a little matinee jacket, just to keep us a little warmer.' Molly passed Rose and Connie a delicate white fluffy jacket each and smiled as they tried them on.

'She's been making these as she lay in bed with the night light burning, I don't know how she's managed it,' Connie said as she pulled her little jacket around her shoulders, knowing it completed her look. 'The last stitch was done at midnight last night. I should know, because she let out the biggest sigh, it nearly blew the house over.' Connie grinned and put her arm around her best friend.

'Oh, Molly, they are so light and delicate but warm; it feels like baby hair and looks so beautiful. How posh do we all look? Blinking heck, you'd never think there was a war on.' Rose gulped and held back the tears as they all stood at the top of the stairs admiring one another.

'All right, come on, enough of this admiration,' Uncle Reg shouted up. 'Don't forget I'm down here and the cars are waiting. It's a wonder George isn't pipping his horn, he's usually got no patience. He's always rushing when he's serving behind my bar.' Winnie's late husband's brother stood with his hands in his pockets at the bottom of the stairs. Even though it had meant having to close his pub on the Shambles, he wasn't going to miss his niece's wedding. 'There's half the street out there waiting to see you, Rose, all leaning over their garden walls wrapped up in their winter coats. The sooner you get on your way, the happier I'll be.' Reg took a sip of whisky from his hip flask and whistled as he watched the girls parade downstairs. 'Bloody hell,

Winnie, you've three stunners here. Like bloody film stars, they are.'

'I know, Reg, they take after their mother.' Winnie pulled her stomach in and smiled at her brother-in-law from underneath the brim of her huge hat, smart in the two-piece suit that only came out of the wardrobe on special occasions. 'Now, let me go and get that bunch of snowdrops and Christmas roses from outside the back door. I've put them there to keep them fresh. I've begged every spare flower from all the neighbours – trust my lass to get married in the coldest month of the year.' Winnie bustled past Reg and opened the back door, reaching for the hand-made bouquet. 'Now, that will just finish you off, our Rose, and these are for you two, just a little bunch for you both to carry.' Winnie passed the flowers to all three girls and folded her arms and looked at them with pride.

'By heck, if I wasn't the uncle to two of you, I'd be running away with you, never mind taking you to church,' Reg joked and then revised his wording quickly as he noticed the look on his sister-in-law's face. 'A choice of four good-looking women, come to think of it.'

'Just don't dig yourself in any deeper,' Winnie advised. 'You always have been a fond old devil, Reg Freeman, it's a good job that I know you. Now, you get my lass and me safely to the church and these two will go with George. We don't want to be late. Poor Ned has waited long enough for this day, and besides, his mother, Ivy, will want the toilet as soon as she sits down, I bet you anything.' Winnie eyed herself in the hall mirror. She wasn't keeping that badly, she thought, as she adjusted the fox fur around her neck and made sure her hat was secure on her newly permed hair. Her daughters were young and beautiful but she was a mature and gracious woman. She followed her daughters out of the small terraced house.

'By heck, I thought you were never going to show,' said Nellie from two doors down. 'I'm frozen to the bone. This wind is such a lazy one, it goes right through you instead of around you.'

'Well, we all had to look just right. There might be a war on, but that's no excuse not to make a wedding day a bit special,' Winnie replied and waved at all the neighbours, feeling like a queen as she sat down next to her daughter and caught her breath. 'Well, they are giving you a good send-off, our Rose. Look at them waving and wishing you well. They think a lot of you, lass, and so they should, seeing that you are a local lass made good.'

'Thanks, Mam, I owe it all to you. We were brought up with love – perhaps not a lot of money, but we were always fed and loved. I hope that I will run my home as well when we have children.' Rose held back her tears. She might have been living at Ned's house for some years now, but this would always feel like home. Especially since at the present Ned lived more at the airbase, but she hoped that now they were going to be a true married couple he would be allowed more time at home.

'Now, Rose, remember what I've told you; sometimes you have to do what your husband wants and you've just to grin and bear it,' Winnie whispered, hoping that Reg wouldn't hear. 'But I'm sure Ned will be a good husband, he's such a grand lad.' They were the same words that her mother had given her on her wedding day, but it was not for a man's ears to hear.

'Mam, you don't have to tell me this, we've been engaged four years. I think I know what he's like and what he's capable of.' Rose blushed and looked out of the car window. She noticed Reg winking in the car mirror and taking another sip of whisky as he navigated the streets of York.

'I know, but I have to say these things, I'm your mother, Rose.' Winnie crossed her arms and decided to change the subject. 'I hope that we have enough food for everyone. It's good of the vicar to lend us the church hall, and for his wife and her helpers to see to the wedding breakfast. I don't know what we would have done without friends giving what they could. I always wanted you to have a posh wedding breakfast, but a Jacob's join is better than nothing nowadays.' Winnie thought about the piles of meat paste sandwiches alternated with sardine sandwiches, and the fairy cakes that she had held back her sugar ration for, as well as a selection of whatever the neighbours could spare for the big day, all laid out beautifully in the church hall.

'Mam, just stop worrying. It will be a perfect day. You've done me proud, everybody has. Ned and I are so grateful.' Rose felt her stomach churn as they neared the church. She had been waiting for this day so long, and now it was here.

'Hey up, the lads in blue are giving you a guard of honour, now don't they look smart?' Reg said cheerily. 'They must be without a mission today else they wouldn't be here.' The three of them looked at the four airmen standing waiting for the couple to arrive. 'It'll be a bugger if Jerry decides to raid us now and they're all at your wedding.' Reg turned and grinned at Rose. 'We'll park up a while and then I'll take you up the aisle.'

'Oh, Ned never warned me of this, everybody is stopping and watching. Oh, Mam, I feel sick,' Rose said. She glanced at the smartly dressed officers standing on the ancient church's steps, straight and proud.

'He's a good lad, well liked,' Winnie said. 'Perhaps he didn't know that they were going to honour you both. Now, I'm going to get out and find my seat. Reg, you'd better be able to walk straight, you've been sipping that whisky all morning. I don't want our Rose being shown up as you walk her down the aisle.'

'I'll not be doing that. Today is one of the proudest days that I've had. It's just a pity it isn't your father that's walking you down the aisle. You'll have to make do with second best.' Reg pulled up in the cobbled square next to the church. 'Right, ladies, let's face the crowds.'

Winnie kissed her daughter on the cheek as she climbed out of the car into the cold winter's air. 'Love you, my Rose. I wish you nothing but happiness,' Winnie whispered and then made her way into the church.

After a few minutes parked up outside the church,

allowing Rose to calm her nerves, Reg decided they had kept Ned waiting long enough. 'Right now, Rose, come on. Take my arm and we'll make this man of yours happy.' He felt her shiver. 'Is that the cold or nerves?'

'A bit of both. There are people here watching that I don't even know, and I never expected a military wedding.'

'They're doing you proud, and everyone gets nervous on their wedding day. I nearly did a runner, but don't let my Betty know. Now, best foot forward. You're the perfect couple and you have all your lives to look forward to.' Reg squeezed her hand as they climbed the steps into the church, where Molly and Connie were already waiting.

The organ filled the air with the wedding march and Rose held tight to her uncle's arm. This was the day she had been dreaming of. The world might be at war, but as she walked down the aisle and saw Ned looking so handsome and dapper in his uniform, with members of both of their families smiling and watching, her cares disappeared. She was marrying Ned, and that was all that mattered. He was handsome and dependable, a good man through and through. She caught his smiling gaze and walked towards him to take his hand.

Both stood nervous in front of the vicar as he asked if anyone had a reason for the two not to be married – even though they knew there was no reason to worry.

The vicar asked them to make their vows to God

and one another, and Ned gently took Rose's hand and gazed with love into her eyes as he tenderly put the wedding ring on her finger.

Rose felt a tear running down her cheek. It was the day they had both dreamed of. They kissed each other softly and turned and smiled at all their guests before going to sign the wedding register together.

'It's like a fairy-tale wedding,' Connie whispered to Molly as they watched the couple come out of the vestry.

'It is. I only hope that they will live happily ever after,' Molly replied.

Rose smiled at Molly and Connie as she and Ned walked past them both to sighs and best wishes from all the guests.

'Well, that's my eldest married. I wonder who will be next? Aye, I wish my old man was with me,' Winnie said, wiping a tear away as she smiled at Ivy.

'Aye, I was just thinking the same myself, Winnie. They would both have been so proud.'

'What a grand spread! Your mother must have been saving her sugar rations to have made a cake like that,' Ivy said as she sat next to her new daughter-in-law. 'She's made a fine job of it.'

'Yes, Mam has scrounged sugar from everybody. She's not let us into the larder while she was icing it, but we knew what she was doing. She's not the most proficient of icers – she should have let one of the piping lasses from Rowntree's have a go at it.' Rose smiled at her mother's wedding cake; it was only one tier high, and in no way expertly iced, but it was made with love.

'Aye, pet, it's grand, and this is going to be the most I've eaten for ages. Those sandwiches look better than all right.'

'Yes, I think everyone along our street has given a little of their ration or made something for us. I don't know how I can ever thank everyone. The meat paste sandwiches were given to us as a wedding present from our butcher, it was more than kind. I can't get over how many wedding presents we've been given. My mother insisted on laying them all out with their gift cards in the hall for people to view, she said it was the done thing.' Rose lipped her arm into Ned's and hugged him.

'We want for nothing, do we, my love? We have a roof over our heads and a loving family and are both employed. All our lives are spread out in front of us. We are truly lucky.' Ned kissed his new bride on the cheek and squeezed her hand, gazing at her with love and pride. It had been her that kept him going when he thought his life was in danger in France.

'Well, some of us are,' said Ivy. 'I'll be lucky if I get to see another Christmas, but then again, none of us might if Hitler sends those doodlebugs over York like he's doing in London. They say they buzz until they get to the place where they're going to drop and then go silent. I daren't go to sleep of a night for listening for them.'

'They haven't got the range to reach York, Mother,' Ned reassured her. 'They only just make it over the

Channel, and they won't be doing that for much longer – our lads are seeing to that. We'll soon have Jerry on the run. They're struggling for fuel and soldiers, the tide is turning in our favour. But enough of this talk of war – it's our wedding day! A time to celebrate, especially as I have two days' leave away from the airbase.'

Rose was already worried about her newlywed husband. He seemed tired after flying late-night bombing missions on a relentless scale over Germany; two days away from flying would do him good. 'I'm going to pamper you something awful.'

'I just wish we could have had a honeymoon, but I'm afraid it's out of the question with the base needing me, and Rowntree's you.' Ned sighed.

'You don't need a honeymoon. You've already got your own home with me,' Ivy butted in.

'I know, Ivy, and I will be eternally grateful. It's been a wonderful day,' Rose said. 'One that I'll never forget.' At that, Molly made her way to the table and stood in front of them all with her latest purchase from her hard-earned cash in her hands, a box Brownie camera.

'Smile, say cheese!' Molly held the little brown box to her eye, peering through the lens and snapping the happy couple and the wedding party. 'Perfect! I can't wait for the chemist to develop these. I hope that they come out all right, I've never taken photographs before. But I thought it's one way for our Annie to see your wedding day, even if she's not here. It's not the same without her; we've always celebrated family things together.'

The hours shot by as guests came and congratulated the new couple, memories were shared and Molly recorded it all on her box Brownie until the film ran out.

Reg came across the hall and stood at the couple's wedding table. 'Are you ready for home? Before the ARP warden shouts at us for having our lights on or making too much noise.'

'Yes, we're ready. It's been a perfect day. Come on, Mother, let's get you home and then you can have a snooze, you must be tired after drinking a sherry or two and all that food.' Ned started to take his mother's arm.

'No, our Ned, you walk out with Rose on your arm. I'll take Reg's, if you don't mind. Besides, he's a lot better looking than you.' Ivy winked at Winnie. 'You've got to keep these fellas on their toes.'

'You'll have Betty after you. Come on then, young lady, take my arm and we'll get you all home.' Reg held his arm out and winked at his wife who was helping tidy the hall up. 'I'll be back before long, love, for that promise you whispered in my ear. It's my lucky day and all.'

Betty grinned, 'Ivy's too much for you to handle. You take care and I'll see you in a while.'

Winnie walked to the doorway with the young couple. 'God bless you two. You make the perfect couple and I'm proud to have you as a son-in-law, Ned.'

'Thank you. I promise I will always love and care for Rose,' Ned said earnestly. 'I have loved her from the first time I set eyes on her. Thank you for giving me the honour of being her husband.' He took Winnie's hand and shook it and then thought a hug for his mother-in-law would perhaps be more fitting. But Winnie got there first, putting her arms around him. 'Thank you,' Ned said quietly as his best man and best friend Peter stood next to the car with a huge grin on his face.

'Mam, thank you for everything.' Rose kissed her mother on her cheek and wiped away an errant tear.

'Go on, get a move on before I make a fool of myself by crying. Ivy's waiting for you, and Peter's been up to some tricks by the looks of it. Haven't you, Peter?' Winnie shouted.

'Certainly have, couldn't let them disappear quietly!' Peter shouted back.

Rose and Ned made their way to the wedding car, where Ivy was settled comfortably next to Reg. Strings of tin cans were tied to the back bumper, making a deafening din as they drove down the street to home, clattering and rattling for all the world to hear them.

'I had to do something to make him embarrassed,' Peter said, looking after Ned with envy as he drove away with his beautiful bride. If only she had met him first, it might have been his wedding today, he thought wistfully. Ned was a lucky man to have such a lovely bride. He was pleased for him, but he couldn't help feeling a little jealous.

4

'Molly, will you come with me to have a look around the flat above the bakery? It's just come up for let and I've got the key from the owner. I think I can just about afford it. Living with you and your mam has been lovely, but now I think that it's time I stood on my own two feet. I thought we could have a look around it this evening?'

Connie and Molly were changing out of their work clothes into their civilian ones, ready to make their way home. It had been a long day of supervising munitions workers along the production line as they filled shells, made them safe and sent them down to the arsenal for storage, on top of their own production roles.

'I don't know why you want to move out. You know you can stay as long as you want with us, Connie. Mam treats you like one of her own nowadays.' Molly thought back to the day when Connie had first come to live with them when she'd been homeless after running away from her abusive stepfather. She'd been a lost soul back then. 'But I'll come if you really need me to and have got your heart set on it.' Molly hesitated for a second. 'I thought that you'd be waiting to see what happens with Chuck? You'll regret it and think that you've wasted money if he returns home when this war is over and wants to take you with him. If you still like him, that is, and want to do that.'

'I don't think that there will be any chance of that,' Connie said glumly. 'He never mentions it any more when he visits me. He used to tell me all the time that he would take me home after the war to meet his parents, but he never even showed his face at Rose's wedding, even though he was asked by me.' Connie sighed. 'Since he's been permanently based at Elvington airbase, I've hardly seen him. At least when he was over in America he wrote nearly every week, but now I only see him when he has time, and nine times out of ten he falls asleep while I'm talking away like an idiot to him. There's not much romance between us at the moment.'

'Oh, Connie, he's just busy. They have flights taking off nearly every night now that they're getting the better of Jerry. He's ground crew, he will always be checking the planes and making sure that they're safe for flight. I'm sure he loves you as much as he ever did.' Molly linked her arm through Connie's as they walked out of the munitions and past the guard. When they'd first started work there, they'd been scared to death of him. Now they just ignored him – he knew their faces and he also knew that they would just give him a load of cheek if he stopped them to be checked. Besides, everyone knew that in a few more months the military would likely be gone, and hopefully normal chocolate production would begin again as soon as possible. 'Oh, I can't wait to come home smelling of chocolate and not have to worry about bloody bombs!' Molly exclaimed.

'I know, but perhaps I'd be better finding somebody else. When I first met Chuck, my head was turned. He was dashing, handsome, American and most of all he came from Montana where my half-brother lives. Now we've got used to one another and the magic has perhaps waned a little. But I still love him.' Connie sighed. 'I don't think I'd be happy with anybody else, but you don't know. I just wish I saw him more often, that's what the problem is.'

'Connie, are you fancying somebody else?' Molly asked as they rounded the corner near home. 'I know you too well, and it sounds as if something or someone is on your mind.'

Connie grinned. 'No, I'll behave myself. I do love Chuck, but have you seen the new man that is helping with carrying the loaded shells? I know he's got a limp, but he is so handsome. I can't help but look at him every time he passes with the detonators to and from the magazine.'

'Well, I can tell you now, he's married and his limp is from being shot in the leg when he was near Calais. You keep your eyes to Chuck. I worry about him, the new fella, only because I think he's got one of the most dangerous jobs, dressed in his leather apron and carrying his bag of detonators. Thank heaven he's always got somebody with him waving a red flag to clear the way – he's not the safest fella to be carrying such like.' Molly reached for the front door handle and yelled, 'We're home, Mam!' but quickly closed the door behind them so that the light didn't escape out into the night sky. The ARP warden was a stickler and didn't mince his words when something was out of line.

Molly turned and whispered to Connie, 'Oh, bugger, smell that – pipe smoke. Ralph Parker is visiting my mother again.'

'They're just friends, it's good for them to have one another,' Connie said quietly as they both walked into the kitchen, to find it empty but with the table set for supper with one extra setting.

'We're in here, you two,' Winnie called through. 'Ralph and I are just listening to the radio. He's staying for his supper. I told him that it's only potato hash, but it's like he says, it will be grand – anything is good when you don't have to cook it yourself.'

Molly pulled a face. She didn't like the elderly man who had become perhaps a little too friendly with her mother over the past few weeks while queuing up with ration tokens at various shops. 'I don't mind Ralph being friends with my mother, but I'm frightened in case he thinks he can replace my father. He will never, ever do that,' she whispered and then shouted back, 'All right, Mam, I'll put the kettle on and check the stove.'

'Thanks, love. We'll be through in a minute when this programme finishes,' Winnie replied.

Molly bustled around as Connie pulled her shoes off and sat next to the fire, smiling at the dark look on Molly's face. Her father might have been dead for quite a few years now, and she was sure Molly could hardly remember him, but she wasn't going to let a usurper into her and her mother's life.

'You know Ralph, he's all right. He's quiet and steady, and he must get lonely since his wife died. They're only friends, Mol,' Connie whispered.

'I hope so. He'll never replace my dad, that's for sure,' Molly growled and then stood up to brew the tea. 'Tea's brewed, Mam,' she called out, 'and I'll get the supper out. Connie and me are going straight out after we've eaten.'

Winnie came through, and Molly asked, 'How long's Ralph been here and will he be staying?'

'He's only been here an hour and he'll be gone by the time you're back. I'm not just here to see to your needs. I was married and running a home of my own when I was your age.' Winnie's face was red and her words sharp; she had been enjoying sitting and having a natter while listening to a radio play with Ralph. But she knew that Molly did not like her relationship with the man who lived two streets away and had been left a widower the previous year.

'I'm sorry, Mam, we're just in a hurry to get out.' Molly was finding it hard to conceal her feelings about Ralph continually being there and knew that she had upset her mother.

'It must be something urgent if you're going out as soon as you've come in. Mind what you're doing out there, you don't know who's about at this time of year.' Winnie lifted the lid on the pan of potato hash that had just been simmering slowly on the top of the stove, filling the kitchen with the smell of onions, gravy, carrots and potatoes, and making Ralph appear from the sitting room.

'There's nothing like your mother's cooking. It always smells delicious.' Ralph smiled at Winnie and stood close to her. 'She's a fine woman, is your mother,' he added, touching her arm gently.

Connie could see Molly's face cloud over.

'Flattery will get you nowhere, Ralph Parker, and besides, your Sissie was one of the best cooks for miles around.' Winnie gave Ralph a loving look as they all sat down around the table with a steaming plate of potato hash in front of them and a loaf of freshly made bread to fill up on. 'Where are you girls going, anyway? It's too dreary to look in the shop windows at this time of night, there's nothing to see.'

'Just going around to see a friend from work, Mam, she needs a bit of cheering up,' Molly answered quickly, not wanting her mother to know that Connie was going to be looking at a new place to live, or at least not yet.

'Well, I hope that she's all right – everybody needs a good friend to listen to their worries. Just take care out in the dark.' Winnie smiled at them both. She was glad that they were both going to be out for a while; it gave her and Ralph some more time together. 'Don't bother doing the washing-up, Ralph and I will do it.'

'Yes, you're all right, girls, your mother can wash and I'll dry. I believe in a man helping out around the house,' Ralph said.

'We aren't that old yet, Ralph, there's still a lot of life left in us.' Winnie tried not to notice Molly shaking her head.

'Thanks, Mam, we won't be long. We just need to give her a few kind words and then return home,' Molly lied through her teeth.

'Yes, just a few kind words and a bit of advice, that's all she will need,' Connie confirmed and put her head down to finish her supper, knowing that Molly would be the one saying the words once they were out of the door, but they wouldn't be kind or anything like.

'He's worming his way in, I tell you,' Molly started as soon as the front door was closed behind them. 'I don't know why my mam can't see what he's doing. I don't like him chatting her up and swarming around her. Mam's always managed on her own before – what does she want a man for now?'

'Happen she enjoys his company,' Connie replied. 'We're always at work and have our own lives, don't begrudge her if she's happy. At least he's not like my mother's fella Bill, now he was a bully, handy with his fists and treated my mother like rubbish. Ralph seems a good soul to me.'

'The top and bottom of it is that I don't like him,' Molly grumbled as they walked down Gillygate, turning into Petersgate, the crowded old medieval part of York with houses so close together that neighbours could nearly shake hands with one another from their top bedroom windows. 'What do you want to live down here for, Connie? It's always so busy and the houses in this part are so old.'

'That's what I like about it, that it's always busy, and the flat is affordable, because it's above a bakery at the moment. They say it's only going to be on a short let. Just long enough for me to make my mind up whether I like living on my own or to know if Chuck is going to marry me. I really hope it's the latter; he's my one chance to change my life for the better.'

'I think you're mad, leaving my mam's for here, but never mind. I know you've always wanted your own place.' Molly watched as Connie stepped up onto the narrow, cracked pavement next to a baker's shop and went up to a hardly visible varnished door that was at the side of the shop. All was in darkness, so she struggled to find the lock and turn it.

'Come on, follow me. There's no lighting on the stairs, but once we're upstairs there is, although it's only gas light. They say that they're going to put the electricity in shortly. I have a torch in my pocket – follow my light until we get to the top and then I'll light the lamps.' Connie shone the light on the wooden stairs that echoed in the silence of the empty house as they climbed them. 'Right, here we go,' she said as she turned the gas tap on and struck a match to light the supply before placing the glass shade back over the flame and then rushing to pull the room curtains so as not to spill any light out into the night. The smell of gas filled the room for a second as Molly gazed around at the small bedsit that Connie was thinking of renting.

'Well, I suppose it's all right, it's a lot bigger than I thought,' Molly said. The floor was covered with linoleum and there was a single bed in one corner, while next to the window there was a table and two chairs that had seen better days. 'At least it doesn't look to be damp, and you'll always be warm if you're living over a bakery. Where's the toilet or bathroom? And you have no kitchen?'

'It's here,' Connie said, indicating a door through to another room. 'There's only a tin bath, and a sink with a gas boiler over it that doubles up as my sink to wash everything in. The owners say that they will put an oven in – look, there's a gas tap here for a cooker or something of that sort.' She felt as if she had been in a dream world when she had looked around it with the owner. It had seemed like everything she had dreamed of when she'd been shown around the first time. Now, with Molly by her side, she was noting all the negative things about it.

'It's all right, Connie. Even though it's a dark January night, it's warm in here. You'll never be cold while they have ovens lit downstairs and the air is filled with the smell of baking and bread. I'd always be thinking I was hungry. At least it isn't the smell of chocolate!' Molly smiled and sat on the stripy mattress of the single bed which squeaked when she moved. 'Everyone will know if you have a passionate night in here with Chuck. You'll have to behave yourselves.'

'Chance of that will be a fine thing,' Connie snorted. 'I hardly ever see him nowadays. All I do is think of him. He's good-looking, strong and has such a warm smile, and I do think I love him. He tells me every time we meet that he loves me, but a girl can't wait for ever, and I need to see him more often. He might come and see me a bit more if I had my own home.' Connie sat down next to Molly and put her arm through hers. 'I don't know what to do. It's a dump really, isn't it? Perhaps I should stay with you and your mother, but I just feel as if I have outstayed my welcome. It was only supposed to be for a month or two, and nearly four years on I'm still relying on your mother's goodwill.'

'It's not goodwill – you pay your way, we have a good life because of your contributions and Mam would miss you. Besides, if you leave, she would entertain bloody Ralph Parker even more.' Molly gave Connie a squeeze. 'It's up to you.'

'I'll have a think about it. I might come back in daylight on Saturday and have another look around. I can't make my mind up.' Connie sighed.

'I'll come with you again. I've never noticed the bakery downstairs before. It can't be that big?' Molly pulled back the thinning curtains and looked down on the street below. 'The street is so narrow. You'd be right in the centre of York, I bet you can see the Minster's spires in the daytime.'

'Yes, you can, and the street is always busy. It's a wonder we've never been to the bakery. I suppose we always go to our local one on Dudley Street, it's handiest for where we live. The one on Dudley Street must be a gold mine, because they close by dinner time every day as they're sold out of produce. Folks only shop where they know the food is good, I don't think here is that busy.' Connie watched as Molly gazed around the room.

'That doesn't take much doing nowadays, flour and suchlike is still hard to get. I bet that's why they're thinking of selling. Trouble is, you might only be here six months, Connie, and then you would have to move. You'd have no security because I bet they would probably sell the whole building, so you would just be turfed out onto the street.'

'Six months is a long time nowadays. The war could be over and then I'd know where I stood with Chuck, and hopefully things might get back to normal. My life is such a mess – it's always a mess, no matter what I do.' Connie sighed.

'Well, at least your man is here and you know that he's safe. I don't know where my Matt is. Last time I heard from him he was somewhere in Belgium and could be fighting for his life for all I know. I pray that he will come back to me. I never thought when we met in the cinema like we did that four years on we would still be writing to one another.' Molly wiped away a tear. She had given her heart to the good-looking soldier who had taken her eye. She hardly knew him, but the letters that they exchanged were filled with love.

'Oh, Mol, he'll soon be coming home; they all will, God willing, and that is when our lives will change. We just have to be strong.'

'Yes, but I still miss my Matt and wonder if he misses me as much,' Molly said quietly.

'Of course he does, even more than you miss him. And he'll soon be home and those Jerries will realize what they have done to the world. Now come on, chin up, let's get threepence worth of chips and share them on our way back. Hopefully Ralph Parker will have gone home and we can listen to *The Navy Lark* on the wireless.'

'That sounds a good idea to me but we shouldn't really, we've already had supper,' Molly said as she followed Connie down the torchlit stairs.

'What the hell, Mol, let's live life to the full. Besides, threepence worth of chips isn't going to harm us. We've been living on hardly anything of late with these blockades at sea. None of the food that we used to take for granted is getting through because of the Nazi U-boats. Those Jerries are trying to starve us into submission, I'm sure. What I'd do for an orange is nobody's business.'

Molly put her arm through Connie's. 'If you go to America, you'll be living on oranges – they grow them over there. Happen not in Montana, though, it'll not be warm enough.'

'Then I'll have to marry Chuck, and Matt and you will have to come over and visit. How does that sound?' Connie giggled as she locked the door to the flat and then put the key in her handbag.

'Perhaps. We'll have to see.'

The following day both girls were back at work when an announcement came over the Tannoy: 'Connie Whitehead to the main office, please.' Connie turned and looked at Molly, shrugging her shoulders as she walked past her to go and see why she was needed.

'Oh, Lord, she must have upset them above, I bet,' said Bridget. 'To be honest, she hasn't been doing her job lately – too much yakking about that Yank boyfriend of hers. Lord knows how she became a supervisor – she can't supervise herself.'

'She's not that bad, is she?' Molly protested. 'I know that sometimes she's a bit careless and short-tempered when somebody doesn't do what she tells them to do, but she's a good worker.'

'We're all good workers, but you have to be special to be a supervisor,' Bridget said and then went quiet.

Molly put her head down and got on with her work, but she wondered why Connie had been called to the offices above and couldn't concentrate until she saw Connie walking back to her station with a look of disappointment and anger on her face.

She turned and mouthed, 'Are you all right?'

Connie shook her head, and then carried on filling her shells, not looking at anybody.

'Could Molly Freeman please come to the main office?' All eyes turned and looked at Molly as she walked out of her workstation. The gods above were playing with people's lives, and something was afoot.

Molly felt her legs shaking as she walked up the stairs to the main office. What was wrong? Were she and Connie in trouble? But she couldn't think of anything that they had done. She stood outside the office and gently tapped on the door.

'Enter,' boomed the voice of the manager from behind his desk.

Molly entered the office that had been taken over by the MOD, and looked at the ex-officer who was her manager.

'Ah, Miss Freeman, thank you for giving me your time. I'll not beat about the bush with my news. Emm . . . I am pleased to inform you that we are in a position to offer you the supervisor's role in your section. It has just become available. Would you be happy to accept? I need the post filling as soon as possible.' Her manager, who still looked very much like an officer, waited and watched as Molly wondered what to say. The offer had come out of the blue and she knew she was stepping into Connie's shoes.

'I don't know. I thought Connie, Miss Whitehead, was our supervisor?' Molly replied.

'I'm afraid she has had to be replaced. Now, the pay is quite a bit better, and we know you are a very conscientious worker, ideal for this position. Now what do you say? Your role would start immediately.' The manager looked her in the eye, making Molly feel under pressure.

'I . . . I . . . I don't know.' Molly thought of how proud her mother would be of her, a supervisor! But poor Connie, she was replacing her best friend. 'I accept,' she found herself saying, thinking about her mother's pride in telling the neighbours and hoping that Connie would understand.

'Wonderful. If you come to my office in the morning, I will give you all the details that you need about your job, although I'm sure that you know them even better than Miss Whitehead. Dismissed,' the manager said, as if he were still in charge of an army unit.

'Thank you,' Molly replied. She couldn't quite believe what had happened, and was dreading telling Connie on the way home that evening.

'Well, what did that bloody manager have to say to you?' Connie asked once they were out of earshot of work and were on their way home. 'I bet he told you that he'd decided that I was not supervisor material and that my stunt of being one was over.' Connie sighed. 'Just when I needed the extra money.' She stopped sharply in her tracks and held onto Molly's arm. 'Did they give you it? I hope they did – you'd be ten times better than me, and don't worry, I won't sulk over it.'

'I didn't want to say, but yes, from tomorrow morning, I'm the new supervisor. I'm sorry, Connie. I didn't really want it,' Molly said, embarrassed.

'Don't be daft. If I can't have it, I'm glad they've given it to you; I only took it for the extra money. I'll still be able to rent my flat, though, if I'm careful.' Connie hugged her friend. 'Now let's go and tell your mam, she'll be so proud!'

'I hope so,' Molly said. 'I'm so glad that you're not upset, I didn't want to lose you as a friend.'

'That'll never happen,' Connie said. 'Friends forever, me and you, no matter what.'

5

There was silence apart from the stirring of a rat nesting in the attic above the sleeping couple's heads. The old farmhouse was at peace, nestled into the Lancashire hillside where it had stood for centuries. It wasn't quite coming light when Annie and Mike stirred, hoping not to be found out by Mike's aunt and uncle as the weak sun peeped through the thin curtains. Mike pulled them back to look at the mist hanging over Pendle and hoped that they were not in for rain. His life had changed completely since he had been discharged from the army because of the injuries sustained to his ankle and leg. Now he was back farming in the job he loved, with a lass he loved.

'Come back to bed, Mike. It's only early, nobody else in the house is stirring. They don't know that you're in here.' Annie pulled on her lover's arm and urged him back into bed with her.

'You are a wicked woman, Annie Freeman. To think when I met you on that train all those years ago when the war was starting, you were so shy and quiet, and now you're leading me astray like this. Butter wouldn't melt in your mouth back then.' Mike pulled his underpants back on and bent down to kiss Annie as she lay sprawled in bed in the spare bedroom in his aunt and uncle's farmhouse at Pendle Farm.

'It's you to blame for this. I was an innocent lass from York until I met you.' Annie smiled and returned his kiss, looking lovingly into his eyes, and then stretched out in her small bed.

'Well, I'm going to my own room now, before Bernard and Lizzie start stirring. It's a good job that you sleep this far away from their bedroom, else I think we would be wakening them.' Mike grinned. 'I'll see you at breakfast after I've milked the cow.'

Annie watched as Mike left her room, sneaking quietly along the passage from the older part of the house to where his bedroom was and that of the Farringtons. She looked up at the ceiling and let her body relax. Her mother would have plenty to say if she ever found out that she was sleeping regular with the nephew of the farm where she was based. She'd probably call her a hussy and make her come back home, but Annie loved Mike, even though sometimes she did think he used her, just slightly, for his satisfaction – but it was a two-way thing, she thought as she hugged her thin, feather-filled pillow. It wouldn't be long before Lizzie would be heard riddling the still-glowing embers from the previous night in the fireplace and shouting for Bernard to move his shanks. Since Mike had been discharged from the army, Bernard was doing less and less, leaving the bulk of the work to his nephew, who now lived with them all the time, much to Annie's joy and satisfaction. Lizzie would often reprimand Bernard, but he would take it in his stride. Show willing for a while and then go back to letting Mike do the main body of the work, complaining that he was getting old and his hip hurt.

Annie smiled, thinking of the love she and Mike had enjoyed through the night. She had been courting him in the broadest sense of the word for such a long time, and she hoped that he would propose to her one day, as he was always saying how much he loved her. He was just summoning up the courage to tell his aunt and uncle that he had fallen for the Land Army girl from York. She closed her eyes, worried again what her mother would say about her relationship. She had been disappointed that a bomb had fallen on the main line from Clitheroe, and sorry she had missed the wedding, but she knew all too well that her mother would have wormed all she could out of her about Mike. Her mother had a knack of knowing things without even being told about them. In the years that she had been billeted with the Farringtons, her family had never visited, and she was thankful for that. She had visited them when she was on leave and had given them a version of her life with the Farringtons that she knew would not cause them concern. Her mother, especially, would be shocked by the state of the farmhouse and the smell of the pigs that were kept nearby. There were no donkey stone-scrubbed steps to be found at Pendle Farm; the step just blended into the general filth of the farmyard. Lizzie was not the best of housewives. And when Annie did offer to help, she was looked at as if she was threatening Lizzie's position as matriarch of the Farrington family. Annie reached for her alarm clock: five a.m., another hour and she would have to stir. It sounded like rain had started to come down outside, but the new batch of pigs would expect to be fed and then cleaned out. But work was easier now that Mike helped. Even though he struggled some days with the pain in his leg and ankle, he never stopped working, although lately he had been at his uncle and aunt's farm more than his own. He had assured Annie and his aunt that everything was all right back at his homestead. He didn't have that much stock on his land, and he had a farm lad doing most of the work there. Everything was better now Mike was here, she thought as she pulled the covers over her head and closed her eyes for a quick snooze.

'You're late up! It's after six thirty, it must have been the rats playing dominoes through the night that made you tired. They keep making a noise at your end of the house,' Bernard said and looked at Annie as she sat down on the wooden stool and laced up her boots.

'Bernard!' Lizzie said sharply and put a strong cup of tea in front of Annie. 'There's always noises in this old house of a night. I swear sometimes we have a ghost.'

'I fell back asleep, sorry, I'll get a move on now.' Annie tried to hide her blushes as she realized what Bernard was hinting at. Mike and her were going to have to be more careful. Although Bernard and Lizzie knew they were courting, she had hoped that their night-time activities had gone unnoticed. 'I'll come back in for some breakfast when I've caught up with my jobs.'

'All right, I'm making porridge this morning, we have plenty of milk at the moment. If you're looking for something to do later this morning, you can churn some butter for the market on Friday.' Lizzie stood with her hands on her hips. 'Tell Mike that his uncle wants a word with him when you see him. On his own!'

Annie wondered if it was to warn Mike to stop visiting her at night-time and felt a stab of anxiety. 'Yes, I will. He should have finished milking by now and I'll clean the cow house once he brings the milk in.'

Lizzie and Bernard looked at one another, and Annie closed the door behind her.

'He's going to have to be told. Now what he does about it is up to him,' Lizzie sighed. Neither of them had slept all night either, but not because of the goings-on at the other end of the house – they had known about the midnight wanderings for months now – but because a big decision had been made between them both and it was going to have repercussions throughout the household.

'I don't know what's going on between Lizzie and Bernard, but there's something happening. They need to see you on your own.' Annie put her hand on the cow's haunches as Mike picked up the milking stool that he was sitting on along with the pail of steaming milk which he poured into the kit that stood next to the shippon's doorway. 'Your Uncle Bernard was hinting that he heard noises coming from my bedroom. I didn't know what to say, I was too embarrassed.'

'He's been acting funny all week if you ask me. They both have, I think they're up to something,' Mike said and put the empty bucket down. 'It will be something or nothing, it always is with them.'

'I hope that they're not thinking of getting rid of me. I never want to leave here, but if the war really is turning in our favour, I'll soon not be needed.' Annie bowed her head and reached for the stiff brush to sweep the cow shed clear after the two cows had been fed and milked.

'It'll not be that; they think too much of you and so do I. We'll see what happens in the next few months, but I don't want to see you leaving. I'd better go and see what the fuss is about, but don't you worry.' Mike pulled Annie close to him and lifted her chin up to look into her eyes. 'I love you, Annie Freeman, now don't worry.'

'I'll try not to.' Annie leaned on the brush and watched as Mike walked across the muddy yard, scraping his boots on the boot scraper, which was a waste of time seeing as the kitchen floor was dirtier than the yard, before he opened the kitchen door and went to find out what was so important that morning.

'Annie says you need to see me, so what's it all about?' Mike sat down at the kitchen table and rubbed his aching leg. Since he had been shot in the ankle and leg, he had constant pain. He watched Lizzie and Bernard and knew instantly that there was something important to be said that morning.

Bernard studied his nephew. They had both regarded him as their own since his parents had died when he was only just in his teens, and what they were going to tell him was not going to be easy. Mike still owned his parents smallholding, but it was hardly big enough to make a living on. They had wanted Pendle Farm to be his one day, but things were not going to work out that way.

'The thing is, lad, me and the old lass are not getting any younger. My hip stops me from doing a lot of things and the housework gets on top of her. I was in Clitheroe the other day and I spotted a house that was up for sale, that would just do us two. We're both going to have a look at it this afternoon and we hope to bid for it when it comes up at auction in another few weeks. The thing is, we will have to sell here, but we know that will be upsetting for you. So we both wanted to tell you first.'

Mike hung his head; their news had come completely out of the blue. He always thought that they would be farming at Pendle until the last breath left their bodies.

'Well, I never expected that. I didn't think that you would ever part with this place. It's always been in your family, Uncle Bernard, it would be such a shame to sell it.' Although it had never been promised, Mike had always hoped that Pendle Farm would be his one day. He had lain awake of a night thinking how he could change it and make it more profitable, and now all his dreaming had come to nothing.

'It's me you can blame, Mike,' Lizzie said. 'I'm fed

up with this sprawling, crumbling house; it's damp and needs money spending on it. I can just see myself sitting content next to one of those new-look fireplaces with nowt to worry about except what we're having to eat for supper. Taking on Annie as our Land Army girl was a boon when you were still in the army, but we are about to upset her life as well. Plus, your Uncle Bernard isn't getting any younger.' Lizzie hesitated. 'You look upset. I know it's going to mean you going back home to your smallholding, but you would have had to do that sometime. You'll have to throw the fella out that's renting there. You might just be able to make a living there if you're careful. I know it's always been dear to you, and your mam and dad managed to make a living there. We would have liked to have perhaps left the farm to you after our day, but we need to move now, while we're still able to.'

Lizzie felt guilty at letting her nephew down, knowing that he had loved staying with them and had even worked for a pittance while doing so.

'It's not for me to say what you do with it, Aunty Lizzie; I'll just be sad to see it being sold. I suppose that will mean Annie will be leaving? Do I tell her or will you?' Mike's world was slowly falling apart and he knew he was going to lose everything dear to him.

'No, we'll tell her,' said Bernard. 'We'll give her enough warning; it will probably be the end of spring when she'll have to leave. You'll miss her, lad, I know you will, it's not been going unnoticed how close you both are. Perhaps too close sometimes.'

Mike studied his hands. 'I'd hoped that the farm would be mine one day, especially now that I'm a bit lame and nobody will want me to work for them. Never mind, I shouldn't have even been thinking it – as they say, you can't always get what you want. And I was wrong to even dream of it.' He got up from his seat and headed for the door; he needed time to himself to focus on what he was going to do next.

Lizzie stood up. 'Mike, if we could we would give you the place, but we still owe the bank and we need to buy the cottage on Preston Road with cash. We can't do anything else.'

Mike turned and stared at his aunt. 'I know. I just need some time to myself, it's been a shock, but I understand.' He tried to smile as he walked out into the farmyard, leaving Lizzie and Bernard looking at one another. He couldn't blame them for leaving Pendle Farm – they deserved a bit of comfort in their twilight years – but he hadn't thought that they would ever move, and he was going to lose Annie if he didn't do something. The two things that he loved the most were slipping through his hands and he didn't know which to fix first, but he had a plan to fix both.

6

'I feel like I've said this a thousand times,' Rose whispered as she nestled her head against Ned's chest, listening to his heart beating as they lay in their marital bed.

'I'll have to go, my love. Another few months and the battles should be won, then I will return and life will go back to normal. That is if Rowntree's will have me back.' Ned sighed and put his arm around Rose and kissed her. 'I've nearly forgotten what normal is, I'm afraid.'

'I think everyone has. Oh, I'm going to miss you so much. I know it sounds daft, but now we are married I will worry even more about you.' Rose ran her hand down Ned's chest and kissed it.

'I'll be fine. You know me, they've tried to get rid of me a few times now and I always bounce back.' Ned wished he had faith in the words he was saying, but he knew that once he returned to base a major operation was about to be started, with all the Allies involved. He couldn't tell Rose, but they had been warned that they were to fly deep into Germany and hit the cities. It was going to cost lives on all sides, but it would hopefully break the spirit of the Germans and make them surrender. 'Now, let's get dressed and have breakfast together before my mother needs our attention. Just me and you over our cup of tea and a slice of toast.' Ned kissed Rose's brow, feeling sick at the thought of the coming missions. She couldn't have an inkling of what was about to take place, or she would never let him out of her sight.

Later that morning Ned sat in the briefing room, along with fellow members of the bombing crew. They were on edge as they were filled in about the new ops to be carried out that night. Dresden, in the very heart of Germany, was their target. No matter the civilian cost, Dresden had to be hit to take out its manufacturing and industry. It was time for the Allies to give Germany some payback. Ned sat back and listened to how the operation was going to be undertaken. His mind wandered to thinking of Rose, who would be busy at work in the offices of Rowntree's and hopefully would have no idea that his life was about to be in the most danger it had ever been. Please let me return, he thought. His and Rose's life was only just beginning.

A dozen Halifax bombers were waiting, the ground crew watching as the pilots and navigators walked across the airfield towards them. It was the first of many missions planned to give the Germans a taste of their own medicine and to try to make them see sense. Ned, now captain of his own plane, patted Peter on the back and wished him luck. They would all need it that night.

The crews waved at one another, stomachs churning with fear, and some of the younger pilots had actually been sick as they walked out of the briefing room knowing that they might never see their homes again if caught in the flak or crossfire from enemy planes.

A full moon shone overhead as Ned climbed onto the wing of his Halifax bomber and signalled the ground crew to remove the chocks from his wheels as he fired up the aeroplane's engines. The smell of fuel and smoke filled his lungs as he pulled over the canopy and thought of his Rose and mother safely asleep in their beds. Unlike the people of Dresden, they would hopefully have a peaceful night's sleep. His orders, and those of the squadrons that were to join them, were to obliterate the industrial city of Dresden in the heart of Germany. Hitler had to be made to see sense, but it would be at the cost of innocent people. Ned kissed his rabbit foot and tapped on the photograph of Rose tucked into his inside pocket. 'Keep me safe, Rose, we have all our lives in front of us,' he whispered and then swung round to face his crew. 'Right, let's give these bloody Jerries a taste of their own medicine.' The ground staff watched as the planes taxied down the runway and then flew out in the direction of the narrow English Channel and to whatever fate had in store for them.

'Bring them all back safe,' Chuck whispered as he watched both English and American pilots and planes disappear into the darkness. 'They need all the luck they can get.'

*

Ned looked out of his cockpit and waved at Peter in the Halifax next to him. They had passed over the Channel without any incidents apart from some flak being aimed at them as they passed over the coast. But now they were going deep into Germany, following the map that had been drilled into them, looking out for certain tell-tale signs on the sprawling land below them. Above them were their guardians, the Spitfires, to keep them safe from German fighters.

'Keep with us, you guys,' Ned said as he took hold of the joystick. They weren't far away now, but Jerry would have picked them up and would soon be shooting at them; despite being short of aeroplanes, they were still deadly.

'There it is, skip. Oh my God, look at that flak that's coming for us,' his second-in-command shouted as shells burst all around them and Stukas appeared as if by magic above them, only for the Spitfires to weave and dodge between them and chase like cat and mouse above their heads.

'We'll do our job and get out of here as fast as we can. Hold tight, we're going to be in for a rocky ride,' Ned said as the bombardier counted down and viewed where they had been ordered to drop their load. The air lit up around them with exploding fire but Ned kept his nerve. From the corner of his eye, he saw Peter swerve to the left and disappear from view; he hadn't time to watch as he concentrated on following his own path.

'Bomb one, bomb two, bomb three, all bombs gone.

Take that, Hitler!' the bombardier shouted as he pressed the release trigger and watched the destruction that was falling on Dresden. 'There's bound to be innocent folk down there,' he said, leaning back against the fuselage as Ned and his co-pilot struggled to keep control of the Halifax. It was being buffeted and knocked about by the shells that were now coming fast and furious at the raiders.

'I know, lad, just like our English homes. Now, let's get the hell out of here! Our job is done for now. Time to go home,' Ned said. He concentrated on evading the flak and prayed that no Stuka would tail them and shoot at them. 'Let's get back to that good old English breakfast waiting for us in the NAAFI.'

Ned looked out across the sky as he started to get clear of the guns firing at them. Below them Dresden stood in ruins, with fires burning and the drone of bombers flying over it. 'Did anyone see where Peter went? He swept left and I couldn't follow him,' Ned yelled back to the rest of his crew.

'No, but he'll be all right, he's always a lucky bastard,' the bombardier shouted.

'I hope that you're right, lad. Tonight has been hell, and we'll have to do it again by the sounds of it.' Ned felt sick at the thought of having to do it all again, but he knew the following night he and his crew would be back in the air, risking their lives to keep England safe and secure. He closed his eyes for a second and prayed under his breath, 'Please let Peter be safe and get us home in one piece.' The following night's raid would be worse. Jerry would be waiting for them; this was just the start. Berlin was to be bombed, along with Frankfurt and most of the major cities in Germany; the gloves were off now amongst the Allies. It was time to put a stop to the war in Europe.

Ned stood with a mug of tea in his hands and looked out into the morning light. It was a cold, grey morning and the sun was just trying to break through the winter sky, making the frost on the grass sparkle like diamonds. His eyes searched the skies, hoping to see a battered Halifax with his best friend in the cockpit come in to land. Another pilot had seen Peter's Halifax shot in the wing, with flames coming out of the fuselage, and had then lost sight of it in the heat of battle. Ned would have done anything to see and hear the voice of his best friend. He was the one with the most experience, the one that everyone looked up to. The squadron would be lost without him and he himself would miss his dearest friend.

The station commander came and patted him on his back. 'Still no sign, old chap?'

'No, but I'm not giving up hope. He's like a bad penny, he'll turn up,' Ned said.

'That's the way, my good man. Never give up.'

Rose had not heard from Ned for five days. Passing the news stand on her way to work at Rowntree's, she bought the morning paper and read the headlines:

INTENSE BOMBING OF DRESDEN LEAVES JERRY REELING

Our lads show just what we are made of as four nights of continuous bombing flattens Dresden, in a show of Allied strength.

Rose felt her stomach churn; she knew that her Ned would have taken part. 'Please let him be safe,' she whispered to herself. He had to be safe; she had some news to tell him. It was a good job that they hadn't waited a minute longer to get married, she thought as she put her hand on her stomach and prayed that her Ned would return to them both safe and sound.

'Ah, Rose, you're with us this morning,' Seebohm Rowntree greeted her as he came out of his office and caught her on the stairs. 'We were all just talking about you. Only in a good way, hoping that Ned was all right. We all know that the lads at Elvington will have taken part in the raids recently.'

'I think he will be,' Rose said. 'I never get to know whereabouts he is flying, and I've had no word from him for a while. When they're on a big mission he stays on the base because of security. I knew he was building up to something big, I could tell by the way he was acting, although he would never say.'

'They keep their secrets, do our military men. No news is good news, my dear, think of it that way. I'm sure Ned will be safe and sound.' Seebohm, patted Rose on the shoulder. 'Speaking of which, we are to hold a meeting in the boardroom, two p.m. sharp. My secretary will be informing the rest of the board. Can you make sure we are not disturbed and that any problems will be resolved in the board's absence? It will be a long meeting, but hopefully a positive one. Since we made George Harris the company chair, he seems to be keeping everything and everyone in line.' Seebohm smiled and then walked off down the corridor, whistling.

Rose opened her office door and looked across at her secretary, who had been assigned to her the previous year. Jane was a young girl, only eighteen, blonde and good-looking and very good at her job, but a little outspoken and a devil for gossiping.

'Ah, Mr Rowntree Senior was just looking for you. He said would you take charge of any problems that might occur this afternoon, while the board hold a meeting.'

'Thank you, Jane, I've already spoken to him. He seems in an exceptionally good mood. I don't suppose he has hinted at what this meeting is about?'

Jane leaned forward and whispered, 'No, he didn't, but I heard that the war ministry might be leaving us, which would mean that our chocolate production can get back to what it was. If we start winning the war, they are talking of moving the munition side down south. Won't that be fantastic? No more bombs being made on the premises and things getting back to how they used to be.' Jane sat back and smiled. 'But you didn't hear a thing from me. It's just that Emma, Seebohm's secretary, said that he's been talking a lot to them in charge, and she's been writing to them as well.'

'Mmm. It's a good job Emma doesn't work for the government – she'd never be able to keep a secret.' Rose gave Jane a meaningful look. 'But it would make sense. I think the war is going our way now, and from what my sister was saying, there's a stockpile over at the munitions plant. Although the way they are bombing Germany at the moment, it will soon be used. It would be wonderful if they did move all munitions down south and we got back to normal.'

'Well, Emma said they're talking of inventing new brands once the munitions factory is closed. She just listens in to things, but she doesn't know much about what is actually going to happen,' Jane said. 'I'm surprised that you don't know all this.'

'They wouldn't tell me any of this, Jane; I'm not a member of the board and I've no money involved in the running of the firm. That is strictly limited to the Rowntree family. I'm just an employee like you, but I'm extremely grateful for my position. They also appreciate my loyalty and my ability not to gossip about what goes on in the firm. If you want to get on in the firm and to stay with Rowntree's, it would be good for you to do the same.'

Jane blushed. 'Yes, Mrs Evans. Sorry, it's just you did ask.'

'I did, and I appreciate you telling me, but don't let it go any further until the board announce something.'

It would certainly be a relief to have Rowntree's up

and running at both plants, if the rumour were true, but it would also mean more work. Molly and Connie would be glad of the news, although since Molly got the position of overseer at the munitions plant she would find it hard to go back to just making chocolate boxes. She had thrived on being put in charge of people and had surprised all the family by her progress since getting the job. As for Connie, she was still a law unto herself, and if Chuck asked her to go with him back home to America, then she wouldn't be seen for dust.

Molly and Connie were just two out of hundreds – what would become of all the workers that had been taken on, like the Polish, Italian and Indian? There was going to have to be a lot of planning and work before things got back to normal, whatever the meeting that afternoon was about.

Rose walked around the factory, going from department to department. Upstairs in the top offices the board meeting was in progress, kept in line by George Harris, now Company Chairman, who had been key in keeping the brand of KitKat and the chocolate dragée going, even through the toughest of the war years. He was married to Seebohm's cousin Friede, which meant the firm was still in the family's hands. It was common knowledge that Seebohm was starting to take a back seat now that age had finally crept up on him.

On her way through the dragrée department, Rose stopped to talk to her friend Mary, as she checked the chocolate levels.

'Here, Rose, what's going on upstairs? All the big nobs are in, and some of them have even walked in here and asked how things are going and do we have any problems with supplies. They're up to something. I hope they aren't thinking of closing this section down. I've just got Joe Junior off to school and I really need my job until his dad comes back from the war.'

'Sorry, Mary, you know as much as me, although I have a feeling that you don't have to worry about the chocolate side being closed down. This half of the firm will keep going, I can tell you that much. Hitler's pack of U-boats aren't as active now, and our lads are getting through with supplies, so our sugar supplies are getting a little easier to secure.'

Rose wanted to tell her best friend that things might soon get back to normal but didn't dare, just in case Jane had been gossiping without knowing the facts. Chocolate production had been hit hard with the onset of war, since the ingredients were no no longer available to make the fancy brands that had caught people's eye pre-war. She was just thankful that they had managed to keep producing the brands that they had and so should Mary be.

'Oh well, I know that you would tell me if I had anything to worry about. It's just with Joe still at sea and my father not getting any younger, then I need my job.' Mary sighed. 'How's Ned? Is he one of those that are taking part in these terrible bombings that we're giving Jerry?'

'I don't know, Mary, he never tells me where he's

scheduled for flying. All I can hope is that I see his face when he gets a chance to leave the base. He's been away quite a few days, but I suppose no news is good news as they say.' Rose looked grave. 'I read about the bombings in the paper this morning, it sounded as if there wasn't much left of Dresden. You can't help but feel for the innocent people, but at the same time the Nazis will be trying their best to kill my man, who is just doing his job.'

'Both our men will come home safe, I just know they will,' Mary urged. 'Now, this doesn't get work done, does it? I'd better leave you and get on with mine, else folk will think I'm getting away with blue murder for being friends with you. You know how it is?' Mary touched her friend lightly. They were the best of friends outside work, but within it was best not to show it.

'Yes. Give my love to your father and little Joe, I can't believe he's at school already.'

Rose caught sight of members of the board walking down the stairs – the meeting must have come to an end. 'Got to go.' She nodded her head in the direction of the group of suited men making their way through the busy work areas, stopping occasionally to look at the process of making chocolate drops from the chocolate left over from producing KitKats.

Rose walked towards the group and smiled.

'Good afternoon, gentlemen. Everything to your satisfaction, I hope?'

'Good afternoon, Mrs Evans,' Arthur Bracken replied. 'Yes, all looks in order as ever on your watch. We've had a good meeting, and I'm sure you will be informed about our decisions shortly. The Rowntree name will be going from strength to strength. Of that we are all in agreement, aren't we, gentlemen?' Arthur Bracken rested his thumbs in his waistcoat pockets and looked around him at his fellow colleagues, who all muttered in agreement.

'Aye, on that we can agree. George Harris is full of good ideas, not unlike your good man used to be,' one of the older members of the board commented. 'It's a pity he left us. I bet he regrets it since the war has grown out of all recognition. We would have made sure that he did not get conscripted, on ethical grounds.'

Rose held her head up. 'Ned is doing what he thought he had to do and risks his life every time he takes to the skies. He's doing so out of the love of his country and for the freedom of us all.'

'Yes, we know, Mrs Evans, and we appreciate his valour. It's just a pity the world has had to endure the evil atrocities of a man like Hitler. But his time is nearly at an end, God willing,' Arthur Bracken said. 'Do give Ned our fondest wishes and tell him that he will always be welcome here at Rowntree's.' He tipped his bowler hat and then urged the group of directors on to the next department, discussing their latest ideas for the survival of Rowntree's.

Rose watched them leave. Whatever Arthur Bracken said, they had no idea how her husband risked his life every time he went into the air – or perhaps they did but couldn't dare to think about it.

*

'Rose, is that you back?' Ivy shouted as she heard the front door close.

'Yes, I'm back, Mother. Are you all right?' Rose walked into the front room, pulling the head square from her head and untying her coat belt. 'Has Ned been home? Please tell me he's been home.'

'No, not heard a word all day, but the neighbours have been in and they've been telling me all about the bombing raids over in Germany. I've worried myself sick all day. Do you think that he's taken part? It's the not knowing what is going on that makes me feel sick all the time.' Ivy held her handkerchief to her mouth, trying not to cry.

'Probably, Mam, but as they say, no news is good news. I just wish he would send a message to say he's safe. If we had the telephone in the house, he could call and let us know. I've been thinking for a while now that we need to have one installed. It is so expensive, but I'm sure it would pay its way in giving us reassurance when we talked to Ned at the base and you could ring me up at work. Not too often, mind.'

'Now, that's a thought. Let's do it. I've some savings, we'll get it out of that. My lad needs to ring home and talk to his mother and wife.' Ivy sat back in her chair. 'Everything's changing and I don't know if I can keep up with it all. I think that it's time for these old bones to be put to rest.'

'Oh Ivy, don't say things like that.' Rose gathered up the tray she had left beside Ivy for her lunch, then paused. 'Was that the front door? Or am I hearing things?'

'What are you moaning about, you old devil? There's life left in you yet.' Ned had sneaked in, and now he stood in the doorway and gazing at the two women in his life.

'Oh, Ned, you are home!' Rose abandoned the tea tray and went and flung her arms around him.

'Yes, I'm home, my love. I'm sorry if you've been worried.' Ned held Rose tight and kissed her, holding her like he had never held her before. 'Oh, I'm so glad I'm home. It's been so hard, these last few days, I just had to keep thinking of my return.'

He went and kissed his mother, then took a deep breath before continuing, 'I have some bad news. Poor Peter is reported as being missing over Germany. I'm hoping that he bailed out safely, but no one knows.'

'Oh, no, not Peter!' Rose stepped backwards, aghast.

'Yes, afraid so. I didn't see him go down, but he's not come back.' Ned sat down in the opposite chair to his mother and reached out to hold her hand as Rose sat on the chair arm next to him. 'I'm hoping to God he's all right and that he's safe somewhere. He'll probably be fine – the devil looks after his own. He'll probably have landed in a haystack and will be sitting eating cheese and sausage in a farmer's kitchen.' Ned tried to make light of his friend's plight as he noticed the worry etched on the faces of his new wife and mother. 'Now, what was this I heard you talking about as I lurked in the hallway? A telephone? That's a jolly good idea, in fact a wonderful idea, but you are not paying for it, Mother, I'll see to it.'

'We worry so much about you, lad. I bet that you've been to hell and back,' Ivy said quietly and wiped away a tear.

'I have, but as long as I have breath in my body, I will come back to you two, I promise you.' Ned pulled Rose down onto his knee and kissed her. 'It's good to be home. I'll always return, Rose, I love you so much.'

'As I do you, my love.' Rose looked into his eyes and cupped his face in her hands as she kissed him and completely forgot about his mother watching them both.

7

'Well, I don't know what's going on, but something is,' Molly said, linking her arm through Connie's as they walked out of the munitions factory on the last shift of the week.

'I hope it's nothing terrible, because I'm going to say that I'll take that flat above the bakery this weekend. Chuck seems to think it will be a good idea, and it will mean that he can come and see me more often. I met him briefly but he was in a hurry outside the Roxie last night. He hasn't been able to get away from the base, they're so busy with the bombings. Oh Molly, I do think I love him. He held me so tight and kissed me so passionately; I stop worrying about if he loves me or not when I see him. It's only when I don't see him that I start thinking that he's losing interest in me. We'll be a lot closer if I get a flat of my own – you know, we'll be more private.' Connie sighed. 'I'll miss your mum's cooking, though, and I've wanted for nothing while I've lived with you.'

'You don't have to go,' Molly said, feeling crestfallen that Connie was making her own way in the world while she was still at home. 'Mam treats you as part of the family now. I'll miss you and all. You've just to say if you need the front room for Chuck to court you in, we would leave you be.'

'No, it's all right, it's time I left you. Anyway, don't be so soft. You'll get even more attention from your mother and I'm only a quarter of a mile away, if that – you can always come and visit. We can go to dances and even the pub and not have to pretend that we're sober when we come home.' Connie giggled. 'I might not have the luxury of your mam's, but I'll have my freedom.'

They turned into their street and Molly said a brisk 'Evening' to the fearsome ARP warden and then returned her attention to Connie. 'All right, when are you going to tell my mother? She'll be upset, you know.'

'I'll tell her tonight, when we sit down to supper.' Connie squeezed Molly's hand tight. 'Don't worry, you'll still see a lot of me. You're not getting rid of me that easy.'

'Well, I have known you've wanted somewhere of your own for a while, but I can't say that I'm not going to miss you because I am, and that's a fact.' Winnie looked at the lass she thought of as her own. 'Is it a decent place, clean and warm, no damp? There's nothing worse than a damp house.'

'It's over the bakery, halfway down the Shambles. It can't help but be warm – perhaps too warm in summer,' Connie replied and watched as Winnie tried to recall exactly where it was.

Winnie's face cleared. 'Oh, I know the one. Ye Olde Bakery, it's called; it brags of having baking just like your mother does. Not that it is anything like your mother's baking. If I remember rightly, they had a notice to change their mucky ways or get closed down if they didn't a while ago. Somebody had complained that there were weevils in the flour. But I don't know how they have gone on since then. It will be the Atkinsons that own it. Don't let them charge you too much!' Winnie reflected for a moment. 'Does it come with furniture? Don't accept their mattress if they give you one; it could be filled with bed bugs. There's a spare up in the loft from when Rose lived here, you can take that.'

'I'll be all right; don't you worry about me. But I will gratefully accept the mattress, if you're sure. The one that's on the bed now is made of striped ticking and looks stained. Thank you.' Connie smiled gratefully at Winnie and then shifted her gaze to Molly, grinning. 'Are you sure you're coming with me in the morning after hearing all that?'

'Yes, I'll come. I want to have a look around the bakery, see what it looks like inside, and spot any weevils or cockroaches just in case the place is crawling with them,' Molly said sarcastically and winked at her mother.

'You can joke, but they did get closed for just that. Mucky, I bet they are. You'd be better off staying here, you're no bother to me.' Winnie sighed. Not long ago, her table was surrounded by laughter, arguments and teasing from her girls. Now she was just going to be left with her youngest, and even she probably wouldn't be with her much longer if Matt returned from the war in one piece. 'I'll find you some bedding and some crockery, because I don't suppose you'll have anything like that. I've too much stuff, anyway. I could do with a clear-out.' Winnie blew her nose and collected the plates, taking them to the sink, not wanting the girls to see her crying. It was stupid of her. Connie wasn't even her daughter; she had just been taken into the family out of kindness.

The following morning, Molly and Connie made their way through York. It was a cold and grey day with only a few people doing their Saturday shopping along the streets.

'You can tell it's February. Everything looks so dreary, there's nothing in the shops and people are war weary,' Molly moaned as she pulled her coat around her and kept up with Connie's fast pace.

'Yes, I'm not moving in the best month of the year, but you have to grab a room when it comes up, and I can't chance missing it. Despite what your mother says about the Atkinsons, they seem right enough. The shop looks clean, although I've never been through into the bakery.'

'I'll grab a loaf of bread and take it home and then we can see what their baking is really like. Mam will make something of it, I'm sure. At least you'll not go hungry if you live over a bakery.'

They reached the narrow medieval street where Connie was going to make her home. The houses were made mostly in the Tudor style, with black beams showing through white plastered walls. 'I always like it here – it's bonny but a bit narrow,' Molly commented as they stopped outside the bakery. The large glass window was bordered by black paintwork and the plaque proclaiming 'Ye Olde Bakery' was painted in gold and red, making it look in keeping with the era of the building. Above the overhang of the shop, Connie's new home was in less good condition, looking a little neglected, but as both women knew, it was dry and warm, and that was all that mattered to Connie. She needed to prove to herself that she could make it in the world on her own, and this was the first step before changing her life after the war had finished, hopefully with Chuck. In the meantime, she and Chuck could have fun together in their own private space.

Molly and Connie entered the shop. The glass counter was clear, although there were plenty of bread, scones and biscuits on view underneath it.

'Morning, Mrs Atkinson, I'm back as promised. I've had time to think about it and I will take the flat above. In fact, I can't wait to move in.' Connie smiled across at the red-faced woman. 'I can pay my first week's rent right now if you want, although I can't move in until next weekend as I'm at work all week.'

'I thought you weren't going to come back at all. I said to my old man, we'll have to give it away at the rate we are going. We seem a bit down on our luck at the moment – no one except yourself is interested in the room and custom is so slow. It makes me wonder if it's worth my while getting up so early.' Despite her plump, rosy-faced look, Mrs Atkinson turned out to be a professional moaner, but perhaps she had every reason to be that way. She yelled to her husband who was back in the bakery, and he walked into the shop looking as miserable as sin and growling at her, wondering what she wanted.

'This lass is back; she's going to have the flat. Do you want to charge her now or do we start next week when she can move in?' Dora Atkinson asked her husband.

While Dora was round and tubby, Wilf Atkinson was gaunt with grey skin and tired eyes. He coughed and struggled to catch his breath before answering. 'Are you on your own – no fellas coming back and forward? And you'll have to put up with us starting baking early. I don't want any complaints now I've made it straight with you from the start.'

'I'm on my own and I have a boyfriend, but I don't see him much. As for early mornings, it won't bother me. I work at Rowntree's on shifts and leave for work early.'

'You mean, you are a canary – both of you are, with skin like that. You don't make chocolate. It's a wonder we aren't blown to smithereens because of that bloody munitions factory.' Wilf Atkinson held onto the counter and caught his breath. 'Half board this week and then you can come back and forward with stuff when you want to. Then it's full board next week, six shillings a week and a shilling for the gas light. I'll get you a rent book, to keep things straight.' Wilf wiped his hands on his apron then went back into the bakery, coughing.

'He's bad with his lungs, the flour has got onto them over the years. Today is a good day if you can believe it; some days he can't catch his breath at all.' Dora Atkinson shook her head. 'Well, it sounds like you're our new lodger. I'll give you the door key and you drop the money in when you're ready, although to be honest I could do with it now. Like I said, trade isn't so good at the moment.' Dora looked downhearted. 'Times might be hard, but they don't seem to want to buy our bread.'

Connie grinned at Molly. 'Then it's no problem; I can give you three shillings if you can give me the key. This is my best friend Molly – she came and looked around with me last time and I've brought her again this morning. I'm hoping that she will make me some new curtains for the window. Would that be all right?'

'Aye, you can do all the changes that you want as long as you pay us the rent on time,' Dora said. She passed Connie the ancient key for the upstairs rooms, taking the three shillings from Molly. 'So you work for Rowntree's? It's a bit of a mixture down there, munitions and chocolates. I don't think I could work there, but I suppose you get used to it.'

'Yes, and we are all doing our bit for the war, in whichever department we work in,' Molly said. 'My sister looks after the production of Jungle Chocolate, for the troops abroad, so we all do our bit for the lads between us. You have to, haven't you?'

'I suppose you do. Now I've to get on with my work. A rent book will be ready for you next time you call in.

Now, you can come and go as you please and we will leave the place to you.'

Dora felt relieved. Ever since someone had found those bugs in their bread, nobody had been giving them trade. At least now with some rent coming in there would be a bit of money in their coffers.

'Don't you think the rent is a bit too much?' Molly asked as she followed Connie up the stairs and looked around her at the state of the flat that her best friend was going to rent. The last time she had been there she had seen it by gaslight, but now, in the true light of day, it was shabby and needed a lot of care to be spent on it.

'No, given a bit of love and some new curtains, it will look nice and warm. It just needs some time and care spending on it. At least it isn't damp, and just smell the air. It's full of freshly made bread.' Connie smiled. 'It will be a place of my own. Much as I love living with you and your mam, I need my own place.'

'I don't know about freshly made bread, it all looked a little stale and there wasn't one customer in the shop,' Molly countered. 'My mam was right about that; nobody wants to eat bread with weevils in it. It's a pity, it could be such a lovely shop. I stood and looked around it while you were talking. It could really make money if it was given a bit of love. And the same goes for this room. You do need some new curtains – these have more holes than material. We have a spare pair of blackout curtains underneath the stairs at home, I know we do. Those will be the first thing you need to go up.'

'Yes, and I'm grateful for your mam's offer of a fresh mattress; this one looks in an even worse state than I saw it last week.'

'I'll help you bring it here, we can both carry it. We can bring most stuff between us. At least you have a table and chairs so we don't have to lug any of them here.' Molly sat down on one of the chairs and blew the dust off from the top of the table. 'You're going to need some elbow grease to get this place looking like anything like a home. No wonder nobody wanted to rent it.'

'It will be right,' Connie said breezily, 'don't you worry. I can entertain my Chuck here – that is when he's not too busy! It wasn't fair on your mother to expect her to put up with our courting.' She stood at the window and rubbed one of the small square panes to clear the dirt.

'She doesn't mind. She's courting herself, anyway, so she can't say anything.' Molly sighed. 'There's only me who doesn't have a fella as such. I hardly ever hear from Matt; at least you see Chuck sometimes. I sometimes think I should write and tell Matt that our friendship is going nowhere, but then I remember how much he loves me, he says so when I do get his occasional letters. So I don't want to hurt him, especially when he's over there fighting.'

'Your mam's not courting, they're just friends. Don't do that with Matt. I know that he thinks the world of you, and you do him, even though you are miles apart.' Connie put her arm around her best friend.

'I'm just scared for him,' Molly said. 'I don't want to be like Rose, on edge all the time waiting for news of her man. I saw in the papers this morning about a battle at Bulge, it must be somewhere in Germany, and that's where he's fighting at the moment. Wherever he's at he will be blinking cold and up against it. Last time he wrote he said the Jerries had young lads fighting for them – just out of nappies, he said, and no fear.'

'Oh, Mol, he'll be fine. Stand by him, love. He will need you.'

'I know, it's just sometimes until I look at his photograph I forget what he looks like, it's been so long. At least Chuck is in this country,' sighed Molly.

'We are a right pair, Molly, but there are thousands like us all over the country, and the war will be won before long, hopefully.' Connie hugged her friend tightly.

'I know, but it's frightening, and sometimes I want to stop the world and get off.' Molly hugged Connie back. She was going to miss her.

8

Winnie sprayed some lily-of-the-valley perfume on and studied herself in the wardrobe mirror. She shook her head as she gently patted her hair in place. She was a silly old fond fool, she told herself as she leaned forward and checked that her lipstick wasn't too daring for a woman of her age. But Ralph was good company, and that was what she was short of, what with the girls working nights and two of them no longer at home. 'He's just a friend and we are having a bite to eat together and listening to the radio, that's all,' she said to her reflection in the mirror and smiled. 'Now, what's wrong with that? We are two people sharing each other's company.' But in her heart of hearts, she knew it was beginning to be more than that. She felt herself getting excited about Ralph's knock on the door, and tonight she had found herself putting on her best perfume and lipstick! She'd not felt as giddy as this since she first went out with Burt, her late husband. Now what would he think of all this? She closed her bedroom door behind her and went downstairs to make sure the corned beef hash wasn't burning on the top of the stove.

The kitchen table was set for two and the radio in the front room was playing some dance music, with the fire lit and welcoming. Winnie stirred the hash and moved her hips to the music. She hadn't felt like this for so long, but she knew her girls wouldn't be happy if they found out that things were getting serious between her and her new man. Guilt shot through her when she heard the front door knocker and at the same time her heart raced. How could she feel like this at the grand age of sixty? She wasn't a slip of a lass at seventeen, she should have more sense.

'Coming, Ralph!' Winnie shouted as she made her way along the hallway and patted her dress down before opening the front door. 'Quick, quick, come in. It's cold out there, come and get warm,' she said, pulling back the large chenille curtain that hung behind the front door to keep the cold from coming in and the light from getting out, and urged Ralph into her home.

'You're right there, Winnie. It is parky and it's as black as pitch; not a soul is out on those streets.' Ralph bustled his way into the house and breathed in. 'Bye, something smells good.' And he smiled.

'It's only corned beef hash. I couldn't get my hands on any fresh meat this morning. Corned beef seems to be all that we live on nowadays, and Molly hates it,' Winnie said as she held her hand out for Ralph's coat.

'I didn't mean the food, although that smells equally as good. I meant you, Winnie, such a lovely smell. It just matches these early flowering daffodils that I've grown in my greenhouse for you.' Ralph handed over a bag with some flowering bulbs that he had lovingly grown with Winnie in mind.

'Oh, Ralph, you are so good to me, and your flattery is much appreciated. I try my best. Now, come in, take your coat off and I'll put this lovely pot of daffodils on the kitchen table. They'll have plenty of light there and they will be warm.' Winnie's cheeks filled with colour as Ralph walked behind her.

'You deserve everything I bring you, Winnie. You have filled that gap in my life since my Sissie left me. I don't know what I'd have done without you.' Ralph put his hand in the small of Winnie's back as he spoke.

'I've done nothing, Ralph, just listened when you've wanted to talk as a friend should. We are both here for one another, and that's all that matters. Now, how has your week been?'

'Aye, quiet really, not been anywhere except for my shopping. Not much to do now, since I retired. I always think February is a dreary month. I can't get out into my allotment and it's too cold for walks. That's why I'm so grateful that you've asked me here tonight. I treasure my time with you, Winnie, I'll be honest.' Ralph touched Winnie's hand. She had taken his heart, if he only dared tell her.

Winnie wondered if she should say something about how she felt too, but in her day it was the man that made the first move. She didn't want him to think that she was a forward hussy, not at her age. 'I look forward to your visits, Ralph. We get on so well, and I love my lasses but I miss a man in my life.'

'Aye, I know, I miss Sissie too, but . . .' Ralph hesitated. 'The truth is, you can't keep loving a ghost forever. I don't like being on my own, and I'm so glad that I've got to know you.' He tried to dig up courage before coyly saying, 'Winnie, do you mind if I kiss you? I've wanted to for a while, but I didn't know how you'd feel about it.'

Winnie took hold of Ralph's hand and held it close. 'I couldn't think of anything I'd like more, but didn't want to show myself as an old fond fool.'

Ralph stepped forward and kissed Winnie lightly on the lips and then kissed her again as she held him close. 'There's no fool like an old one. But who cares, when we have one another?'

'Aye, we have that, lass. I think we can say we are courting now. But we won't tell your lasses just yet.' Ralph smiled and watched as Winnie stepped away and blushed.

'No, but they will have to know sometime, and they've started to comment already.' For a brief second, Winnie wondered if she was doing the right thing. Molly definitely had no time for the new man in her life, but she had to hope that she would eventually accept him.

Connie and Molly stopped for a second to rest with their load. It was Sunday morning and the Minster's bells were sounding out around the city as well as the other church bells. However, Molly and Connie had no time for church; they were lugging the mattress that Winnie had given to Connie for her new home above the bakery.

'I'm shattered, Connie. Let's just put it down for a minute.' Molly rested the striped mattress on the side of the pavement and watched as well-dressed people made their way to church.

'Come on, Mol,' Connie pleaded. 'Everyone's looking at us. And it's that cold I want to get it on my bed before it gets damp.'

'Just give me a second to get my breath,' Molly said grumpily. 'We're going to be going back and forward all day as it is with all your stuff. But I'm not complaining, as that blinking Ralph is coming around for his dinner and he'll probably be staying most of the afternoon. Why my mother had to ask him on my only day off, I don't know.' Eventually she picked up her end of the mattress and helped Connie to pull it along the street.

Connie put the key into the lock when she got to the door that led up to her flat on the second floor. It felt cold. There was no warmth from the bakery, with it being Sunday, and instead of it smelling of freshly baked bread the room smelt musty as they dragged the mattress in to replace the old stained one.

'I'll take these old curtains down. Mam has found the pair for you, but she needs the curtain hooks from these if they have any.' Molly reached up to the curtains and started to unpin them from their hooks. 'Somebody must have taken some pride in living here else there would just have been a bit of tape holding them up,' she said. 'These are no good for keeping the light in. You can nearly see through, and I tell you what, the windows look dirtier than ever, and just look at the cobwebs!'

Connie grabbed a brush from the corner of the room

and started sweeping the floor. Dust flew up all around them and Molly was tempted to open the window but knew the cold air would not be welcome in the already parky flat.

'The muck in here is nobody's business, although look, it is starting to look better already. In fact, the oil-cloth on this floor doesn't have any holes or tears in it, and with new curtains up at the window and the rug I bought off the rag-and-bone man on the market, it will start looking like home.' Connie leaned on the brush and beamed. 'I'll be snug as a bug in here when I get all my knick-knacks together and start making it like a real home.'

'I'd choose my words more carefully than snug as a bug, seeing that they've had weevils in the flour. You don't know what might be lurking behind these skirting boards and walls.' Molly grinned. 'But yes, if there are no creepies, then you will be all right here. It looks better already. I'll finish taking these down and then we'll go and have dinner with my mam and Ralph and play gooseberry.'

'He's all right is Ralph, he's just lonely like your mam now we're all at work. He'd brought potatoes, leeks and some Brussels sprouts, I noticed, so that is one consolation of your mother having him as a friend. He comes bearing goods from his allotment.' Connie put her head down and continued brushing out every inch of her room as Molly put the curtain hooks in her pocket and folded the thin curtains up into the throwing-out pile for the rag-and-bone man along with the soiled mattress. Everything was recycled; what was one person's rubbish was a boon for another. Any rags were sold on to make shoddy, which was partly how the rag-and-bone man made his living.

Molly picked up a cloth duster and polish and applied a great deal of elbow grease to polish the few items of furniture as she continued to complain about Ralph.

'I don't care, he'll never replace my father, and I'm going to make that clear to my mam. He thinks he can creep his way into our lives, well, he has another think coming.' Molly stood and looked around her. 'It looks better already, but we'd better get back else there will be no dinner left for us two, the way he eats.'

'Molly Freeman, you are not showing yourself in a good light. You should be thankful that your mother has found somebody at her age. Instead, you just moan about her, and yet it's quite clear that she has got a wiggle in her step since Ralph has started visiting. I would be glad that she is happy – after all, if Matt comes back and you start courting, she'll be left on her own if you decide to get married.'

Connie swept the dust and dirt into one heap, then picked up some newspaper which she dipped in vinegar and used to clean the windows, wiping each pane vigorously until it glistened clean.

'I don't think Matt will ever ask me to marry him. We only write to one another, it's not like you and Chuck. When Chuck can get time away, he does at least come to see you. I bet he'll never be away now that you have a place of your own.' Molly sighed. 'I'm just worried that if my mam does decide to do something daft and remarry, she'd throw me out, and then what would I do?'

'You're an idiot, Molly Freeman. Your mam would never throw you out and you know it. Now come on, let us go home, sit and be polite while your mam and Ralph play footsie under the table, and then we'll come back with the bedding and your mam's curtains and that pegged rag rug which I am so happy I bought from the rag-and-bone man. It will look just grand on the floor there. Then next week, I'll get some shopping in, or what I can with my ration book. Your poor mam's going to miss my contribution to the shopping. Hopefully the rationing won't go on for much longer.'

'I'm going to miss you and all, I've never been on my own at home. I've got used to our Rose and Annie not being around, but I'm going to be totally on my own when you leave.' Molly felt as if she was being left behind while everyone else made their own lives.

'Don't be so daft. You know you can come around here anytime, and Rose always makes you welcome and you know it.' Connie flicked a duster at her. 'Now stop feeling sorry for yourself and let's get a move on, else all the sprouts will have been eaten or will have been boiled to mush. We'll all have to fight over the piece of belly pork as it is. Your Annie would probably turn her nose up at it; she'll be used to the best cuts with living on a farm. I know it's a cheap cut of meat, but your mam makes it so good.'

'That's the other reason Ralph comes, to fill his belly,' Molly said primly, pulling on her coat.

'Stop moaning! Come on, I'm hungry, and we can put up with Ralph for an hour.'

'So, you girls are back, are you? I was just telling Ralph that you're moving out, Connie, and that I'm going to be lost without you. It's a good job Molly isn't going anywhere fast, else I would be lost.' Winnie pulled up her chair at the dinner table and looked round at everyone.

'Aye, Winnie was just saying that you had set yourself up with somewhere to live. I've told her that will give her more time for herself and not to worry, we can soon find things to do together.' Ralph gave Winnie a knowing look and Molly noticed a slight blush come to her mother's cheeks.

'I'll still be here, and Annie will come back when she gets leave, so you aren't on your own, Mam,' Molly said quickly, staring at Ralph.

'I know I'm not, love. And I'm hoping to be a grandmother soon, if Rose and Ned are blessed. But happen not yet, until the war ends. It's no good bringing a child into a world in turmoil like it is – although if one comes, it comes.' Winnie sighed. 'Now, enough talk, let's get this dinner eaten. I know there's not a lot of meat, but Ralph's veg makes it a real treat.'

'There's plenty more where that came from and in another month, I'll start to turn my allotment over and will be planting all sorts. I'll keep you supplied all summer, Winnie my love.' Ralph smiled and then tucked into his dinner. He'd missed his wife's dinners and was glad that he had his feet under the Freemans' table.

'Connie and I are going as soon as we've had this, Mam. We're taking another load of things to her flat. Do you have the curtains ready? I've got the hooks in my coat pocket. We'll get out of your way and make Connie's flat more of a home.'

Molly felt her life was mundane compared to Connie's. Nothing new was happening for her, unlike everybody else. Every day it was go to work, get on with production of the shells, watch for any irregularities in production, grab lunch when able and then go home to bed and supper. It was monotonous.

'Yes, we've had a good tidy-up before and we'll take some more of my stuff back this afternoon,' Connie said. 'I'm so grateful for the curtains, Mrs Freeman; I wouldn't want the blackout wardens after me as soon as I move in.' She looked anxiously at Molly. She was going to have to get used to Ralph being around her mother. Anyone could tell that there was a quiet romance taking place between them.

'Bloody allotment, bloody vegetables, I'll keep you well stocked, Winnie. He's creeping around my mother – next thing you know, they'll be getting married,' Molly moaned as they lugged the second lot of Connie's belongings through the quiet Sunday streets.

'She might not marry him; she might take him in as a lodger,' Connie said, making Molly even more angry.

'Over my dead body! If he comes and lives with us, I will leave and you will have a lodger.' Molly lugged the eiderdown and sheets that her mother had given them up the stairs and put them on Connie's bed. 'Two of us could fit into this bed at a squeeze.'

'Two might, but I wasn't thinking of sleeping with you. I had other ideas,' Connie said with a grin and put the folded blackout curtains on the table.

'Connie Whitehead, you'll get a reputation if you have Chuck staying here regularly. Folk will talk!'

'Chance would be a fine thing. Like I said, I never hardly see him. Apart from when we go to the pictures or snatch a meeting in between us both working. Of course you can come and stay whenever you want, but not too often as that bed is very small. Perhaps I should keep an eye out for a double bed, it would make a lot more sense.' Connie didn't want to upset Molly too much – after all, she was her best friend. However, she had no intention of sharing the bed with Molly: it was to be for her and Chuck. She was hoping that she would see a lot more of him now that they had their own space.

9

Annie lay back in Mike's arms and studied the crack running the length of the bedroom ceiling which was becoming more visible in the grey morning light.

'This place needs a lot of money spending on it, Mike. I'm not surprised that Bernard and Lizzie want to sell it.' Annie had been giving the situation a lot of thought. 'Trouble is, it will mean me finding a new placement, and I love this place and I love you.' She sighed and cuddled up tighter to him. Even though Lizzie would soon be setting in motion the business of selling the property, they were trying to stay with one another as long as they possibly could.

'Aye, I don't quite know what to do,' Mike said. 'But I'll tell you this, I'm damned if I'm going to lose either of you. I think I'll have a word with Bernard this afternoon before he goes to the bank in Clitheroe. I've been thinking of a way to perhaps solve all our problems. That is, if Bernard and Lizzie will be patient with me and just wait a bit while I see what I can do. I don't want them to lose the house they have set their heart on, though.' He turned on his side and reached for his pack of Woodbines and matches and lit one. They both watched the smoke that he exhaled disappear into the cold bedroom air.

‘What are you thinking of doing, Mike? I wish I could help.’ Annie watched as Mike got up and pulled his shirt and trousers on, yanking his pullover over his head, then sitting on the edge of the bed to put on his socks.

‘I’m not going to tell you anything, Annie, not yet, not until Bernard and Lizzie hear what I’m thinking of doing. It’s only fair that they hear it first and that I don’t raise your hopes. It will change our lives, if I do what I’m hoping, I can tell you that. But for now, I’d better make myself scarce. I’ve to plough the tattie fields today, ready for planting, in the hope that it will be us harvesting them this autumn. That will show the old bugger how serious I am.’ Mike stood up and looked down at the lass who had stolen his heart. He didn’t want to lose her. It was time to make decisions.

He bent down and kissed her before walking out of her bedroom and going downstairs to put his boots on.

‘I heard you getting up. You forget that the outhouse is under Annie’s bedroom, my lad.’ Lizzie took Mike by surprise as she walked out of the pantry carrying a handful of kindling. She gave him a knowing look as she knelt down and added them to the dying embers of the previous evening’s fire. ‘You’ll get caught out if you’re not careful, so I hope that you think something of her,’ Lizzie said sharply, as she blew softly into the fire to make a spark catch on the dry sticks.

Mike reached for his jacket from the back of a kitchen chair. ‘I do, Aunt Lizzie. I’m not taking advantage of her. We do think a lot of one another; it’s just that

I've never got on with telling her exactly how much I think of her. I'm a bit shy of becoming a married man; it brings a lot of responsibilities with it.'

'Aye, well, the way you are both carrying on you will be walking down the aisle before you know it with a baby on the way. I'm thinking that it's perhaps time to settle down, Mike, and stand by Annie. She's a grand lass.' Lizzie added some small pieces of coal to the flames and then stood up and wiped her blackened hands on her apron.

'Leave me be, Aunt Lizzie, we both know what we're doing. I'm off to check over the tractor. I'm going to make a start on ploughing today, but I need to talk to you and Uncle Bernard before you go into Clitheroe. I've something to ask you both. And I do love Annie, it's just me who needed a kick to make me act.'

Lizzie's light blue eyes had a way of looking into your soul when she wanted them to, and this morning was no exception. 'Oh, happen, my lecture has done some good?' She shook her head. 'I blinking hope so.'

'You'll have to wait and see, I'm saying nowt until I can talk to you both. You needn't go quizzing Annie, because she doesn't know what I'm going to be saying either. So you will have to wait.'

Mike pulled on his cap and walked out into the fresh morning air. The frost on the fell side of Pendle glistened in the rising sun as he crossed the yard to the beast of a tractor that the War Ag had persuaded Bernard to buy, even though he couldn't drive it and was in no way inclined to be mechanical. It was a good job that the army had not wanted him back. He bent down next to the grey Fordson tractor that had made life so much easier on Pendle Farm and filled it with red derv, ready for the work he was to do that day.

The tattie fields were ploughed in no time, not like when a horse and harness were used. Progress needed to come even faster to Pendle Farm, he thought. He watched Annie come out of the farmhouse and make her way to the pig pens. He did love her, he wasn't using her, and hopefully by the end of the day he could tell her just what she meant to him.

Annie filled up the trough for the farrowing sow to eat from. Soon there would be ten or more young piglets feeding from her, all pink and sweet with their tails wagging as they took milk from their mother. This was the time of year that Annie loved, new life on Pendle Farm and the warmth of the coming spring to look forward to. She had never thought, in the days when she had been boxing chocolates up at Rowntree's factory, that she would be here, slop bucket in hand, taking delight in a big fat sow about to give birth. It was such a pity Bernard and Lizzie were going to sell up – unless a miracle happened, she would be leaving Pendle Farm by summer. Leaving her heart at the farm along with Mike, who she hoped would not wash his hands of her when he went back to his own smallholding as well as getting a job to keep the wolf from the door.

She looked across to the implement shed where Mike was busy checking the tractor and plough. He obviously had a plan, but he wouldn't tell her anything. He was like that, keeping things to himself, even when it came to the way he felt about her. He was good at gestures but not with words – typical northern man, she thought, as she moved on to the next pen. Whatever he was going to do, it sounded as if it had implications for the farm and all involved with it.

Bernard, Lizzie and Mike sat in the front room of Pendle Farm, the door closed behind them. This was obviously family business that needed to be discussed, Mike had made that clear over the breakfast table. It had all left Annie feeling a bit miffed as she was told by Bernard to bed down the latest family of piglets while business was sorted, and the three of them walked into the house when the grandfather clock struck ten.

'Now, what's this all about, our Mike?' Bernard said. 'You've been skulking around ever since I told you Pendle was going to be up for sale. You know that I can't do anything about it, and I know that you've always loved it here.' Bernard could tell that his nephew needed to get something off his chest.

'I don't know where to begin. You are either going to love me or never talk to me again – especially Aunt Lizzie. It's her I should have been straight with from the beginning of all this.' Mike chose his words carefully, addressing the couple who had virtually brought him up as their own.

'Well, get on with it, lad, we'll let you know where

you stand when you've got us told your tale.' Bernard had a worried look on his face as he glanced at Lizzie.

Mike lowered his head and clasped his hands. 'When I first enlisted, I feared that I might never make it back home alive. Mother and Father had left me the family farm, but I thought there wouldn't be much point in me leaving it empty and neglected, with me perhaps being buried in an unmarked grave. I just thought that I genuinely would not return, so I decided to sell it. I know I should have said, but I couldn't bring myself to tell you both.' Mike caught his breath, dreading the shock he would find on his aunt and uncle's faces. 'Stockdale hasn't been mine for nearly six years, but I never dared tell you, because I thought it would upset you. Especially you, Aunt Lizzie, as it was originally your family home, like Pendle is yours, Uncle Bernard. I've had no home but here ever since I got injured. This is my only home and I hope not to have to leave it.'

Lizzie wiped a tear away from her eyes, remembering the days of her youth at Stockdale, the dairy farm near Whalley. 'We thought that you had rented it out to them at Borins Farm next door. Especially when you used to say, "I'll just pop over and see how things are doing at Stockdale" and disappear for a day. You never said a word to either of us; we never had an inkling of what you had done. Why did you do that? Your parents left you that farm so that you would have some security. That's why we thought you had rented it to someone you knew.' Lizzie didn't know whether to feel sorry for Mike or to be angry.

'Like I said, I didn't think I'd be coming back,' Mike said awkwardly. 'I thought I'd be dead on some battlefield, but instead, I got injured and so I've been living with you both ever since. Plus, I got a good offer from the farmer at Borins and it made me quite wealthy. I went back and stopped with my old neighbours a night or two, as I knew that you thought it was being farmed by them in my absence. I was always made welcome by them.'

'How much did you get for it, lad, and what have you done with the money?' Bernard asked. 'Not wasted it, I hope? Not that you go anywhere to waste it.'

'I would have liked to have known my family home had been sold. There might have been one or two things of my mother's that I would have liked out of the house,' Lizzie added sharply.

'I got a good deal and I've not touched a penny of it, so it's been making interest in the bank. Which leads me to my next confession.' Mike took a deep breath. 'I'd like to buy Pendle, if you will let me. I think that I have enough and it would save you crawling to the bank, and you'll be able to buy that terraced house outright, cash in hand.' Mike took in the surprise on both of their faces. 'I've been thinking about it ever since you said you were having to sell, but I didn't know whether I dared tell you what I'd done.' Mike's stomach was churning and his heart was beating fast; he had deceived the two people he loved the most after losing his parents. However, he was hopeful that his suggestion would be helpful and outweigh any hurt that he had inflicted on them.

'Bloody hell, you're a sly one, Mike, we had no idea.' Bernard paused, taking it all in. 'I can't believe what you've just said. And you say you can afford to buy us out? That you'll offer us a decent price and take it on as it stands? What do you think, Lizzie?'

Lizzie shook her head. 'I don't know what to say. I'm flabbergasted.'

Bernard brightened as he took in the implications of Mike's offer. 'It would work out grand, lass. You'd not have to bother about folk coming around viewing, and I'd know that I wouldn't have to sell all my pigs. It was going to break my heart.'

'I don't know; I need time to think about it. It does seem a solution to everybody's problems, but it's a shock. I can't quite believe what you've told us.' Lizzie was finding it hard to forgive her nephew for being underhand with her. Why hadn't he told her that he had sold the family farm?

'It's what you wanted, woman, a smaller place in Clitheroe and less work, and your Mike gets to live here, which is what we both wanted. Just as long as he comes up with the money.' Bernard sat back in his chair.

'One thing, lad, if you take on here, you do right by Annie. Either leave her be or get wed.' Bernard had seen what was going on underneath his nose and decided to let it run its course without his interference, but now things were different. If Mike was going to farm Pendle, then it was time he got married to the Land Army lass who had lost her heart to him and the farm.

'Well, yes, that's the next thing I've set my head to do, but I don't want her to know until I've bought this place,' Mike said. 'I do love her, but first I want to have a home to give her, and I know she loves it here. You'd never think that she used to make chocolate in York. She's a farmer now.' He grinned.

Lizzie's face cleared. 'By heck, Mike, you are a deep one, but I've always thought a lot of you. If you are going to be right with that lass that loves you, then I'll wish you well, and like Bernard says, as long as you take care of Pendle, I'll be happy that it belongs to you. It does work out right for us all, especially that slip of a lass. She'll love keeping my house clean and tidy, but it will never look as good as I have it.'

Lizzie realized that it didn't matter that she didn't have some of her mother's knick-knacks – there were more than enough for her new terraced house in Clitheroe already, and she wouldn't have the smell of pig muck every day in her house. Bernard was right; Mike buying Pendle Farm would be a weight off their shoulders and they could go and buy their retirement home without any worries.

She smiled warmly at her nephew. 'Thank you, Mike. We'll have to sort all the legal stuff out, but think of Pendle as being sold and still in the family.'

Mike knew his Aunt Lizzie was disappointed in him for not telling her earlier that he had sold the farm, but he could see that she had been completely won round by his proposal.

'I think you should talk to Annie now,' Lizzie

continued, 'tell her what we have decided upon. She will only think that something is going on behind her back otherwise. It'll be news for her family – I hope that they will be happy for her.' Lizzie sighed. 'I've never met them. They've never been here, even after all these years.'

'Do you think I should? I must admit, she's been wondering what's been wrong with me of late, although I have let slip a thing or two. I just didn't know how everybody would take my news and I was worried about how I was going to tell you two. I'll go and tell her how I feel now, tell her I'm buying this place and propose.' Mike swallowed hard. His days of being a single man were at an end, but he wouldn't have it any other way.

'Aye, lad, everyone knows that she loves you – you can tell that even though neither of us have ever commented. Go and do it now, while she's out there on her own,' Bernard urged.

'Take her somewhere a bit more romantic than out in the yard, lad,' Lizzie recommended. 'This one here proposed to me over a pig trough. I've always remembered and thought what a spot, and that I should have known what I was in for.' She grinned as she walked around to her nephew and gave him a peck on his cheek. 'Go on, get what you want said to her. I forgive you for not saying that you'd sold my brother's farm, but I'll not forgive you if you don't look after this place or marry that lass.'

Mike's confession had come completely out of the blue, but she should have realized that he didn't show his feelings easily. After losing his parents, he wouldn't want to lose what he loved the most again: Annie and Pendle.

Mike walked out of the farmhouse feeling as light-headed as if he had drunk nine pints of the pub's best. An hour sat with his aunt and uncle and his life had turned around, not to mention theirs. However, now the biggest question had to be asked.

He found Annie strewing the bedding for the new piglets out in the pens.

'It's blinking cold this morning. Do you fancy a walk up Pendle to warm up? It might be frosty, but the sky is blue and we would soon warm up once we get walking.' There wasn't an ounce of doubt in Mike's mind as she turned around and grinned at him, running her hand through her dark hair.

'I think Bernard will have something to say if I just down tools and go walking with you.' Annie kissed him, wondering what had brought about his suggestion of a walk.

'No, he won't. They're not going to Clitheroe now, and I told him I was going to ask you to walk with me. Come on, it'll be grand up there this morning. Spring is on its way – let's get up there and look at it all while it's sparkling in the morning sun.' Mike pulled on Annie's hand. 'Leave them pigs, come on. Honestly, neither Bernard nor Lizzie will mind; they have too much to think about this morning.'

'I'm beginning to think that you've lost hold of your

senses,' Annie replied, but she didn't need to be persuaded any more as he took her hand and guided her out of the farmyard through the gate that led to the steep incline of the pastures.

'I think I have, but I'm hoping I'll be the happiest man in Lancashire once we get to the top of this hill.' Mike looked behind him down onto the farm that was shortly going to be his and the lass who was following behind him, rosy-cheeked and excited as she caught her breath and smiled at him.

'Mike, I don't know what this is about, but you are crackers.' Annie held his hand as they climbed to the summit of the sleeping giant of a hill and looked out at the valleys, sparkling and shimmering in the early spring frost. 'You are right, it is worth Bernard and Lizzie having words with me, just to see this.' Annie held her breath. The air was clear and sharp and hurt her chest when she breathed in, but the view was spectacular in all directions as she stood secure in Mike's arms.

'Annie, I couldn't think where to take you, but this is the place we both love, so it seemed fitting. Bernard and Lizzie won't be mad with you; they know what I'm about.' Mike gazed at Annie with love in his eyes and dropped to one knee on the white frosted hillside.

'Will you marry me, Annie Freeman? Will you be my wife and farm Pendle Farm with me? Because it is about to be mine – I'm going to buy it and I need you by my side.'

'Mike, you are joking! Pendle can't be yours and you can't be asking me to marry you, I can't believe it!' She paused, taking in his expression. 'You can't be serious; you've never even hinted anything like this!'

'I've no ring yet, but I mean every word and I've just agreed with Bernard and Lizzie to buy Pendle Farm. So please, Annie, say that you will marry me, else I'll be doing all this for nothing.'

Annie looked down at the man she had loved ever since she had met him on the train on her way to work at Pendle Farm nearly five years ago.

'I can't believe it, but yes, Mike, I would be honoured to marry you. I love every inch of you and always will. Now get up from off your knees, and I'm not worried about a ring. I love you with or without.'

Mike stood up, and as he did he picked a piece of frosted moorland grass that was covered with frozen sparkling dew and tied it around her ring finger.

'This will suffice for now, but a proper diamond is what I will buy you,' he said as he bent down to kiss her.

'This is worth more than any diamond, Mike; it is given with real love. I will never forget this moment.'

10

It was a frosty Monday morning in the middle of March as Winnie sat down and looked again at the letter that had just been delivered from Lancashire with the news that had shaken her morning. It had been posted nearly three days ago but had only just landed on the doormat.

She sipped her tea. Her Annie, the one with all the attitude and a mind of her own, was to get married. She had hardly mentioned this Mike when she had written home, let alone given a hint of a romance with him. Winnie put the letter down on her knee and gazed into the fire. Her Annie to marry a farmer – she shouldn't be surprised; she always had a wild streak and hated her job at Rowntree's. However, before her lass did get married, she wanted to see what exactly she was marrying into. Annie was always headstrong, and knowing her, he would be a character of some sort. Her description of the farm she was billeted at had left nothing to the imagination and now she was saying that she was to make the rest of her life there. 'Oh, our Annie, you always have been the one I worried about the most. You always were the headstrong one,' Winnie whispered.

It was no good, she was going to have to visit her daughter, see exactly what was going on. She would write a letter and put it in the afternoon post, telling

Annie that she would come up to Clitheroe to see her the following week. The visit was long overdue anyway – she should have visited the place ages ago in all honesty – but she was not one for travelling. Especially these days, when train tracks were easy targets for German bombers offloading unused bombs. Still, she would go and see what Mike and his family looked like and offer to help with the wedding. Winnie sighed. Another one gone, and a long way from home; she was going to be a lonely old lady if she wasn't careful.

Still, Molly would be at home for a good while longer yet. Her fella didn't write as much lately, and Molly didn't seem that bothered nowadays. Hopefully Connie would put her move on hold and stay with Molly until she returned; she would be company for her and that would work out well. But before writing her letter she would go and tell Ralph, see what he thought; he was her shoulder to lean on nowadays. Not yet used for crying on but she was sure he would be one day. She blushed at the thought that filled her head as she pulled on her thick winter coat, banked up the kitchen fire and put the fireguard up, before putting her second-best hat on and heading out to visit Ralph in Gladstone Way.

She walked quickly past the White Cross Hospital and looked up to Fossway – at least the River Ouse hadn't broken its banks and flooded the streets in the area that year. Sometimes it was impassable along Fossway, the river was so deep. She pulled her coat around her as she walked down the end of the terrace that led to Ralph's door. His street was much like hers but had the busy Huntington Road leading directly into Monkgate running past it, making it busy with people and traffic, talking and going about their business despite it being a cold March morning. She stood on the doorstep of Ralph's two-bedroom terrace and hoped that he'd be in. Looking down at the doorstep, she noted that it must not have been scrubbed since his wife had died and wondered whether to offer to do it. Then changed her mind as she heard Ralph coming to the door.

'Winnie, what are you doing here? You don't usually visit until a Friday. I was just pulling some leeks up in the back garden and wondering whether to bring them around for you.' Ralph stood on the doorstep looking sheepish and uncomfortable at his unexpected visitor.

'Never mind your leeks and your belly, Ralph, I've had some news and I'm just looking for your advice. Now, are you going to ask me in or what?' Her distress made Winnie speak sharply, but she managed to stop herself from pushing past him into the warmth of his back kitchen.

'Yes, come in. I've Mabel from next door in the kitchen; she just came for a bit of a banter when she saw me in the garden. Her Tom is at war and she gets lonely.' Ralph spoke quietly to Winnie as she pushed her way past him, giving him a questioning look.

Winnie walked into Ralph's kitchen and eyed the woman that was sat at his table. She was blonde and buxom and was older than she was trying to be made out to be.

'Who's this, Ralph? Is she your sister?' Mabel from

next door said and crossed her legs, looking hard at Winnie. 'You said you have an older sister, so it's nice to meet her.'

Winnie folded her arms and decided that she did not like Mabel from next door.

'No, Mabel, this is Winnie. We're just friends, she's come around to have a natter.' Ralph looked at Mabel. 'Perhaps I'll see you later, Mabel, your lass will be coming home from school for her dinner.' Ralph hoped that Mabel would get the message.

'Oh, you still have one at school. I thought you looked too old for that?' Winnie got her own back and smiled as if butter wouldn't melt in her mouth.

'I know when I'm not wanted. I'll get home. But don't forget my offer, Ralph. You know, any time,' Mabel stood up. 'Have fun.' And with that she walked down the hallway and out the front door.

'What did she mean by that, Ralph? She's a bit common.' Winnie wrinkled her nose at the smell of cheap perfume Mabel had left behind and sat down in her chair. 'If I didn't know better, I'd think she was a bit fond of you.'

'Oh, that's just Mabel, she's a bit of a one. Her mouth will be glad when she goes to sleep at night because she comes out with all sorts and never shuts up.' Ralph reached for the kettle and tried not to look at Winnie, hoping that she would not cotton on to the arrangement with his neighbour.

'Well, I'll tell you this right now, I don't like her,' Winnie said and folded her arms.

'No, I didn't think you would. She's just the opposite to you, my love.' Ralph smiled and sat down next to Winnie. 'Now, what's worrying you? I'm all yours.'

'It's our Annie; she's sent me a letter saying that she is to marry the nephew of the ones that she works for. It's come completely out of the blue. I think that I'd better go up and see her, Ralph, just to make sure things are all right. I don't know the first thing about him, but she seems to be happy there and fed well.' Winnie was hoping that Ralph would show her a bit of support.

'Well, you know best, Winnie. It's a long way to go, but you'll be all right. Is it a rushed wedding, did she say? It's just with it coming out of the blue, I thought there might be a reason for it.' Ralph saw Winnie's face cloud over.

'I don't know, she's not said, but she wouldn't, would she? I don't think they've even set a date or place to marry. Oh Ralph, I wonder if that is the reason. I hope not, I've always brought my girls up to behave and have respect for themselves no matter what.' Winnie sighed and looked around the kitchen. There was no sign of freshly dug-up leeks; perhaps they were still in the garden, she thought, as Ralph reached for her hands.

'I know you are a stickler, but as long as it makes them happy, does it really matter? You go and see her, Winnie, put your mind at rest, and I'll be waiting to hear your news when you return.'

'I came here for you to put my mind at rest and now you've made me even more worried. Perhaps I'm going to be a grandmother. I always thought Rose would be the one that made me that first, but perhaps not. Our Annie could have got herself in trouble, the silly head-strong lass.'

'Now, Winnie, you don't know until you've seen her. Stop fretting. It's good news that you have received. A wedding in the family, and she's to marry a farmer – she'll want for nothing.'

'He's a pig farmer, Ralph, not a lord or an earl. She will want for some things but perhaps not bacon or ham.' Winnie scowled.

'Well, I think she's blinking lucky, there's nothing better than a bacon sandwich,' Ralph replied with a grin and looked longingly at the empty frying pan hanging up on his kitchen shelf.

'You and your belly – it's all you ever think of, Ralph Parker. Now, I'll get home and write to tell her I'm coming down to see her. I just hope I get there and back safe and sound.' Winnie decided that she wasn't going to get much in the way of comfort with her new friend. 'I'll not be visiting on Friday, Ralph, too many things to do, and I'll not be here for Sunday dinner, so you'll have to make something with your leeks.' Winnie spoke sarcastically and turned to let herself out of the house, which still smelt of Mabel's cheap perfume.

'I'll miss you when you are gone, Winnie. You tell me as soon as you're home.' Ralph pecked Winnie on the cheek.

'I will, and you behave yourself. That Mabel is far too young for you; it'd take more than a handful of veg to keep her happy, you old fool,' Winnie looked hard at the fond old man. Had her Molly been right? Perhaps Ralph was chancing his luck with her and Mabel. She should have had more sense, she thought, as she picked up her pride and walked out, partly devastated and partly mad with herself.

'Don't know what you mean, Win, I've only got eyes for you, you know I have.'

'Aye, and my dinners. I'll see you when I'm back,' Winnie snapped. Ralph Parker was a fond old devil, but she had found herself liking him more and more lately. She should have known better. He was only interested in her to feed him and look after him; there wasn't much love, and that was beginning to hurt.

'Now Mam, you will be all right, won't you? I've never known you travel so far before.' Molly stood on the platform at York and watched as her mother climbed on to the train with an overnight bag and a basket with some home baking.

'I'll be fine, don't you worry about me. I'm more worried about leaving you and Connie on your own. At least Connie is going to stay with you until I get back. Now, there should hopefully be enough to eat in the pantry, and I'll be back before you know it.' Winnie closed the train door behind her and leaned out of the carriage window. 'I just need to put my mind at rest and see what this fella is like that Annie says she's to marry. He could be anybody, knowing our Annie; she never has had good taste when it comes to men.'

'Oh, Mam, she will be fine, she's often written about

him to me. Give her my love, won't you, and tell her we are all hoping to be asked to the wedding and that we can get time off from the war effort,' Molly yelled as the station master blew his whistle and the train built up steam.

'That's the other thing. I hope she doesn't think I can afford to give her a lot towards her wedding; I'm only just recovering from Rose's.' Winnie looked worried as she waved goodbye to Molly until she could no longer see her daughter standing waving on the platform, and the train made its way out of busy York station and into the surrounding countryside. She sat back in her seat and watched her fellow travellers, holding her belongings close to her and praying for a safe journey.

'Your mother could have given us a bit more warning. I've never had such a tidy-up in my life.' Lizzie stood with her hands on her hips and contemplated the cleanly scrubbed kitchen floor, thanks to Annie being on her hands and knees with a scrubbing brush while she had cleaned the windows and scrubbed the kitchen table. 'Her bed is made up and I've put an extra blanket on it – she'll not be used to our winters, towns are always warmer. Now, are you happy with everything, because we want to make a good impression. She's to know that we are good folk and that our Mike will be the perfect husband.' Lizzie was nervous; she had never met Annie's mother but thought that she would be posher than herself.

'Please, she's just my mam. She's not used to farm

life, but she's not a snob. I know now that you will both get on. I am surprised that she's visiting, though, she hates travelling. She'll be a nervous wreck until she gets here.' Annie sighed and checked around the kitchen, which now looked nearly acceptable. However, give it an hour or two and Bernard and Mike would be bringing half the farmyard in on their boots when they came back. Old habits die hard, but when she was in charge of the house there would be a different regime. Boots would be taken off at the door – little did Mike know.

'Aye, well, the fire is lit in the other room and it's all dusted. You know, you'd think it was the queen visiting the way I feel. I only hope she likes our Mike, else what are you going to do?'

'She'll like him, I know she will, and if she doesn't, it makes no difference, it's me that's marrying him.' Annie held her breath; she knew that she was going to get a grilling from her mother for not saying how close her relationship with Mike was. She hoped that Bernard and Lizzie would show a little decorum. 'We'll soon find out, because they're here now – that's the sound of the gig with Bernard and my mam in. She will be wondering what sort of home this is, knowing her.' Annie rushed to the farmhouse doorway and out into the cold, followed by Lizzie. She waved as the gig and its occupants pulled into the yard.

'Oh heavens, how good it is to see you! What a journey I've had.' Winnie slid along the seat of the gig and then lowered herself down gingerly with the help of Annie's hand. 'Folk forever on the train and I didn't realize that you lived so far out in the country and that it was so blooming cold.'

'This is nowt, lass, only a bit of hoar frost. Get your arse down and into the kitchen for a warm-up, and then you will be all right,' said Bernard as he climbed down and regarded the woman who was going to be the nearest thing to an in-law he was ever going to have. All she had done was comment on how cold it was and moan about the country smell. She was a townie, not used to the country.

'Oh Mam, it's lovely to see you. The train is always busy. Come on, come in. You've met Bernard, this is Lizzie, his wife.' Annie introduced Lizzie to her mother as they picked their way through the yard to the farmhouse doorway.

'Nice to meet you, Mrs Freeman. I hope you didn't take any notice of our Bernard; he doesn't edit what he's saying, bless him. He is more used to talking to his stock.' Lizzie gave Bernard a black look. He had been told before he went to the station to be polite, and already he was saying what he thought.

'Don't stand on ceremony, my name is Winnie, and yes, Bernard does say it as it is, but that's better than being mealy-mouthed. He's told me all about here and shown me the house which you are hoping to move into as we drove past. It's not unlike the one we live in at York, you should be happy there.' Winnie took in Lizzie's appearance: her hair was tangled and her cheeks were bright red; as for her dress, she would never have dared to walk out of the front door dressed like that in York. But these were farmers and she had been prepared for their lives to be different to hers.

'Well, I'm sorry, Winnie. You know what it's like, you can talk until you are blue in the face, but do these men listen?' Lizzie said as she ushered Winnie through the front door into the kitchen. 'Here, let me take your bags. Mike will take them to your room when he comes in; he's just finishing cleaning the pig pens out and then he will be with you.' Lizzie reached for Winnie's bags.

'There's some scones in that basket, I thought they might come in handy and I didn't know what else to bring. You seem from Annie's letters to have no problem with food like we do in York.' Winnie spoke quietly as Lizzie took the basket off her arm.

'Oh, Mam, they will be lovely. Here, give me your coat and we'll go into the front room. It's warm in there, the fire is lit and I'll put the kettle on.' Annie took her mother's coat and gave her a big hug and kiss as Bernard sat in his usual chair and proceeded to take his mucky boots off to reveal socks with more holes in than wool. Annie's heart was brimming over with the love she felt for her mother. She hadn't realized just how much she had missed her until she had seen her and smelt her usual violet perfume. She was here to give her blessing, and Annie knew that her mother must be feeling the loss of her and Rose.

'It's a good-sized kitchen, I wish mine was as big at home,' Winnie said, gazing around her. 'I bet you spend most of your time in here, a right home.' She looked at the pot board of the dresser which was weighed down with china, ornaments and letters that had come in the post only to be put to one side. The Yorkshire Range burnt bright and the kitchen table looked as if it had been cleaned in honour of her arrival, but nothing could make the smell of the pigs disappear. Yet Annie's face was happy, and she thought that as long as she was happy she'd not comment. 'If this is where you usually sit, then it will be right for me. Don't go out of your way to do anything different just because I'm here.' Winnie touched Lizzie's shoulder gently and pulled out a chair to sit upon around the table. 'Our kitchen is where everything gets discussed; I think that's what happens with all families, probably.'

Lizzie smiled. 'Aye, we are right proud that Annie is going to be part of our family. I only hope that you will feel the same way about us and that you will like our Mike – he's a good lad. He and Annie were meant for each other from the moment they clapped eyes on one another.'

Blushing, Annie sat across from her mother and watched her looking around the kitchen; she knew that she would be saying what she thought about it all once they were together in private. 'I do love him, I really do,' she said quietly.

'Well, out of all my girls, Annie was the one I never thought would settle down. She always had a bit of wanderlust in her blood, so your Mike must be special.' Winnie looked up as the kitchen door opened and in walked Mike himself. He wasn't how she had expected, even seeming a little reserved and quiet as he walked towards her.

Annie pushed back her chair and went and stood by Mike, linking her arm through his and holding his hand. 'Mam, this is Mike.' She smiled at the dark-haired man with so much love as she stood by his side, hoping that her mother would approve.

'So, young man, you want to marry my daughter, I understand?' Winnie smiled but tried to look serious at the same time.

'I do. I love her, Mrs Freeman. I knew that on the first day I saw her when she looked lost and lonely coming on the train to work here. It was fate that she came and worked for my uncle, and I even thank the Jerry that shot me and made me lame so that I could come home to her.' Mike faced the woman that Annie loved and respected, hoping that he would get a nod of approval.

'Well, she only has eyes for you, my lad, that I can see. But you've got to promise me that you'll look after her and look after her well. I expect her to be respected, and you make sure that she goes without nothing if you can.' Winnie noticed a quick glance from Annie and knew she was cringing, hoping that her mother would not pry too much into their affairs.

'I would put my life on the line for her, Mrs Freeman, and as for money, I'll make sure she wants for nothing. I've just agreed to buy the farm from Uncle Bernard and Aunt Lizzie, so this will be our home.'

'Annie said so in her letter to me. It must feel good

taking on your uncle's farm – a lot of work, mind.' Winnie could see why Annie had fallen for the lad. Not only was he tall and good-looking but he was obviously deeply in love with her and was willing to take on the farm for both of their futures. 'Now, what date are you thinking for this wedding, and where is it to be? York or here? It should really be York, as it is traditionally held at the bride's home.'

'We thought Easter, Mam, and I know it isn't tradition, but I think it will need to be here, at Chatburn, which is the little village that you came through on your way here. We can't leave the pigs and the farm for too long, they need regular feeding, and there's a lovely church there. It's a country church, just small and quiet – we don't want a big fuss. As long as I have all my family and Mike's aunt and uncle are there, that's all that counts.'

'That's a bit sudden. Is there any reason for such a quick wedding?' Winnie looked her daughter up and down.

'No, Mam,' she said, blushing. 'We just thought Easter would be nice, a spring wedding; the daffodils will be blooming in the churchyard.' Annie frowned at Bernard as she heard him mumble under his breath something that nobody could quite catch. However, both Lizzie and Mike had a good idea what it was.

'And bridesmaids? Are you not going to have bridesmaids? And you'll need a dress, won't you?' Winnie asked but at the same time thought of the money involved in getting her second daughter married.

'We aren't bothered, Mam; we don't need any of those trappings. But of course I'd love Molly and Rose to come if they can. It's just a long way for them to come and everybody is so busy. They have their jobs to think about, and you never know where is going to get bombed next – travel is dangerous nowadays. It doesn't seem right to have a big day when the war is still raging.'

'I've told her that your wedding day is only once in your lifetime,' Lizzie put in. 'You celebrate and make a big day, but she's not having any of it. I've also said I've got my old wedding dress up in the loft, it will just fit her. My mother made it for me, took her nights of work because she made all the lace upon it.' Lizzie beamed at Annie. 'At least have my wedding dress, and I'm sure your sisters would really like to be with you on your special day.'

'Lizzie is right. You know your sisters will want to see you get wed, and I know they want to meet Mike. I'm sure you want to meet them too, Mike?' Winnie smiled.

'Whatever Annie wants is right by me. But yes, I would like to meet the rest of your family, of course.' Mike knew that it was best to have his mother-in-law onside from the very start of the marriage.

'Oh well, if you think they can get here, it would be nice to see my sisters, and I suppose Connie, because she will no doubt want to come along as well.' Annie sighed.

'Right, well, Winnie, don't you worry about a dress or the wedding breakfast. I'll book Chatburn village hall and will boil a ham and serve it with some salad, so everyone will get fed. That can be our wedding gift; it's as good as anything and we are at hand. So we are sorted. We'll try the dress on, book the church, organize the wedding breakfast, ask Annie's sisters to be bridesmaids. That is if everything sounds all right with you?' Lizzie quickly added, not giving time for Winnie to reply before moving on to her next suggestion. 'We wondered if you would like Bernard to give Annie away, what with her having lost her own father? He would be honoured to do that if you would like.' Lizzie beamed at the pair of them, who were slightly bamboozled by all the organization, but Annie nodded gratefully. 'Just the vicar to see and the banns to be read.' Lizzie sat down opposite Winnie, folding her arms. 'Now, wasn't that easy, and we will all have a grand day. Your family can all stay here, Winnie. We will have moved into our terraced house by then, so there will be room.'

Lizzie had taken everything into hand whether Winnie liked it or not, and Annie was sure that on her return home her mother would have plenty to say about it. However, she was happy for her to do so – after all, her mother had just paid for Rose's wedding and she knew money would be tight.

'That's very kind of you, Lizzie. It's a lot to ask of you and you are doing so much already.' Winnie smiled and tried not to show how she truly felt. That she should really have a bit more say in her daughter's wedding.

'It's no problem. Now, Annie, show your mother her bedroom, then she can have ten minutes to herself and get herself settled for the evening. Bernard thought before you go home in the morning he would show you the church where these two lovebirds are to be married, and then your mind's at rest.' Lizzie had noticed that Winnie looked a little tired after her journey and knew that she would need a little time to herself.

'You'll like it, I'm sure.' Mike smiled. 'It's a lovely village, is Chatburn, just on the outskirts of Clitheroe. It's where I spent a lot of my time when I was growing up.'

'I'm sure it is. Annie is lucky that she's going to be part of such a close family; I can tell that you have taken her in under your wing.' Winnie patted Lizzie on her hand and then followed Annie through the kitchen and up the creaking stairs.

'It's an old house, is this one, Annie, I bet it's been cold in winter.' Winnie looked around at the discoloured wallpaper as she climbed the stairs and followed her daughter up onto the landing.

'Yes, it's sixteenth century; it was standing when the Pendle witch trials were being held at Lancaster. I often think about that when I'm lying in my bed.'

'Pendle witches – I've heard about them but never thought about it until now. I hope I can sleep tonight for thinking about them.' Winnie laughed. 'Poor devils, they would just be harmless old women that folk took a dislike to.'

Annie showed her to her room next to Bernard and Lizzie's bedroom. It was in need of redecoration but it was clean and tidy, Annie had made sure of that. 'Here you are, a bit basic but you've plenty of covers on your bed and you can look out of the window down across the fields.' She hesitated for a moment. 'Is everybody all right at home? I miss you all and I'm sorry I didn't get to Rose's wedding.'

'Everybody is fine, love. Rose is happy but worried stiff every time Ned goes on a bombing run. Molly, all she does is work, and as for Connie, well, she's just the same.' Winnie saw her few belongings had been put on the bed. 'Now, how are you? Still happy to be getting wed? Now I've met Mike, I'm a lot happier about it, and the Farringtons seem a good lot.'

'Mam, I've never been as happy. I love Mike and I love living here. Although I sometimes do miss you all.' Annie walked forward and hugged her mother. 'Be happy for me, Mam, this is where I want to stay for the rest of my life if I can.'

'That's all I wanted to hear. You have my blessing, and you know no matter what happens, me and your family will be there for you.' Winnie held her tight and lingered for a moment, remembering when she was just small and had shown her independence even then. 'Now, I'll have a lie on the bed and then I'll come down and join you all. The train journey was a long one, and I worried that we might be bombed at any time.'

'Yes, you would have two changes and you never know what Jerry is going to do. I'm just glad that you made it here safe. Just enjoy the peace, Mam, and the silence – it's wonderful here.' Annie closed her mother's bedroom door and sighed. She loved her mother and her family so much, but she was about to make herself a new life with the man she loved.

Winnie lay on the bed and thought of her Annie and the life she had chosen. It was going to be a hard one: the house was an old, rambling home and outside was just a mire of dirt and the smell of pigs. She closed her eyes and pulled the eiderdown over her; she was tired and now she was safely here she felt able to relax. Downstairs she could hear Lizzie in the kitchen and Annie and Mike were talking outside her window. This was Annie's new family, she thought, as sleep caught up with her.

The late evening light lit up the room as Winnie stirred and looked at the alarm clock next to her bed. It was just after six o'clock, she saw, and she raised herself quickly off the bed. The house was filled with the smell of cooking from the downstairs kitchen and she could hear that the family had gathered around the kitchen table. She quickly tidied herself and made her way back downstairs to her hosts.

'Are you all right, Mam? We thought we would leave you and not wake you until you were ready. Anyway, you've just made it in time for supper.' Annie was putting out five plates around the table as she spotted her mother at the bottom of the stairs.

Winnie yawned. 'I overslept – how rude am I?'

'It's the country air. It doesn't matter – we're not going anywhere. We are in for the night now. Everything's fed and watered, and it's time to sit and reflect on the day and to fill our bellies,' Bernard said, watching Lizzie placing a bowl of boiled potatoes, cabbage and a plate full of pork chops for everyone to help themselves from. 'Come on, lass, sit down and tuck in; you are part of the family now.'

'Thank you, I can see why Annie loves it here.' Winnie pulled a chair out and looked at the faces around the table. It might be a rough and mucky farm and it might smell of pigs, but the folk around the table were the salt of the earth. She knew Annie would be happy with them.

'Aye, she's fit in since the day she landed. You've no worries,' Lizzie replied and pushed the bowl of potatoes Winnie's way. 'Tuck in, we're not on rations when it comes to potatoes and pork.'

'No, I can see that.' Winnie smiled across at Annie as she put a chop on her dinner plate. 'No wonder Annie didn't want to come home!' There was the equivalent of a month's worth of meat ration on the table in front of her if she'd been back home in York. Life was good at Pendle Farm.

Early next morning, Winnie, Annie and Mike climbed into the trap. Bernard and Lizzie stood outside the farmhouse and waved goodbye to their guest.

'Now, remember you all come and stop with us when it's the wedding, we'll fit you all in,' Lizzie shouted.

'Thank you, I'll let you know what we plan. It will soon be here.' Winnie held onto her seat before giving a final glance around the farmyard. She had been made more than welcome, but the farm smells made her stomach churn, especially when Bernard had come in from mucking a pig pen out and sat at the table to his breakfast. The outside toilet left a lot to be desired and she couldn't see Ivy sitting on that.

'You all right, Mam? Mike's just going to take us via Chatburn and then you can see the village and the church. It's not much out of our way.' Annie sat in the back of the trap and hung on to the sides as Mike urged the horse on down the lane.

'I'm fine, thank you, Annie. It's a bit bracing today, but at least the weather is keeping fine for us. It is bonny country around here, a bit wild but lovely.' Winnie wrapped her coat tightly around herself.

'Not far now, Mam, and then we'll get you to the station. You'll be home before Molly finishes work.'

'Aye, we're entering Chatburn now,' said Mike. 'It's a bonny little village. Look, it's got a butcher's, fruit shop, post office and that's the little shop that's known for its famous ice cream and café. There's the church just over there, it's got a grand spire but it's not that big once you're inside.'

'Oh, it's lovely here. I didn't know what to expect.' Winnie gazed around her. 'And is that the village hall where the reception will be held, just across the road?'

'It is, Mam. Are you going to get down and just have a quick look in the church? It's got a lovely stained-glass window and is just the right size for our wedding; we would have been lost in the big church at Clitheroe.'

Annie jumped down from the trap and helped her mother down, then they walked along the path towards the studded oak doors. 'I'd better not walk into the church – my boots are mucky.'

'I don't know how you put up with the muck and dirt. I don't think I could,' Winnie whispered as she opened the church door. She stood at the end of the aisle, taking in the magnificence of the small village church as the early morning sun beamed through the ancient stained-glass window. Annie was right; the church would be perfect, small and simple but beautifully looked after. Winnie returned to Annie and Mike with a sense of relief that her daughter's wedding was going to be held in such a beautiful place. But now she had to catch the train and get home and report her findings to Rose and Molly.

'You take care of yourself, Annie my love. If there's anything you need, you let me know.' Winnie hugged and kissed her daughter. 'And don't worry, we'll all make it to your wedding,' she whispered before turning to Mike and hugging him.

'And you look after my daughter, although I know you will. It's been so nice to see you at long last, and it will be even better when you are part of our family.' Winnie kissed Mike on the cheek as the train whistle blew.

'Right, I'll be on my way home now. Remember, if you need anything, write and let me know.'

'We will, Mam, you get back home safe.' Annie gave

her mother a final kiss as she slammed the train door shut, holding back her tears.

Mike put his arm around her waist and they both waved until the train had disappeared down the track. She'd miss her mam, but she had Mike now – and soon a family of her own, if she was right.

Winnie alighted from the train at York, thankful to be home. Annie might be happy living on a pig farm, but it was definitely not for her. The first thing she was going to do was bring the tin bath in from the back and have a bath. What a life Annie had chosen for herself, Winnie thought as she walked quickly down the street. The pigs, the smell, the house stuck in the middle of nowhere. She herself couldn't put up with it, but Annie seemed happy, and that was all that mattered. Four years in the country had made Annie forget her town ways, but then again Annie never had been one to follow the pack. At least Mike seemed a decent sort, and perhaps once Annie got run of the house, things would be a little tidier. They couldn't be any worse, Winnie thought as she turned the key in the lock of her much-loved home. She hung her coat up and breathed a sigh of relief.

She would ask her girls to try to get time off for Annie's wedding, but perhaps give excuses to not stay at Pendle Farm. On the first night there she had been kept awake all night by rats running along the loft space, and the smell . . . she never would forget it. How Annie lived with it she would never know. A soak in the bath while Connie and Molly were at work and a cup of tea would put her right. Then she would have to catch up with what had been happening while she was away and see what Ralph had been up to in her absence. Two nights staying at Pendle Farm had seemed like a lifetime to her. Annie must be smitten by the lad, else she surely would have come back home rather than work there, she thought as she filled the boiler up with water for her bath.

The pots had been left unwashed in the sink by Connie and Molly. She would have to have words with them as well, she thought, and then set about tidying it all as if she had never been away.

11

'Oh, Mam, it can't be that bad, surely!' Rose listened to the woeful tale of Pendle Farm as her mother gave her a quick visit on Saturday afternoon.

'Oh, it is, Rose, but our Annie seems to be so happy and I must admit, Mike is a lovely lad, and if the house was made tidy and looked after it could be a wonderful home. It's just the pigs! The smell, the muck. I don't think any of you would want to stay there when we go to her wedding.'

'She's getting married, down there at Clitheroe?' Ivy gasped.

'Yes, at a little church at Chatburn, which is a village not far from the farm. It's nice, I rode past it on the way to and from the farm. I'd always envisaged my girls would all be married here at our local church, but Lizzie, Mike's aunt, seems to have taken everything in hand and Annie is happy to roll with it. To be honest, living as far away as I do, I'm grateful for the help and the generosity. I don't think Annie would complain at getting married anywhere, even in one of the pig pens, she seems that head over heels in love with Mike.' Winnie smiled, remembering the tender looks of love.

'That's all that matters then, Mam, but if the farm is as bad as you say it is, I don't fancy staying there.

Besides, Ivy here is going to find it hard no matter what we do.' Rose gave a quick glance at Ivy, who looked a bit put out by her comment.

'I'll be all right, I'm not that precious! A bit of muck won't put me off.' Ivy folded her arms – she wasn't going to miss another wedding.

'There is one good thing – I don't seem to be expected to pay for much. I did offer, but she was having none of it. Lizzie has the breakfast sorted and everything in hand. I'm glad about that, as we've only just got you and Ned married; I haven't that much money spare, and Connie is about to leave. I'll be short of her rent money, not that I charged her a lot.' Winnie sighed.

'We won't need any new clothes, anyway, Mam. Connie and Molly can wear the clothes that they wore at my wedding, and the same goes for you and Ivy. Would we be able to go there and back in the day by train, instead of staying on the farm, do you think? Although Annie, I'm sure, would like us to stay. Or perhaps Ned could come up with a solution. He could always take two of us in Peter's car, if he can get the petrol. Bless Ned, he's got the use of it at the moment; Peter had left a letter saying if anything happened to him, it was his. We would both rather have Peter back with us, but I must admit the car is an absolute boon to us. Poor Peter.' Rose looked sadly out of the window, thinking about the good-looking pilot friend of Ned's who had also fallen for her – but that was her secret, and now with Peter gone, it would stay that way.

'No news still?'

Rose shook her head grimly.

'That's awful.' Winnie said. 'He's a grand lad, not that I know him that well. How's Ned doing? Are they still putting in as many bombing flights? Surely Hitler knows he can't win now. His country is being bombed beyond belief and the Russian army and the Allies will soon be knocking on his door.'

'Ivy and I never hardly see Ned of late with the bombings being so regular, and when we do, he's exhausted and comes home to sleep. Not knowing if Peter is alive or dead has affected him deeply, I think. Like all of us, he's had enough of this war. Everyone wishes it would just end.' Rose sighed, trying not to cry.

'At least he's not a prisoner of the Japs,' Ivy commented. 'They are brutal and terrible. Hilda's lad down the road got captured when they took Singapore back. He's working on the Burmese Railway, starved and near death every day – vicious little devils, they are. I never know what to say to poor Hilda. I doubt her lad will ever come back, and if he does he will only be half the man that he was.' Ivy shook her head. 'I thought we had seen enough of war the last time around, let's hope the world finds more sense after this one.'

'It won't, because there's always some dictator that thinks they need a bit more than they already have. We can only live in hope. I'm glad that I'm the age I am. The world is changing so fast.' Winnie rose up from her seat. 'Right now, I've given you my news, I'll go and see Ralph, see what that old fool has got to say for himself.'

'It is changing, Winnie, we are changing; we're both

old dinosaurs nowadays. It's up to the next generation to make this world a better place now.' Ivy grinned. 'At least you have a man in your life.'

'We're just friends, Ivy – in fact, I don't know if we are even that, sometimes. We just keep one another company, that's what we do. I do a bit of baking for him and he brings me veg from his garden. It works well. So you needn't think that there's more in it than that.' Winnie's tone was sharp. She was seeing Ralph in a different light since she had met Mabel.

'That's how it begins, but I'm only jealous. Whatever makes you happy, Winnie, there's enough sadness in the world. Now, I'm going to have ten minutes and Rose, you do the same. I heard you tossing and turning all night until you heard the squadron arriving back to base in the early hours of this morning. Ned will be arriving this afternoon and you need to look your best, add a bit of colour to those cheeks of yours.' Ivy pulled her blanket up around her and started to close her eyes even before Winnie had left the room.

'Well, that's you told.' Winnie grinned as she stood on the step of Rose's home. 'She is right, though, you do look a bit pale and tired. Are you all right?'

'I'm fine, Mam, just busy with one thing and another. I worry about Ned all the time, and the raids are relentless at the moment. Germany is getting a taste of its own medicine in the hope that it will surrender, but I dread every evening because I know Ned and his crew are putting their lives at risk.'

'It'll end soon. We just haven't to weaken. Paris is

taken and the Russians are taking back what Germany pillaged. Happier times are on the way, my love. We have to pray that Ned keeps safe till it's all over. Now, go and have ten minutes like Ivy; the world won't stop turning without you for a few minutes.' Winnie leaned forward and gave Rose a kiss on her cheek.

'Love you, Mam,' Rose called after her mother as she watched her go down the garden path and close the gate behind her.

Her mam never gave in, no matter what was thrown at her, resolute in her faith in a better future. Rose only wished she was as strong.

'Oh, you're back, are you?' Ralph greeted Winnie. 'How did you go on in deep and darkest Lancashire? It's all cotton mills and factories, isn't it?'

'No, it isn't, Ralph. In fact, it's lovely countryside where Annie is, if you can overlook the pigs that they keep. I don't like the mucky animals; I couldn't farm them myself.'

'Then you'd have no bacon or ham, Winnie, and there's nothing better than a bacon sandwich. Although that is getting to be a distant memory,' Ralph said sadly.

'Well, you'll be in luck then, because Lizzie sent me back with a good packet of bacon rashers. You can come and have your supper with us, if you can supply the potatoes.' Winnie hadn't forgotten the way Ralph had acted around Mabel and didn't trust him like she used to. But at the same time she enjoyed his company and had missed him. 'What have you been up to while

I've been away? Has Miss Floozy been around while I've been gone?'

'No, she hasn't. You talk like I entertain her regularly. I can assure you that I definitely don't. What time do you want the potatoes for? I'll look forward to a good frying of bacon. I'm only allowed two rashers a week in my ration book and that is if the butcher has got any. Your lass has fallen on her feet good and proper, if you did but know it,' Ralph said.

'Perhaps you're right,' Winnie admitted. 'The lad she is to marry, Mike, is buying the farm that they live on. She'll be a farmer's wife and it's in a bonny part of the world. I just wish she didn't live so far away, I miss her. Although I was glad to be back and to get clean. They have set their wedding day as the thirty-first of March, Easter Saturday, and she's getting wed at Clitheroe, or a little church just outside. I wish it was here, Ralph, you could go then.'

'Sounds to me like she has found a good one in him. He must be worth a bob or two and she's not going to go hungry, is she? Annie's landed on her feet. You are going to be left with only Molly. Will you be all right, you two on your own?' Ralph wondered whether to suggest something he had been thinking of for a while but didn't dare say.

'It will be quiet, but Molly isn't going anywhere just yet and Connie only came because there was nowhere else for her to go. To be honest, it will be nice to have a bit of time to myself. Once this war is over, work at Rowntree's will get back to normal and Molly will be on ordinary shifts again. Twelve-hour shifts are too long for anybody. There's rumours that it will be sooner rather than later that the military will be pulling out. I meant to ask Rose if she knew anything, but I forgot. She's so worried about the continuous bombing that her Ned is taking part in, so I didn't get to ask her this afternoon.' Winnie was hoping that Ralph would offer her a cup of tea, but no offer came her way.

'Oh, as long as you will be all right. You will find it hard, you know, seeing you have been used to having a bit more money coming in.' Ralph plucked up the courage to suggest his idea. 'What if I came and stayed – as a renter, nothing else? It would save us both money.' He immediately regretted even thinking it let alone suggesting it as he watched Winnie's face turn bright red.

'Ralph Parker, that would get the whole street talking about us,' she replied sharply. 'They would have us living over the brush, and I dread to think what Molly would have to say about it. So, no, over my dead body. Perhaps at one time I might have been persuaded, but no, you are just a friend, and that's what you will remain.'

'I didn't mean to upset you. I just thought it would save us both brass and I must admit, while you have been away I have missed you. You know it's cold and miserable on your own in a house rattling around trying to find something to do every day. Since my Sissie died, I've had nobody to keep me warm at night or to talk to. I'd be no bother.' Ralph gazed at Winnie with his soulful eyes, hoping he might win her over. 'I do think a lot of you, my love.'

'You've her next door, I'm sure she would keep you warm. But it will not be me.' Winnie hesitated. 'I don't know if I want a man living in my house, I'm used to my independence nowadays.' She smiled and patted Ralph's hand. 'Just friends, Ralph; you keep to your house and I'll keep to mine for now. Perhaps when we really need one another, when we are ageing and not coping alone, then we will see.'

Ralph muttered something under his breath as he turned and looked out of the window, gazing at the vegetables that he'd been using to bribe Winnie.

'What's that, Ralph?' Winnie asked, standing behind him.

'I was just saying my leeks are at an end. Good job it's coming spring; I can get re-planting and perhaps look for a fresh plot to keep me out of mischief.' Ralph sighed.

'That sounds like a good idea to me. A fresh plot is just what you need.' Winnie decided it was time to leave. The man had obviously been expecting a bit more than a bite to eat from her.

'Yes, right. Oh, Winnie, if I can make it for a sandwich, I'll come round sometime this week.' Ralph didn't bother turning around. He'd let Winnie see herself out – he'd wasted enough time on her as it was, and for what? A quick peck and a bit of food.

Molly sat at the kitchen table. She hadn't bothered going with Connie to her flat which was starting to be her pride and joy; she wanted to have some time to herself with her mother. Since she had finished work and had supper, her mother had seemed a little quiet, so she wanted to know what was wrong, although she knew that Winnie was missing Annie and worried about the distance between them now.

'Mam, are you all right? Annie will be as happy as sin living on a farm – she always was one for doing what she wanted to do – and as long as Mike seems all right, then what is there to worry about?' Molly said quietly.

'I know. They're in love, you can tell they are. I just wanted her to marry and live here, where she belongs, and it is going to be such a carry-on getting there and back. But I suppose as long as she's happy, that's what counts.'

'She might be happy, but you don't sound that happy this evening. What's wrong, Mam?' The supper had been burnt and nothing seemed to be right in her mother's world since she had returned from Clitheroe.

'I'm sorry, but I'm worried about Annie, Rose looks ill with worry over Ned and I'm going to miss Connie's contribution towards the rent. I've just a lot on my plate at the moment. There's only you that keeps me going.' Winnie sighed.

'Thanks, Mam. I try my best no matter what is going on in the world. I'll always be here for you; you should know that. There's no chance of me disappearing, I haven't heard from Matt for weeks.' Molly felt as glum as her mother when it came to her relationship with the man she'd thought loved her.

'Men, don't you mention them! Even an old duffer

like me gets taken in with them. I don't think we will be seeing Ralph Parker for a while now. Do you know, I honestly think he was working his way into living with us? Even though I suspect that he's not as faithful as he made himself out to be. There was not a sign of a ring or proposal of marriage. He's led me on and I cottoned on this afternoon after he suggested he came and rented with us and then in the next breath saying his bed was cold. What does he think I am? I'm no tart, not like his next-door neighbour; he'll have to find comfort with her.' Winnie shook her head.

'Well, you know what I thought of him from the start, but I'm truly sorry, Mam, if you thought he was going to bring you some happiness. You know I'm always here for you. I never did like that Ralph, sorry.'

Molly picked up the evening newspaper and read the headlines. **British and Allied Troops Cross the Rhine.** She thought of her handsome Matt and wished that he would write just to say he was safe if nothing else. That's all it would take to make her feel happy, but not a word had been sent and now she was wondering if he was even alive.

'I know you didn't like him one bit, did you? I was just flattered; it's nice when a man gives you the time of day, no matter what your age. You have plenty of men and years ahead of you, so there's no need for you to worry. If anything has happened to Matt, that will be a big loss for you – I only hope that he's all right. But you mustn't lose hope; another man who is just as good for you will come along, especially after this war has ended.

And the end is in sight, by the looks of the headlines this evening.'

Winnie sat down in the chair next to her daughter and took her hand and squeezed it.

'I know, Mam, but it hurts, doesn't it? Being in love really hurts. I sometimes wonder if it's worth it.'

'When you find the right man, it is worth it, and he will be out there if you haven't found him already. But yes, love hurts and there is nothing you can do about it.'

12

'Has your Rose not said anything about what this meeting is about? I should know better than to ask. She never tells anything to anybody, does she? Perfect management material,' Connie said sarcastically as she and Molly lined up along with their fellow workers at the munitions factory. Just for once, production had stopped. The relentless music from the Tannoy and the chit-chat of workers had become silent, and the endlessly moving belt of munitions being filled had halted, making everybody speculate what could be going on in the world of Rowntree's and the Ministry of Defence.

'Rose tells me nothing. I hardly see her nowadays anyway. She's either in the boardroom with the big nobs or looking after Ivy. Even my mam was saying that she hardly sees her. Although Mam was around at her house the other day about Annie's wedding and she came back worried. She thought that Rose looked ill.' Molly and Connie shuffled along with the crowd of workers making their way into the NAAFI where they had been told to gather. 'Don't you think it's funny we haven't been told to get into our civvies before we head there? We've never been allowed to go into the NAAFI in our working clothes before. It's always change and a check-down in case we're hiding anything or have enough TNT powder on us to be combustible.' Molly looked around at everybody in their uniforms and with their hair covered by their turbans, lined up talking and looking worried.

'It must be something urgent if they can't give us time to change,' Connie said. She was chewing on some gum that Chuck had given her, and her breath smelt of mint.

'Don't let the bosses smell that on your breath, else you'll get reprimanded. You aren't supposed to eat while you're at work.' Molly thought her friend's habit of chewing with her mouth open was a little bad-mannered.

'They'll only be jealous. It isn't everybody who can get gum, nylons and cigarettes at the drop of a hat. There have to be some perks to dating an American airman.' Connie grinned. 'And that's just the one I can mention now I've got a flat of my own.

'I knew he was only keeping away because we had no privacy. It might be a bit of a dump and I don't half miss your mam's cooking, but the other perks more than make up for it.' Connie winked. She had only been living in the flat for a few days, but Chuck had called in whenever he could sneak away from the base.

'It is a wonder that he's not too busy,' Molly said. 'Rose never hardly sees Ned at the moment; he's always on a mission. Mam says she looks tired out with worry; it must be awful to think every evening that her husband might never come back.'

'Yes, at least when the planes are up and flying that is

Chuck's job done, and he faces no danger at all unless the airfield gets bombed. With being ground crew, his job starts again when they arrive back. He hates it when they come back shot at with injured on board and even more so when they go missing. He's been saying that the Allies are winning now and that Germany is a broken country. He's even begun to feel sorry for them; Hitler has had such a hold on them. Imagine a whole country believing in every word their leader tells them, like faithful sheep!'

'I'm sure some saw the evil in what he's been doing,' Molly replied. 'If they didn't, they soon will by the sound of the atrocities that have been going on behind ordinary people's backs. The camps they are starting to find are horrendous – those poor people! Anyway, we have our own worries. My stomach is churning, wondering what this meeting is about. Perhaps we're all going to be given our marching orders, or dare I even think it, get our old jobs back. I swear I will never moan about the smell of chocolate ever again. I will make as many chocolate boxes with that stinking glue as my fingers will let me if that's what we're back to.'

Molly and Connie continued to shuffle along with the crowds of munition workers and waited for the board of management and the officer who always made announcements on behalf of the MOD. At last they arrived: George Harris, Seebohm Rowntree and the pompous Major Booth, whom everyone had to acknowledge as he walked around the munitions factory with his swagger stick under his arm.

A hush came over the hall filled with workers and everyone held their breath and looked nervously at one another.

'Good afternoon, everybody, thank you for attending.' George Harris looked nervous as he took in the room of workers dressed in their munition uniforms instead of the usual white overalls of the chocolate production department.

'I'm sure that you are all wondering what this meeting is about and that you have probably heard rumours circulating around the factory. Well! Let me put your fears and concerns to rest.' George Harris took a deep breath.

'Major Booth and the MOD have decided that the way the war is proceeding, they will no longer need the production of munition here at Rowntree's. That is to come to a gradual end over the next few months.'

The hall was filled with an excited rumble of voices and Molly and Connie looked at one another and hugged tightly. The days filled with endless hours of assembling shells bound for killing would soon be over. The war must be nearly at an end. They would all hopefully be returning to their previous work with much relief.

'Oh, Mol, we must be winning, else they wouldn't be closing us down.' Connie sighed and then listened intently as the three men in charge of every worker's life explained to the excited crowd that the production of munitions was to be moved elsewhere in the country, and the production of chocolates would begin again as soon as practically possible.

Molly was grinning from ear to ear. 'This is the best news I've heard in months. No more ginger hair and worrying about blowing myself up every day. Back to chocolate making and proper working hours, not terrible twelve-hour shifts, one week working days and the next working nights that make you feel half-dead all the time. Oh, I'm so glad. I can't wait to tell my mam. I bet our Rose has known for weeks but she's never said a word – she's a deep one.' It was wonderful news, but Molly noticed that her friend had sighed deeply despite everyone else rejoicing.

'It is good news, but I've just rented my flat thinking that I could afford it on my munitions pay. I've got some savings, but I will struggle unless Rowntree's have altered their pay, and I can't see that's going to happen. If anything, wages will be even tighter.' Connie was thinking out loud. Her heart had ruled her head when it had come to the flat, and if the war was coming to an end, that would mean Chuck would be returning home. She hoped that now he would ask her to marry him.

'Connie Whitehead, you must be the only one who isn't celebrating this good news. Britain and America are winning the war, or else we would still be making munitions – is that not enough for you? I can't wait for life to get back to normal. Do you know what I want more than any chocolate? I want a big, fat, bright-coloured orange. I can just imagine peeling it and the juice spurting at me. Oh, I can just taste it now. It has been so long.' Molly closed her eyes and dreamt of what she had missed most.

'An orange – all you can think about is an orange, Molly! What about Matt coming home and you making a life with him? I might be losing my Chuck and all you can talk about is a bloody orange.' Connie looked around at everybody as they started taking the news in and chatting about how it was going to affect their lives.

'Matt hasn't written for so long, and to be honest, there wasn't much romance between us,' Molly admitted. 'A kiss and cuddle when we were together, and letters to one another. I did once think that I loved him, but I'm not so sure now. I don't even know if he's alive or dead, and I should care more than I think I do. Anyway, I'm happy as I am. But Chuck loves you, he will find a way to stay with you, of that I'm sure. Isn't he always telling you that he'd like to show you Montana? That was the original attraction to him, as I recall, and then you really fell in love with him. Even though you were full of it that he came from the same state that your little brother Billy had been adopted to.'

'That was when we first met, he never mentions it any more. He used to talk about his home so much, the high, snow-covered mountains, the huge forests and the rolling prairie as he calls it. Now all he does is worry about if he's fixed the planes right and if the flight will return home. I know that is his job and that pilots' lives are in his hands and that it is a heck of a responsibility, but he never seems to talk now about his family and home. Although he does love me, I know he does – he's just tired like everyone else.'

'Oh, he loves you, I know he does,' Molly reassured her. 'Now come on, smile, the war must be nearly at an end and I can't wait for the morning when I don't have to handle a shell case or powder ever again. Bloody lovely!' Molly swore so loudly that the women around giggled.

'Yes, it is, I know it is, sorry. Things will be fine; I just don't want to lose Chuck and be left on my own in my flat,' Connie said quietly as they walked back to their work stations.

Frida came over to them. Their friendship with the Italian girl who had come to work at the munitions family at the start of the war had grown. Her English had improved immeasurably since she had started working next to Molly and Connie.

'Good news, yes? I will be going home soon, back to Italia. Back to the sun and my mamma. No more rain and dreary British weather.' Frida beamed.

'Hopefully, Frida, but everything will take a while,' Molly replied, returning Frida's hug.

'What wrong with you?' Frida asked Connie. 'War nearly over. You should be happy!'

'War might be nearly over, but that means my Chuck will be going home and I will never see him again,' Connie said. She hugged Frida but she still didn't feel as joyful as everybody else.

'He not leave, he'll stay here, or you go with him, back to his home. If he loves you, he not leave you,'

Frida said, holding her close. 'Happy times are here, smile.'

'I'll try to, Frida, and yes, I know I should be grateful just like everyone else. A whole new beginning and who knows what lies ahead of us all. See, I'm smiling now.' Connie grinned. 'Back to chocolate-making and packing, that's got to be better than bloody bomb-making.'

'Well, isn't that good news, Molly? The government must be confident that Hitler and his Nazis are on the run, else they wouldn't be closing the munition side of Rowntree's down. I didn't expect you to come home and tell me that. Our Rose hasn't given us any hint of what's been being discussed, but she must have known. You'd think she'd tell her own mother.' Winnie shook her head.

'She probably couldn't, Mam, and knowing Rose she would be thinking of Ned and Ivy more than work at the moment. I bet she's glad, because all the foreign workers will eventually go home; she's been struggling explaining things to them in their own language. Hopefully things will return back to normal. Saying that, I'm really going to miss one or two of them, especially Frida. She made me laugh when she told Connie to stop thinking of herself today when we got the news. All she could think about was what was going to happen between her and Chuck, never mind that we were winning the war.'

'Well, he's a Yank, he'll want to go back home – no wonder she's worried. It's a shame, just as she's just moved into that flat as well. You can tell her she can move back in with us if she likes, her rent payment would be welcome. Not that I'll have any of their hanky-panky under my roof. She'll have to behave herself here.' For the first time in ages, Winnie thought there might be a future for all her family.

Molly gave her mother a penetrating look. 'Is Ralph, the earnest courter, not here tonight?'

Winnie kept her eyes on her darning. 'No, I think my friendship with Ralph may have come to an end. We had a difference of opinion, and besides, he was a fond old devil. Thinking he could get around me with his allotment vegetables, it'll take more than that for me to turn my head and look at another man. I married the best one when I married your father and I'll not be looking at one to replace him.'

'Oh, well, as long as you're happy, Mam. I can't say I'm not pleased to hear that, I never did like him.'

'By heck, Molly, I never had a clue that you didn't like him.' Winnie grinned. 'You might as well have put a notice on our door, "Everyone welcome except Ralph Parker", it was that obvious.'

'I was just thinking of you, Mam,' Molly said quietly.

'I know you were, love. As I always do you. On that note, the lad at the butcher's shop was asking about you this morning. I told him you were fine, single and still at home. He's a nice lad – it's a wonder he hasn't got a girlfriend. He stood behind the counter making all the rest of the queue wait while he asked about you. I felt quite guilty, the woman behind me was starting to lose her patience as he kept smiling at me.' Winnie tied off her darning. 'No word from Matt?'

'No, Mam. I don't know if he's alive or dead, and it's been so long I've nearly forgotten what he looks like.'

'Perhaps time to move on, Molly love,' Winnie advised. 'Anything could have happened to him. With the end of the war will come change. Look to the future, my love.'

13

'I'll have to go, Con, the base will be missing me. There will be hell to pay if I'm not back on time. We have another night-flight tonight.' Chuck stood up and pulled his vest on, then leaned down to kiss her.

'I know you've got to go, but I could do with you staying tonight, I get so lonely,' Connie said longingly.

'I can't, doll, you know I can't. Lives rely on me. When this war is over, I can stay with you every night and we'll have a life together. But right now my arse belongs to the base and Uncle Sam.' Chuck buckled his trousers and pulled on his jacket before kissing her again. 'I love you, doll, but I have to go, you know I do.'

Connie pulled the cover over herself and watched him go. She was on her own again. She had wanted him to stay so much but she knew he couldn't, not when lives depended on him. Without him and the Freeman family, some nights could be quite lonely. She picked up a copy of *Woman's Own* but put it back down with a sigh after flicking through a few pages. She had made a mistake in moving out of the Freemans' home – she missed the banter, the meals and the playing of the radio. In the flat on her own, the nights were long and there was nothing to do except sleep, eat and go to work. Even making herself a meal was draining, she thought as she turned on her side and studied the crack that ran the full height of the back wall. Still, she told herself, she was seeing more of Chuck than she had ever done, and that made up for the nights when she was alone. She picked up his photograph from her bedside table.

'Look at the life I'm living just for you. I would have been better off with Fred at the shoe shop, you big American idiot, and I bet you leave me just as fast as you came into my life. Then what will I do?'

Chuck was full of life when he wasn't exhausted from aircraft repairs, taking her to the flicks, as he called them, and bringing her chocolate, nylons and other things that the British could not get their hands on, but she knew that she would be naive if she counted on him being with her forever. Her lifestyle with him would end just as quickly as it had started once the war was over. And over it would be shortly, if the news from Rowntree's was anything to go by. It had been good news, but everyone knew that along with peace came change, and Connie was feeling a little afraid for the future.

'You look half dead this morning. Are you not sleeping in your new home?' Molly asked her best friend the next morning as they changed into the hated uniforms for making munitions and stepped into the prohibited zone.

'No, I didn't sleep a wink. I don't know what's going to happen between Chuck and me. Perhaps you're right in not writing and worrying about Matt any more. But

I think I love that big, useless hunk of mine, and my heart will break when he goes back home. It will never be the same writing to one another. He'll find someone else and I'll be stuck here making bloody chocolates until I'm an old maid.' Connie looked around at her fellow workers. 'In a short while this will be gone, along with half the people we know. It will feel strange, as if we've been living in a dream or a nightmare. Then we'll be back to making boxes for chocolates, replacing the dust of TNT with the awful smell of those glue pots.'

'You are being a misery! Living by yourself isn't doing you any favours. Now, come on, stop grousing and let's get to work. I'll go and ask for something bright and cheerful to be played over the Tannoy, some Glenn Miller or something we can all wriggle our hips to. That will cheer you up.'

Molly watched Connie enter the box that had been her workspace since they had both started to work there. She had only progressed in her job briefly, becoming a supervisor for a month or two before being put back on main production. Connie had not been suitable as a supervisor, having no patience and being sloppy with the loaded shells, unlike Molly, who had for the moment replaced her as a line supervisor. She'd been recommended for taking care in her work and for helping others, but above all was especially cautious when the filled shells had to be taken to the safety of the bunker storage. She'd felt chuffed to be given the supervisor's position, and her mother had beamed with pride when she had gone home and told her about it.

'Now I know I've brought my girls up well – cream always rises to the top,' Winnie had said, and she had hugged Molly closely to her once she and Molly were on their own. Even so, Molly had felt bad that she had replaced her best friend.

She opened the door to the manager's office for her floor and smiled at Jeff, who was sitting with his head down, looking through the worksheets of those who were going to be leaving once the factory was reclaimed for chocolate making.

'Morning, Jeff,' she greeted him. 'You look busy. You aren't usually in here this early. I've just come to change the radio station, to find something a bit livelier, else Connie is going to slit her wrists with the mood that she's in.'

'You should know I can't play any other station than the Home Service, Mol, but once the seven o'clock news has been on there's an hour of Will Bradley and his swing band, that'll cheer her up.' Jeff leaned back in his chair and grinned at Molly. 'Good news for you lasses – you'll soon be up to your arms in chocolate again. Me, I don't know what I'll be doing; this leg of mine is going to mean I need an office job for the rest of my life. But there will be hundreds of soldiers coming back looking for work.' Jeff rubbed the knee joint where his false leg was attached. 'This war has just caused so much heartache for so many. I hope they hang that bloody Hitler when they capture him.'

'You'll keep your job, Jeff, Rowntree's will make sure

of that. They're a good firm, loyal to their workers,' Molly said.

'Well, we'll see.' Jeff sighed. 'I'm going through the list of people that are either going to be moved on to other munitions factories or who have no longer got employment here, and it's worried me. Things are going to be so different when the lads are home.'

'I'm sure you'll be in employment, Jeff. I just hope Connie and I aren't on that list. I'm looking forward to going back to chocolate box making.' Molly smiled and left Jeff with his list of employees who were going to have their lives changed through no fault of their own. He hadn't said anything to Molly, but he had just noticed that Connie's employment with Rowntree's was being reviewed along with a few others from the chocolate box department. Rowntree's were going to downsize their staff and bring in new production methods; nobody was as safe as they thought they were going to be. There would still be heartache even after the war had come to an end.

'I'm glad the day is over, my heart's not in it any more. What's the point of making munitions if the war is coming to an end? Hopefully they'll never have to be used.' Connie pulled out a packet of Senior Service cigarettes and lit one as Molly and she began walking home.

'Well, they are starting to change everything over next week, so I've heard, so it won't be for much longer that you have to endure shell packing. Jeff was looking at the new employment list when I was in his office this morning – a lot of people will be looking for work. I can't see Rowntree's keeping on the staff that they had before and we have so many people making munitions because of the demand.' Molly watched as Connie breathed out a cloud of smoke. 'How long have you been smoking? You never did when you lived at my mam's.'

'I only started last week, it passes a few minutes and calms the nerves,' Connie replied. 'Are you all ready at your house for Annie's wedding? I'm so looking forward to it, if we can all get there! It's good that we've got the bridesmaids' dresses from Rose's wedding, we can both wear them again. At least nobody will recognize them except your mam and Rose.'

'Ned says he's got the transport sorted for us. A way we can all go together and it won't cost a penny. Rose had a devilish grin on her face when she told us, so Lord knows how we are going to get there. Just as long as we do and can come back the same day, although it will be a long one, because Mam says she will definitely not be staying, and you should have seen Ivy's face when Mam told her about the pigs.'

'Ah, well, it will be nice to see Annie. I'm glad that she's got her man, pigs or no pigs.' They had reached the corner where they now parted ways, and Connie sighed. 'See you tomorrow. Enjoy your mam's supper. I will go home to my tin of sardines and my evening alone.'

Molly watched as Connie made her way down the

street until she disappeared into the darkness. She should never have left her home with them. Since living on her own she had been nothing but negative. Although it had only been a few weeks, a lot had happened and everybody's future was up in the air. She had moved at the worst possible time. Good times were coming and Molly was sure that Connie would not be left high and dry by Chuck, but nothing was certain when it came to the Yanks. A lot had come over and lived life like a never-ending party, leaving some women pregnant and heartbroken. She just hoped that Chuck wasn't going to be one of them, for Connie's sake.

'How's Connie today? Regretting leaving here?' Winnie asked as she watched Molly tuck into her supper of Spam fritters.

'You could say that, Mam. She's worried that Chuck will leave her high and dry. The Yanks are going to be leaving soon, now the war is being won.'

'It isn't over yet. They might think they are winning, but I wouldn't trust these Nazis and I doubt the Japs will ever submit.' Winnie sighed. 'She needs to be careful with that fella of hers, she doesn't want to be like her mother. Letting him have his cake and eat it and then jiggering off back home with not a care in the world. Don't think I don't know now why she moved out. She knew that I'd not allow any of that going on in my rooms!'

'She's not that daft, Mam, but she has started smoking, she says to calm her nerves. I only hope that we've both kept our jobs. Jeff was going through the list of employees to be kept this morning and I couldn't help but feel he was being a bit shifty.' Molly had been thinking about the look Jeff had given her all morning. The management upstairs weren't that keen on Connie, and even Rose had her reservations. Connie never put her name forward for anything and hadn't been giving her best to her work recently. It would be the last straw for poor Connie if she had no job and Chuck left her high and dry.

'Well, as long as they keep you on, else we will be struggling. I might even have to ask Ralph Parker to move in with us yet!' Winnie tried to keep her face straight as she took Molly's clean plate away.

'Mam, never – don't even joke about that! Over my dead body do I want that man to live here!' Molly gasped.

'I think you're safe, my love. I saw him outside the butcher's this morning and he was arm-in-arm with Minnie Platt. Minnie Platt of all people! She's got a face like the back of a bus! So much for being smitten with me. I'm glad I saw through him. They always say there's no fool like an old one. Unfortunately, I nearly fell for his charms, but I realized in time.' Winnie shook her head and leaned against the kitchen sink. 'William Allen at the butcher's was asking after you again. He's a grand lad. I'm glad that he never got conscripted. His father says he gets asthma, so he'd be no good on the front line.'

Molly yawned. 'He's all right, I've not seen him

for a while. He always was chesty at school. Don't you go saying anything to him, Mam, I can't be bothered with men in my life at the moment, and besides, I still don't know what's happened to Matt. I can't rest until I do really.' Molly knew perfectly well what her mother was up to. Just because her own love life appeared to have come to an end, it didn't mean she should dabble in hers.

'Only saying, Molly, there's a lot worse out there and he's a butcher, you'd never go hungry.' Winnie grinned.

'Mam. Stop it!' Molly protested. 'I'm going to bed. Before you know it, I'll have to be up for the next shift. I'll be glad when these twelve-hour days finish – I seem to have been working them a lifetime. Eight hours a day will feel like heaven.'

14

The front door opened unexpectedly at the Evans home and Rose rushed into the hallway.

'Ned, you're home! Thank the Lord for that,' she gasped, running to put her arms around him.

Ned held Rose tight and ran his hands through her hair, breathing in deeply, just glad to have survived the night's bombing raid and be back in her arms. 'It's good to be back, Rose. I love you, so much.'

Rose led him into the front room. 'Sit down, you're absolutely done in. Let me make you a cup of tea and you just close your eyes.'

'Sorry, my love, it's been one hell of a night. I didn't think I was going to make it back. I couldn't get out of debriefing fast enough. I haven't even changed out of my flying jacket.' Ned slumped in the armchair and gazed into the welcoming warmth of the open fire. 'Where's Mother? She's usually up and about, is she all right?'

'Yes, she's just gone upstairs for her midday nap. She's fine. We didn't expect you back yet. It's usually later in the day after your briefing that you return. Was it really bad last night?'

'It was. I honestly didn't think I was going to make it back. We might be winning, but the Germans are far away from surrendering. It was poor Frankfurt that took the brunt of it last night. Thank God the briefing was short and I could come home early. I hate it, Rose, I hate it – those are innocent people that we are bombing. This isn't what I signed up for. I joined to protect our shores, not murder everyday citizens.' Ned closed his eyes and leaned his head back, hoping that he could blot the memories out with sleep. 'It's horrific what's going on out there. Why don't they surrender and save lives?'

'Oh, my love, I'm so sorry. But you are home now, just try to put it out of your mind for now.' Rose kissed her husband's brow and sighed. She was just glad he was home safe and sound for the time being.

'You never told me Ned was home, you should have woken me up!' Ivy grumbled as Rose helped her downstairs an hour later.

'Well, he's fast asleep, dead to the world in the front room. I've just put a blanket over him; he's even still in his flying jacket, he came straight from the base. So you haven't missed much. Now, watch your step and let's sit down at the table and if I close the front room door, you can listen to the radio.' Rose took Ivy's arm and guided her into the kitchen. She was getting worse at walking and becoming more cantankerous and forgetful by the day. She was not the Ivy that Rose had first met, the twinkle in her eye had dimmed, although on good days the sense of humour that Ivy had always had still shone through.

'What have we got for our Sunday tea, Rose?' Ivy asked. 'I'm right hoping for a good slice of roast beef.'

'No roast beef, I'm afraid, Ivy. I was lucky to get some lamb's liver, it's braising in the oven for dinner. I think there should be enough for the three of us. I didn't know Ned was coming home today – you never know from one day to the next what the base needs him to do. I'm going to use these bread crusts and make a custard with dried egg to make a bread and butter pudding – that should fill us up.'

'What! No roast beef! We always have roast beef. Liver, tah! I don't like offal.' Ivy shook her head. 'I thought that you'd make a better wife than this, Rose. Why didn't you get some beef? You know how much my Ned and I like beef,' she groused, forgetting about the rationing that was in place.

'I'm sorry, Ivy, I can only buy what's in the shops. I queued for that for an age before I went to work as it was.' Rose tried not to give in to the tears that could have easily have fallen if she had let them.

At that moment, a sleepy Ned entered the room. 'Are you causing upset, Mother? Rose does the very best she can for you and us. She works full-time, she cleans and runs this home, and she puts in a lot of hours looking after you.' Ned made his way to his mother and hugged her. 'There's rationing on, Mother, have you forgotten? She can't get what we all fancy, a Sunday joint or anything much else. It's good that we have liver and mashed potatoes.' He smiled at his mother as she looked up at him, confused.

'Oh, I'm sorry, I did forget; this old head of mine plays up from time to time. I'm sorry, Rose, I didn't mean to complain.' Ivy smiled at Ned. 'I'm glad that you're back, I do nothing but worry about you when you're away. The house isn't the same when you're not here.' Ivy clung to Ned's arm as he sat down next to her.

He rubbed his face with his hands and yawned. 'Well, I'm back now, I've got two whole days to stay with you. A break from the flights before I start to lose my concentration and put my crew at risk. We've had a hard few weeks.'

'Two days, oh that will be wonderful, Ned. Two days of not having to worry that you are safe.' Rose beamed with relief – two days to have her Ned home. He would see how his mother had aged, and to be safe in his arms would be a rare luxury.

'Yes, and I've made sure that I've got March the thirtieth and thirty-first as leave,' he added. 'They'll have to find somebody else to do their bombing over Easter, I'm not missing your Annie's wedding. I've also managed to get some transport lined up. We'll be going to Clitheroe in style, all together and there and back in the day, so your mother doesn't have to worry about having to stay over. It will be a long day, but we'll all be together.'

'I'm not flying; I'm not going in one of your bombers,' Ivy said, shaking her head.

'You'll not be going in a bomber, Mother. The RAF don't think Annie's wedding is that important, but it will be in style, trust me. It's all in hand. It's not what you know; it's who you know sometimes.'

'What are you up to, Ned?' Rose smiled at her husband who looked full of mischief.

'Never you mind, you have enough to worry about. Just be aware that you and your family have to make an early start as we'll have a long day, but it will be one we'll never forget, I can assure you. Now, that liver and onions is just what I fancy for dinner. Doesn't it smell good, Mother? At least we have food on the table – some people have absolutely nothing, not even a home. York has come off nearly unscathed, so we should be thankful for small mercies.'

'Yes, Ned, you're right. It is good to have you back home. I miss you,' Ivy said ruefully while looking blankly at Rose.

'Your mother is getting really forgetful. I do worry about her, but it does make caring for her more challenging. I don't think she is right well. She's struggling with her walking as well.' Rose wrapped her arms around Ned as he held her close.

'She is forgetful,' he agreed, 'I've noticed that lately. She was very short with you as well, when she had no need or right to be so. That is completely out of character. Perhaps she should have a visit to the doctor. It wouldn't hurt.'

'Let's arrange that after we've been to the wedding,' Rose suggested. 'Perhaps she's just feeling a little weary. Winter always does drag when you have aches and pains, and this blasted war is dragging on so long. The wedding is bound to cheer her up. Tell me, how are you going to get us all there?!' She snuggled up to her man, taking comfort that he was with her and not flying over some distant part of Germany.

'Ah, that's my secret, but it's a good one. Now, are you all right? Mother isn't the only one looking a bit under the weather. You look worn out too.'

'I'm fine, just tired. I haven't had a chance to tell you that the Ministry of Defence is leaving Rowntree's – no more County Industries! The munitions factory is going to close and chocolate-making will hopefully resume throughout the factory. Although I think that a lot of the munition workers will be moved with that part of the firm, and Rowntree's will be cutting back its employees. I'm just hoping that Molly or Connie won't be on the list of employees to be made redundant. I haven't seen it yet.'

'And there was me thinking of returning there when the war came finally to an end,' Ned said. 'I was hoping to come back as a manager. I'm tired and I have no desire to remain a pilot, especially after what happened to Peter.'

'I know, poor Peter, we both miss him so much.' Rose paused, then continued, determined to be positive. 'But I'm sure they'd take you back at Rowntree's. They're looking to the future and redesigning and reinventing at the moment. You always were a forward thinker; they will take you back, I'm sure. That's why I'm worried about Molly and Connie's jobs – they were on glueing boxes, but new machinery will be replacing them if the new director of the board, George Harris, has his way. He's also suggesting that they brand the chocolate dragées as Smarties and box them in a cardboard tube or small box. The chocolate boxes are going to be standard and pre-produced, unless they're for a special sale. Nothing is going to be as smart or as costly as it used to be. The firm is economizing.'

'Enough of work and worries, we have better things to do tonight.' Ned kissed Rose and pulled her closer. The night was not going to be wasted talking business; there would be time for that in the future.

Connie entered her flat, lighting her small gas light as soon as she had pulled her blackout blind, and glanced at the letter that had been lying waiting for her behind her front door.

It was the run-up to Easter and Rowntree's had posted their intentions of employment to each of their employees. Over the Easter period, part of the munitions factory was to be dismantled and the NAAFI was to be reclaimed as the main dining hall. Everyone was on tenterhooks to find out if they were keeping their jobs, and not all of the Rowntree's Board were happy with the decisions. Job losses were against the beliefs of some of the stauncher Quaker board members. Rowntree's had been there to help the people of York, not to turn their backs on them in time of need.

Connie was confident that the letter would be offering her re-employment within the chocolate factory, so she didn't bother to open it. After all, she had always worked hard, even though they had not thought of her as the right material for being a supervisor. She was still good at her job. She and Molly would definitely have jobs; it would be those who had just been taken on to make munitions who would be let go. She was sure of it.

The following morning, Connie was running late. She sipped a fast brewed cup of tea, then hastily tied back her hair and picked up the letter. She would read it at work and see where she and Molly had been allocated within the different branches of Rowntree's. Boxing chocolates, dragée making, KitKat wafer department – it didn't matter what it was, even box storage. Anything was better than making munitions. She knew she had moaned about the smell of the glue pots, but at least they didn't endanger your life every day, whereas a simple trip with a loaded shell could have ended her life.

She folded up the letter into her coat pocket and ran down the road. She was late, so there was no time to admire the daffodils that were braving the cold in the park or say hello to the postman as she fell into line with her fellow workers to register and go through the usual body checks to enter the munitions building.

Molly was sitting waiting for her in the changing area, as Connie came through the door and started to take her coat and civvies clothing off to change into her munitions uniform.

'Thank goodness you're here. I was so worried you might have had bad news in your letter like some other of the girls and decided not to come,' Molly whispered as Connie changed in the so-called contaminated area before re-joining her in the clean area.

'Don't be daft, of course I'm here, and of course they will have taken me back on. I haven't even checked my letter. I've worked here before, of course they'll be keeping me on.' Connie pulled on her white turban. 'Have you read yours? There's no doubt that they'll keep you on – you were their special one, making boxes for Queen Mary.'

Molly looked a little anxious, hoping her friend was correct. 'Yes, I've read mine, I'm to start in the Black Magic department mid-April, learning how to work with the new box-making machine that they are going to buy. I wonder if you'll be with me?' Molly was a little disappointed that she wouldn't be back to decorating the lovely chocolate boxes which she had taken so much pride in. Still, it was better than having no job at all. Beatrice, who they had both always worked with, had been told that she was not being re-employed and had walked in to say a few choice words and tell the guard on the door exactly what he could do with his shells before picking up the contents of her locker and leaving.

'Well, we can soon find out. Wait a minute and I'll open my letter and read it.' Connie re-opened her locker, pulled her letter out of her coat pocket and tore it open with an expectant smile on her face.

But that smile soon disappeared. There was a horrible silence while Molly waited to hear what she had feared. 'No, no, they can't be serious, they can't lay me off! I'm a local lass, I know the job, I've worked here before. They must have got it wrong, they must have done!'

Molly went to comfort her friend, sitting next to her on the hard wooden bench, and read the letter herself.

'Oh, Connie, I'm so sorry. What a mess.'

Her friend, as she had feared, now had no job and had just taken on her new flat. What was she going to do with no wage coming in? There was next to no employment in York, except for Rowntree's and Terry's, and both were going to struggle in the coming months.

Connie looked up in horror. Even if the war was coming to an end, she could see no future for herself. She would have to hope she could go crawling home to the Freeman household and find some way to pay her rent there. She was back to square one. She screwed up the letter and tried to stop the tears from falling as Molly hugged her.

15

'I never knew I had so much stuff, and I've left a lot behind.' Lizzie Farrington looked around her new front room and beamed the biggest smile. 'Doesn't it all look grand, Bernard? That three-piece suite that we got from the second-hand shop is so comfortable, and the table from the old end of the farmhouse has shone up a treat. We're going to be happy here, I can just tell we are.'

'Aye, perhaps. It's going to be quiet and I'm going to be lost for a while with nothing to do. I can always go and help out at the farm occasionally, Mike said he'd need my help.' Bernard pulled back the lace curtain and looked out into the back yard. 'You know that out-house next to the lavvy would just hold a pig – it would be grand if we could still have our own bacon.' Bernard turned and smiled at Lizzie.

'Bernard Farrington, there will be no pigs coming to that yard. I have lived with the smell and dirt of pigs since the day I married you and here, in this lovely terraced house, is where it stops. At Pendle, it was never worth my while to do the cleaning, but I aim to have that doorstep donkey-stoned every week, the floor clean and the furniture polished. Else folk will talk about us; they always do when you live in a town.

There's bound to be a gossip along this row and I have a fair idea where they live. I bet she will be the first one to make herself known.' Lizzie stood with her hands on her hips, determined to fit into her new neighbourhood. 'My head doesn't know if it's coming or going, what with this wedding and moving into here.' She saw that Bernard was about to make himself comfortable in one of the new chairs. 'Don't you dare sit down. You can carry one or two of those heavy boxes upstairs; they are cluttering the floor down here.'

'Is there no peace for me, woman? We moved because I was suffering with aches and pains and now you have me lifting and moving all sorts. Bloody hell, I should never have mentioned this place was up for sale. I was as happy as any fella could be living at Pendle.' Bernard picked up one of the large boxes filled with bedding and started making his way up the stairs.

Lizzie read the list of things she still had to do for the upcoming wedding, Bernard was right: they should have waited until the wedding had taken place before moving, but it had freed up some bedrooms at the farm for Annie's relations, and they had to move sometime. Thank heavens Annie only wanted a quiet wedding and all was in hand. Banns had been read in both churches, the village hall at Chatburn had been booked and Annie had looked a treat in her old wedding dress. It might have been forty years old but it was the one thing that she had taken care of, hoping that one day a daughter of her own would be wearing it. The silk had cost her parents a small fortune and the lace had been hand-made by the seamstress who had designed it. Those were the days when her family had been wealthy landowners, gentleman farmers, and they had been absolutely horrified when their daughter announced she intended to marry a pig farmer from Clitheroe. Love had no boundaries, she thought, as she remembered the good-looking farmer that Bernard had once been. She came back from past dreams to the present day when she heard a knock on the front door and heard the letterbox open as somebody peered through it.

'Cooee! Hello, anybody there?'

Lizzie put her list down, straightened her apron and looked quickly in the newly hung wall mirror before putting a smile on her face. This would be the next-door neighbour she had been expecting since they had moved in the previous day. Her net curtains had never stopped twitching as she had watched the cattle wagon that had moved them in and taken note of what was being unloaded. She had done well to have waited twenty-four hours before her visit to vet them.

Lizzie opened the door to the woman standing on her step. She was about the same age as her, with a crossover pinny covering a pink knitted jumper and tweed skirt. She stood in her pom-pom slippers and smiled a sickly smile.

'I just thought I'd pop around and welcome you to the street. I live next door at number nineteen. I thought I'd bring you a jar of my homemade crab-apple jelly – it's a bit tart seeing sugar is in short supply, but my Trevor loves it.' She put her foot over the threshold and looked down the passage to the kitchen. 'I'm Kath, Kath Benson, and my husband is, as I say, Trevor. Have you got settled in? Anything I can do for you, anything you need to know?'

'Nice to meet you, Kath, I'm glad that you've made yourself known to us. Thank you for the jelly, I'll pop it in our kitchen cupboard.' Lizzie stepped back as Kath nearly pushed her way in.

'Well, I thought it would come in useful. Now, is your kitchen like ours? I've not been in here for an age. Ben Foster never let anyone into his house, grumpy old devil, he never mixed with anyone. It will be good to have a couple as neighbours. I take it you're both retired?' Kath said as she walked past Lizzie into her kitchen and looked around, taking in every detail.

'Yes, we've just retired from our farm, under Pendle, time for the young ones to take over. Our nephew is about to get married to our Land Girl. They make a lovely couple.' Lizzie filled the kettle, put it on top of the stove and lit the gas with a pop as the flames ignited.

'Oh, are you keeping the gas in? I don't like it, I don't feel safe with it. A Land Girl, now do you think that will work? She'll be from out of a town and not used to our ways.' Kath pulled a face and then turned around as she heard Bernard coming down the stairs.

'Annie is a grand lass. She took to farming straight away, we have no concerns on that front.' Lizzie saw Bernard as he caught his breath and took in the woman who was standing in his kitchen. 'This is Kath, from next door, our new neighbour, she's brought us some apple jelly.'

'Oh, aye our first visitor, grand. It's a pity I can't stop to make myself known to you, but I'm off to see a man about a dog. So you'll have to excuse me, I'm sure you two will find plenty to talk about.' Bernard tried to ignore the dirty look that Lizzie gave him as he felt for some change in his breeches pocket. He'd leave her to making the new neighbour welcome; Lizzie had been right, she was the nosy one, with her tight permed hair and smarmy smile. He was off for a pint to get out of the way. He'd only put his foot in it anyway, with what he had to say.

'He's not really going to see about bringing a dog here, is here? The walls are fairly thin. We couldn't do with the barking, my Trevor is such a light sleeper.'

Lizzie poured the tea and urged Kath to sit at the table which had seen better days, despite the polish that it had just recently had.

'No, he's going for a pint at the Dog and Gun, it's his way of getting out of any jobs. He's suffering from a bad hip, that's why we've moved into Clitheroe.'

'Drinking in the afternoon! Now my Trevor would never do that; in fact, we hardly ever drink, just a sweet sherry on special occasions, that's us.' Kath sipped her tea and looked around. 'The dustbin man calls on a Tuesday, the paper shop keeps open until eight at night and there's a man comes in a van from Fleetwood with fresh fish on a Friday, but he's not to be relied on, just depends if he has any petrol or not.'

'Thank you, Kath, that is all good to know. We aren't used to having everything to hand; we only used to come into Clitheroe once a week to go to the market and to pick the pig slops up,' Lizzie said without thinking.

'Pig slops, you were pig farmers. Oh, I thought you were sheep farmers; I should have guessed when I saw the state of the cattle wagon that moved you in.' Kath wrinkled her nose and decided that she had heard enough. 'Anyway, I'll have to get back, Trevor will wonder where I am. Just one more thing, we usually scrub our steps on a Monday after we've done the washing – we try to keep up appearances along this row.'

'I'm sure you do; I'll do it when I see fit. Now, I need to do more unpacking, but do call in when you need to know anything else or when you want to come and see the pig we are going to be keeping in the back yard. It won't be any problem. Pigs are clean animals really.' Lizzie couldn't help herself, the sight of Kath's face when she had mentioned they were pig farmers had just made her say it.

'A pig, in the back yard! Oh, no, I don't think so, at least I hope not,' Kath chuntered as she went out of the door.

'It'll keep the whole row in bacon, especially if I get a pair,' Lizzie shouted down the garden path and then grinned as she closed the door behind her. That would get the gossips going and give the nosy Kath Benson something to talk about. Bernard's idea had been a good one, but there was no way she would put it into practice.

*

'This letter's a bit vague. Mam says that none of them are staying the night of the wedding. They are all coming and going back in the same day. But she doesn't say how, it sounds as if she doesn't even know herself.' Annie passed Mike the letter she had just been delivered in the morning's post. 'Still, it means that I don't have to get the spare bedrooms tidy. They aren't ready, especially Bernard and Lizzie's old room which needs a good cleaning. The back bedroom has more holes in the roof than there is roof. The rain just pours in at the old end of the house. Bernard kept saying he was going to repair some slipped slates, but he never got on with it because of his aches and pains this winter.'

'Aye, come the better weather, that is one of the first things that I'll look at fixing. Pendle Farm has needed a new roof for all the years that I've been coming here. Bernard wasn't one for spending money; he'd rather have it in his bank. I'm going to rearrange the pig pens too, perhaps not have as many next year.' Mike quickly glanced at the letter and then decided to tell Annie more of his ideas for the future. 'The tatties are profitable at the moment because there's none coming from abroad, but if the war comes to an end, that will stop. I might even change that land to grow something else. It's back-breaking work and I'm sure there's other things we could grow that would make our farm more profitable. Uncle Bernard was a bit set in his ways.' He looked across at Annie. 'Are you feeling all right, lass? You look a bit peaky.'

'I feel a bit sick; I have done all morning. I think it's

just nerves and excitement. It's our wedding next weekend and we have so much to do. At least if my family aren't staying here, I need only get downstairs tidy and clean. I could tell by my mam's face she thought the house was a mess, but she was too polite to say anything.'

'As long as it is just that. You were sick yesterday morning. I'm starting to think that I'd better get a move on with the roof being fixed – we may be in need of those spare bedrooms.' Mike smiled and took Annie's hand.

'I didn't want to spoil our wedding day, but yes, I think we may be in need of those bedrooms, or at least one before the year is out.' Annie blushed. 'Thank heavens we are to be married soon, else I don't know what I'd have done.'

'So, I'm going to be a father. Aye, it's just as well that we are getting married. Don't worry, Bernard would have got his shotgun out if I didn't stand by you, and I suppose we have chanced our luck, sleeping together like we have.' Mike held Annie close and put his hand on her stomach. 'Not too much bending and scrubbing, and definitely no feeding the boars. If they knock you, it would do you and the baby damage. I love you, Annie Freeman, and we're going to have the bonniest baby ever born. A bouncing boy, one that has his father's looks.'

'Oh, we are, are we? Well, I might want a bonny girl that takes after her mother.' Annie buried her head in Mike's shoulder, relishing the love that they shared. 'It's a good job we are getting married. At least you can't tell yet. Your mother's wedding dress is cream and loose over my hips, but it fits lovely.'

'You'd look lovely in a potato sack and I'd still marry you even if you were having as many piglets as our best sow has just had.' Mike kissed the top of Annie's head. He loved her so much, and now he was going to be a father.

16

'I still don't know how Ned is going to get us to this wedding and back, but we're certainly having an early start. Six o'clock in the morning and we're all expected to be in our finery and ready to go. I bet Rose is cursing him, having to get Ivy up and dressed so early. You know it sounds daft, but I'm half expecting an aeroplane to land in our street to pick us up, Ned has been so secretive about it.' Winnie adjusted her hat and pushed her shoes on.

'No, I've no clue how we are getting there, I've just got the same instructions as you, be ready for six and make sure Connie is with us.' Molly stood up in front of her mother. 'There, how do I look? I feel a bit guilty at not having a new dress for Annie's wedding, but she's only seen these bridesmaid's dresses on a photograph, so I'm sure she won't mind, especially when times are so hard.'

'You look lovely, darling, you always do. Now, where is that Connie? She's late, she'll miss going with us if she isn't careful.' Winnie had no sooner said the words than there was a gentle knock on the front door.

'I know, I know, I'm late,' Connie said breathlessly. 'Sorry, I just can't get motivated. My mind's on other things, now I don't have a job.' She hurried inside and flung her handbag on the kitchen table. 'Annie was never that keen on me. I was surprised she wanted me as her bridesmaid, although it is good of her to.'

'You have to be her bridesmaid,' Molly told her. 'Rose is looking after Ivy, and seemingly this Mike that she is marrying has hardly any family. Besides, it goes without saying that she asked you. Although I must admit I feel like the old saying, always a bridesmaid never a bride.' She sighed and straightened Connie's headband. 'I wondered whether to dye my hair, to get rid of this ginger tinge, but people say not to do it else my hair will drop out.'

'All right, rub it in. I've been watching them dismantle our production lines and the people I've worked with gradually disappear all week, and I'm left standing there feeling sorry for myself. I know I should be happy that the war is coming to an end, but my life is falling apart.' Connie just wanted some sympathy. She was in no mood for a wedding, especially since she hadn't seen Chuck for a day or two.

'What on earth is that noise coming down the street? I was only joking when I said Ned must be taking us in an aeroplane.' Winnie made her way to the front door and peered out into the early light. It was Easter Saturday and all the workers were having a lie-in and were fast asleep, or should be if it wasn't for the sound of the huge khaki bus that had just crunched its gears at the top of the street and was now pulling up outside her front door.

'Howdy, ma'am, your taxi is ready. Next stop

Clitheroe, thanks to the American Air Force.' Wearing his US Air Force uniform, Chuck shouted out of the already open bus doors from the driving seat. 'We'll get you there in style and in good time, providing everybody is ready.'

'Oh, my Lord, we are travelling in this! Will it get us there?' Winnie exclaimed.

'Course it will, ma'am. We have jerry cans of diesel in the back and there's a crate of beer and a picnic hamper made up by our NAAFI – I thought that we might need to eat before we get there.' Chuck grinned as he saw Connie come out of the house. 'What do you think, doll? We have sort of borrowed it for the day! I couldn't let you all down, now could I?'

Connie squealed and tottered over in her heels to admire the khaki painted bus with an American white star on the side and the stars and stripes on the bonnet. 'Oh lover, just look at it! I can't believe that we're going all those miles to the wedding in this.' She climbed on board and bounced up and down on the brown leather seats before getting up and throwing her arms around Chuck's neck. 'I love you, my man.' She kissed him on the cheeks as Winnie and Molly closed the front door behind them, wedding presents and flowers in their hands.

'Isn't he the best man you could ever have?' Connie beamed.

Molly and Winnie glanced at one another. Connie changed her mind about Chuck as often as she changed her knickers. 'Yes, he'll do, but it's a long way to go in a bus, I hope it gets us there.' Winnie climbed in, followed by Molly.

'Morning, Chuck, this is a surprise. I'm glad that you'll be driving us to the wedding.' Molly had always admired him in his uniform and she understood exactly why Connie had fallen for him. He was dark and good-looking and he came from Montana, a place where Connie wanted to go to find her half-brother, even if the state was huge and he probably wouldn't even remember her.

'I sure am, Molly. Wouldn't miss an English wedding. It'll be something to tell the folks back home when I go back.' Chuck glanced at Connie and saw a cloud cross her face. 'I don't know when that'll be. We're still busy at the base, so I guess we'll be here a while longer yet.' Chuck put the bus into gear and then made sure everyone was seated. 'Right, we'll pick Ned and his family up and then it's on to Lancashyer. Never been there – I hope it's as scenic as Yorkshyer and that Ned has plotted our course accurately.'

'On a bus, we're going to Clitheroe on a bus and with a Yank driving us!' Ivy took Ned's hand and climbed the step into the bus, then slumped down in the seat next to Winnie.

'He never told me that we were going like this. What if I need a pee? I can't wait to have one all the way to Clitheroe or wherever it is,' Ivy moaned.

'You'll be all right, Ivy,' Winnie reassured her. 'We'll stop for you and it won't just be you that needs a wee.

There will be cafés, won't there, Chuck? We can stop for a comfort break.'

'There sure will be, ma'am. It's only sixty-one miles away, just three hours and we'll be there. This old bus will get us there and back. I've done all the maintenance on this old girl myself, she's to be trusted.'

'Stop worrying, Mother, sit back and enjoy the journey. It's not everyone that gets taken for a trip out in an American Air Force bus.' Ned patted his mother's shoulder and sat down behind her beside Rose. 'Are you all right, love? Nice surprise, eh?'

'You can say that again. It's a long way to go on a bus, but it will be worth it to see Annie get married. Do I look all right? Molly and Connie look beautiful.' Rose looked in her compact mirror and hung on to the seat as they started off on their journey with a jolt. She hoped that Chuck had got permission from his superiors for the use of the bus.

'You look wonderful, my love. Now enjoy your day. I know exactly how to get there, I mapped it out the other day. We just go across the Pennines. It will be lovely scenery but we'll have to try and get back before dark, because of the restrictions. There's a small airfield at Warcop near Clitheroe; I've flown over it many a time. It takes less than an hour in a plane, but I think this trip is going to take a while longer. Best we sit back and enjoy.'

'No wonder you didn't say much about how we were getting to the wedding. I'm sure Chuck will get us there safely, and besides, it's making Connie's day. She looks and sounds so happy. I feel for Molly, being on her own. I wish she could find herself a good man. That Matt that used to write to her hasn't been in touch for weeks now,' Rose whispered.

'Sounds like bad news there. Something's not right, it's to be hoped that he is still alive. But it's best not to give up hope. Our lads are winning, hopefully this war will soon be over.' Ned breathed in deeply. He had lost too many friends and colleagues over the last few years.

'I can hear you two,' Molly said, 'and I know that you're only concerned. I'm fine on my own, I promise. But I do wish I knew what had happened to Matt. I've got his home address, I think I'll write to it next week, just in case something has happened to him. Surely his mother will let me know where he is, and if he doesn't want to write to me any more then I'll accept it. I haven't seen him for months anyway.'

'Sorry, Mol, it's only because I care about you.' Rose smiled at her youngest sister. 'There might be a good-looking man at the wedding today that takes your eye.'

'Well, I've given up with telling her that she's got one that asks after her every week, but she won't listen. The lad at the butcher always asks, every time I go in, regular as clockwork,' Winnie quickly pointed out.

'Mam, William Allen is not for me,' Molly said firmly. 'I haven't hardly seen him since I left school. Now please let's change the subject.'

'You'll always have something to eat, Molly, if you marry a butcher. You could do worse,' Ivy piped up.

'Yes, Mrs Evans, so my mam has told me time and

again. But William and I sat next to one another at school. I know him too well, like the way he used to pick his nose and hide pig's tails in his pocket to frighten us all with. So please, everybody, forget the idea that William and I will ever be a pair.' Molly crossed her arms and decided to concentrate on watching the countryside go by as the flat fields of York made way for the more rugged scenery of the Pennines. They finally crossed the border into Lancashire with a cheer from everybody on board as Chuck pulled into a lay-by and let everyone stretch their legs and Ivy and Winnie rush to the café to use their toilets.

'Not long now, folks, we're nearly there.' Chuck lit a cigarette and offered one to Ned, then leaned against the bus with his arm around Connie. 'You look a million dollars, girl. I'll have to fight the men off from looking at you today.'

'I don't think that there will be many men here, Chuck. Besides, you know that I only have eyes for you.' Connie kissed him on the cheek.

'Aye, leave him alone. You might as well have been sitting on his knee when he was driving us here you were that close,' Ivy said as she came out of the café with Winnie taking her arm. 'You were such a distraction, I thought we were going to be in the hedge a time or two.'

'We're nearly there now, ma'am, I'll not put you in a hedge, let me assure you. Nobody has cracked the crate of beer open yet or helped themselves to the hamper – are none of you hungry or thirsty?'

'On the way back, old man,' Ned said. 'We'll celebrate on the return trip.'

Everybody nodded and Chuck started up the engine.

'Annie and Mike, here we come. I'm so pleased the sun is shining for their big day!' Chuck yelled.

They could see a town in the distance, set at the head of a long, sprawling valley with mountains on either side.

'Chatburn is just on the outskirts, Chuck, it should be signed. It's a lovely little village,' Winnie shouted over the noise of the bus.

'I'll find it, don't worry,' Chuck assured her. 'We're in good time.' He smiled at Connie as she stood next to him, clinging to a handrail and chatting to him while he drove.

Ten minutes later, they were lost. 'We should have taken that turn back there. It's not this side of Clitheroe, I'm sure of it. I don't recognise any of these roads or houses.' Winnie looked worried and couldn't help but sound frustrated as Chuck tried to reverse the bus in the smallest of spaces along one of the many country roads. 'Perhaps if you had concentrated instead of talking to Fanny Anne here, we wouldn't be lost!' she sniped, looking at Connie.

'I'm not distracting him. There's no road signs and everywhere looks the same,' Connie bit back.

'You've never shut up. Perhaps if you stopped talking to him for a while we would get there.' Molly gave her five penn'orth and got glared at by her best friend.

'Molly, that doesn't help,' Rose chastised her. 'We will find it, stop flapping. It doesn't help that some of the signposts are missing or changed around. It's nobody's fault, we will get there.'

'There's a young woman walking down the road in front of us. Pull up and ask her the way, else we're going to be late,' Ned suggested as he ran his fingers through his hair in frustration. They had been past the same farm three times now and all the small roads looked the same.

'I will, Ned, the doll is sure to know,' Chuck replied.

'Doll, who are you calling a doll? Chuck, you can't say that! You should only have eyes for me,' Connie yelled.

The young woman looked up in surprise as Chuck opened his window and leaned out.

'Are you lost? Are you looking for the Yank munition hiding place, because you've taken the wrong turning.' She smiled at Chuck.

'Thank you, miss, but no, we're looking for a little place called Chatburn. But if you don't mind my saying, you shouldn't be telling us about munitions. You could cost our boys' lives.'

'Well, you aren't exactly undercover in this big monster with your flag and a star on the side. Besides, everyone around here knows where it is, supposedly hidden under the trees down the Trough of Bowland. It's hardly a secret around here despite no road signs. You lot are always buzzing about. Anyway, you're on the right road. Chatburn is three miles further along.

Drive for two miles, then turn left and carry on for about a quarter of a mile and then you should be able to see the church spire.'

'Most grateful, miss, that's exactly what we are looking for. We're late for a wedding!'

'A wedding! In that?' the young woman exclaimed.

'Yes, that's where we're going, thank you, miss,' Chuck said hurriedly as Connie and the rest of the bus urged him to drive on. They were going to be late and Connie wasn't having him talking to the local lass for a minute longer.

17

'Do I look all right? I feel like I'm going to be sick,' Annie said as she stood shivering in her wedding dress. It was a lovely long cream satin dress, in a simple cut, but Lizzie had obviously been married in summer, not at the beginning of spring. Annie clutched her simple bunch of primroses and violets as she stepped outside Bernard and Lizzie's new home. She had slept there overnight, leaving Mike alone on the farm, adhering to the tradition of it being bad luck for the bride and groom to see one another before their wedding day.

'You look lovely, absolutely beautiful – our Mike is a lucky lad. Not that you've got a bad catch with him.' Lizzie pulled the small net veil over Annie's eyes. 'Now, go on, you get in the back of the car and I'll sit in the front. It's good of the landlord at the Brown Cow to lend it and he's even put a ribbon on it. Although I think Bernard will have part shares in his old car with the amount of money he's spent over his bar. Bernard is so chuffed that you've accepted his offer to give you away. He's polished up quite well for once.'

'Are you two going to gas all day? Don't you know that we have a wedding to go to?' Bernard shouted, keeping the engine running. 'Oh Lord, we're going to be late at this rate,' he muttered as he saw the neighbour's front door open.

'I had forgotten it was the wedding today!' Kath Benson crossed her arms and looked Annie up and down.

'Yes, this is Annie; she was our farm girl but she's about to marry our nephew.'

'Oh, good luck, my dear. All the best for the future. You must not have any problem with pigs, else you would be foolish to be getting married to a farmer of such.' Kath pulled a face. 'I can't abide them.'

'No problem at all, they are lovely creatures, unlike some humans,' Annie replied and stepped into the car. She hadn't time to talk to the neighbour that Lizzie had been worrying about; she had a wedding to get to.

'What the heck! Do you have some Yanks at your wedding, Annie?' Bernard exclaimed as he pulled up in a space next to the church and looked across at the bus parked up at the opposite side of the road.

'Not that I know of.' Annie climbed out of the car to the chiming of the church bells from the small bell tower. The vicar was waiting for her in the church porch, and she saw her mother standing behind him with a huge smile on her face. Annie's eyes started to fill with tears. She remembered her mother's hugs and kisses and the love her late father had given her and the days growing up with her sisters. She was getting married, and she would never return to York to live at home again. All her emotions clashed as Lizzie straightened her dress and veil and smiled at her.

'Oh no you don't, no tears, even if they're tears of happiness. You make a lovely bride and I hope our Mike realises how lucky he is. We are so proud of you both.' Lizzie dabbed her eyes and looked across at the vicar and Winnie.

'Now, come on, Bernard Farrington, take this bonny lass's hand and take her down the aisle.' Lizzie smiled at Winnie as she came across to them. 'Isn't she bonny? Never seen a bonnier bride.'

'She is, Lizzie, you have done her proud and the church looks beautiful.' Winnie took Annie's hand. 'You'll always be my daughter and I'll always be there for you no matter how far away we are. Never forget that. Now, before you go down the aisle, put this around your neck. It used to be Grandmother Annie's necklace, so I thought you should have it on your wedding day.' Winnie hunted in her handbag for the small silver locket that had been her mother's pride and joy, a token of love between mother and daughter, then placed it around Annie's neck and kissed her on the cheek. 'I hope that you and Mike will always be happy.'

'Thanks, Mam,' Annie wiped back a tear.

'Hey, none of those tears,' Winnie chided softly. 'Now, chin up, smile, and that good-looking man of yours is waiting for you, along with your family. We've all made it together in that bus over there – what a carry-on! But none of us would have missed your wedding.

You should have known that. Us Freemans are a family and we never let any one of us down.'

'It's you lot that are in that Yank bus?' Bernard exclaimed. 'How did they get away with that, then?'

Without replying, Winnie simply gave him a sly smile then set off with Lizzie to take their seats in the church.

Bernard took Annie's arm. 'Right, lass, welcome to the family. Let's get this job done.'

Annie glanced around at Connie and Molly as they stood behind her looking absolutely beautiful in their hand-made dresses. Molly had so many skills and she should be proud of herself. Annie breathed in and steadied her nerves.

The daffodils were blooming in the churchyard and the wedding march was playing as they stood in the church entrance. Annie smiled nervously at Bernard – even he was shiny, clean and well dressed. It was her perfect day. She stepped over the ancient threshold and made her way down the aisle to her handsome farmer who was standing next to the vicar with a huge smile on his face. She took his arm and gazed into his eyes, loving every inch of him.

Mike mouthed silently, 'I love you.'

'Dearly beloved,' the vicar said loudly, looking around at the small gathering that had come to celebrate a joyful wedding in his ancient church. Love would always find a way, he thought, as he looked down at the farmer and the Land Girl who had come together because of the war and fallen in love. Out of bad came some good things. He asked the congregation if there was any reason for these two not to be married and breathed a sigh of relief when none was given.

Annie's voice quivered as she promised to love, honour and obey, and watched, her hands shaking, as Mike placed the small golden band on her finger.

They walked down the aisle, and Annie beamed to either side at her new relations and the old ones. It was the start of a new life for her and her family. The war was coming to an end, she had the man she loved and a baby on the way – although she hoped the latter would remain a secret for a while longer yet. They walked out into the spring sunshine and heard the bells ringing high above them.

'Smile! Say cheese.' Molly dashed in front of them both with her camera. 'One for the family album.'

Winnie took it back from her for a group shot. 'Come on, line up, let's have one of us all together. Chuck, you stand next to Connie – it won't be every wedding that has a Yank in uniform in their wedding picture.' She organised everybody before the vicar came and took the camera out of her hands, insisting that she too should be in the shot.

'It might be March, but it's still cold,' Ivy moaned as she stood next to Ned and tried to smile.

'We're going across the road to the hall soon, Mother, you'll get warm and have something to eat there.' Ned took his mother's arm and watched as the sisters lined up together and Connie captured them on camera.

'It's going to be a long day for me. But it's nice to see everybody happy,' Ivy said as Ned walked slowly by her side. 'I remember when I married your father. There wasn't any of this fuss, just your grandparents from both sides and us two. We had no brass, but your father was determined to make us a better life.'

'And he did, Mother, we wanted for nothing,' Ned replied.

'Aye, he was a good 'un, taken too early, but we've managed.' Ivy looked at the wedding party coming down the church path, with Connie throwing tiny pieces of torn-up paper over them as a form of confetti and the vicar giving a disapproving look, thinking of the mess it was going to leave behind. 'If they're as happy as we were, they'll not want for much.'

'I'm sure they will be, Mother. Or at least I hope so.' Ned smiled as Rose came and joined them.

'Doesn't she look a picture? This farming life is suiting her well. Now, let's make our way to the village hall and get you seated, Ivy. It's cold standing in this sneaky wind.'

'Aye, I'd like to get in and get something to eat. It's been a long day already and we're only halfway through it. It will take me weeks to get over all this excitement.' Ivy took Rose's arm and shuffled across the road towards the small village hall. Once inside, she settled herself down at the nearest table and looked around the decorated hall with its Union Jacks flying from the beams and a bunch of daffodils upon each table.

'It's grand in here, Ivy, and just look at the spread on the long table over there. It's a help-yourself do.' Rose pulled her seat up next to her mother-in-law while Ned took their plates to load them up with food and to stop his mother from moaning.

'Aye, it's all right, isn't it? Your Annie has done well for herself, I'm glad for her. Your mother looks relieved that the day is going well.' Ivy watched as Winnie came in, all smiles, following the newly-weds and laughing with Lizzie and Bernard.

'She will be feeling it, if I know her. She knows that Annie has a new home now.' Rose watched as the wedding party sat down around their table. 'She's only got Molly left to get off her hands now, and that will break her heart.'

18

'Oh, Lizzie, you've done my lass proud. It was a lovely wedding and the reception at the village hall was wonderful; we couldn't have provided half of that over in York.' Winnie climbed down from the bus into the farmyard.

She had vowed she wouldn't stay there and had secretly hoped that Chuck would never manage to drive the bus up the narrow track to Pendle Farm when Mike and Annie had begged them to come back with them before they returned home. But manage it they had, and now all the family, dressed in their Sunday best, was looking around the place Annie called home.

'Aye, well, us farmers club together and if it's a wedding everybody raids their larder. It was only like a Jacob's join but it was better than nothing.' Lizzie watched the young couple as Mike picked up Annie, her hands clasped around his neck, to carry her over the threshold of their home. 'That's grand to see – new life in the old farm – and it looks like they've been busy tidying up already. I know Annie loves living here, so don't you worry about her.'

'I know she will, she never has been a city girl. Always going for walks and wanting to be somewhere else than sat at home. Mike looks as if he truly loves her, I know I needn't worry about her.'

Ivy leaned on Ned's arm and stepped across the newly cleaned yard, eyeing the pigs without going near them.

'My father used to have a pig when I was a girl, up in the North East,' she said. 'You never go hungry if you keep a pig. We used to butcher them and then share with our neighbours. I'll always remember pig-killing day. My mother used to make me go to my aunty's house to stay while the dirty deed was done. Mucky creatures, but bonny when they are young.' Ned helped her into the farmhouse.

'Ivy's getting more and more frail and taking more and more looking after,' Winnie mentioned quietly to Lizzie. 'My poor Rose has her hands full what with looking after her, working at Rowntree's and worrying about Ned returning from his bombing missions. She's my main worry at the moment; you always have worries if you have children.' Winnie sighed.

'I've never been blessed,' Lizzie replied. 'Although Mike is as near as I can get. He's a good lad, so I'm glad that he's married your lass. He does love her and he'll always look after her, that I'm sure of. He had it hard when his parents died and I thought he might go off the rails a little, but he didn't. He's a hard worker – he can be a bit secretive, but I think your lass has found that out already.'

Lizzie's attention switched to Molly as she laughed with her sister. 'Your Molly seems a nice lass. Has she no fella?'

'She has, but he's in the army and she hasn't heard

from him for a while, so we don't know where he is. I think she's just accepted that he's no longer interested in her, so it's a good thing that she didn't get to love him too deeply.'

Connie and Chuck walked up the yard and admired the young piglets that still looked so sweet, Connie giggling about them and their antics.

'She's going to have her heart broken when he goes home if he doesn't take her with him,' Winnie commented, 'and it won't be long before he does go home, as it sounds as if the war is coming to an end. About time. We've lost enough folk and have suffered enough.'

'Come on,' Lizzie urged. 'We'll go in and have a cuppa tea. Are you sure that you won't be staying the night?'

'No, no, we can't – Chuck has to have the bus back by dark and Ned is back at his base tomorrow. But thank you, Lizzie, you have done more than enough for us.' Winnie knew that she was leaving her daughter with a good family.

'Well, we will treat her as our own, so you have no worries,' Lizzie assured her. 'I'm sure she will invite you to stay whenever you want, now that she has her own home. And I bet it won't be long before you are made a grandmother if I know them two.'

They walked into a spotless farm kitchen that both women hardly recognised. The walls had been whitewashed, the stone floor had been scrubbed and rugs laid down, furniture had been polished and a vase of spring flowers was set upon the table.

'Lord, I've only been away a few days and just look at the difference!' Lizzie exclaimed. 'It's hardly the same kitchen. Except I see you, Bernard Farrington, have made yourself at home next to the fire as usual.'

'Aye, I wouldn't mind coming back to live here if it was always kept like this.' Bernard sipped his tea and winked at Annie.

'You're coming home with me. It could always have been like this if you had shifted yourself and kept the yard and farm tidy.' Lizzie flicked a tea towel at him, but she couldn't help but smile. 'It's lovely, Annie, well done.'

'Thank you.' Annie sat on a kitchen chair, still in her wedding dress. 'We're going to work our way through the rest of the house and Mike is going to mend the roof in the summer so that the far bedrooms won't be damp. Everybody will be more than welcome to stay then. Molly, you could come on holiday when you take some time off from Rowntree's. Rose has just told me that the munitions factory is closing and that you are back shortly to making chocolates or boxes. You must be glad about that?'

'I don't know if I am,' Molly confessed. 'I'd become a supervisor in what I was doing and I was enjoying my job. I might be like you and change what I do. As you used to say, there's more than chocolate in the world.' Molly didn't dare look at her mother's face.

'You've got a good job there, Molly Freeman,' Winnie retorted. 'Rowntree's have been good to this family. You have a job for life if you stay there, just like Rose.'

'Just toying with the idea, Mam, I'm not saying I'm leaving.'

'I should think not! It's a good job and at least you have one. Poor Connie, she's not so lucky. She looks worried to death. Is there nothing you can do for her Rose, a good word here or there?'

'No, Mam, I don't have the influence, and they've got rid of so many people anyway, ' Rose looked at Ned for support.

'Maybe when things get back to normal, there might be more leeway,' he suggested. 'There's bound to be ingredient shortages until the shipping lanes open up again properly and work resumes as usual. This war is going to take some time to get over. Even I don't know what I'm going to do when the war ends.'

'Mmmm . . . well, hopefully she will find something else. She'll have to move back in with us. She's not a bad lass, always has bad luck though,' Winnie said quietly.

It was getting to be late afternoon; they would have to be thinking of returning home soon and leaving the newly-weds. It would be a long trip and Ivy was already nearly asleep in the rocking chair next to the window. At least they would know their way this time, Winnie thought as she sipped her tea. Hopefully they would be back before dark.

'Oh, Chuck, aren't they lovely? So pink and cuddly.' Connie watched as the piglets buried themselves under the straw and put her arm through his.

'They are,' Chuck agreed. 'We have one or two on

our farm back home, but mainly cattle and horses. Wow, I miss home so much. I'll be glad when we get our orders to ship out. I miss the big open ranges, the smell of pine when you wake up in the morning and the snow-capped mountains when winter arrives.' He leaned over the pen, his head bowed. 'I'm not going to stay in the Air Force if they'll let me leave. I'm going to go back home and hope that my father welcomes me back to run the ranch with him. I was headstrong and thought I knew everything when I left home, but my time in this country with you has changed me.'

Connie put her arm around him and kissed him. 'I'll miss you, Chuck, because I love you. I've never felt this way about anybody. I tried not to love you but I can't help it. I know I'm asking for heartbreak, I've known that all the time. Everyone warned me that you Americans were all right to flirt with but not to give our hearts to.' Connie wiped a tear away from her eyes. He was going to leave her as soon as the war was over, as she had always known he would.

'What do you mean, Connie? I love you too, I've no intention of breaking your heart. I've been thinking for a while now that we should get married; you know I've always wanted to take you back to Montana with me. But would you be happy to come over to America when I get my orders home and when I've sorted things out with my parents? They will love you, I just know they will, and my younger sister has always wanted a sister to share things with. Connie, I've never felt this way before and I've never loved anybody like I do you. Say that you'll marry me and come back home to Montana with me?' Chuck held Connie close and kissed her.

'Oh, Chuck! Marriage! Montana! America! A rancher's wife! Oh, I love you so much, how can I ever say no? A new life for both of us away from the war and all the worries.' She shook herself, beaming up at him. 'I can't believe it! Do you really mean it?' She wrapped her arms around his neck again.

'I sure do, Connie Whitehead. Will you marry me and make me one happy American?'

Connie squealed with delight, 'You know I will, you big hunk, Chuck Lawrence. I can't wait to tell everybody.' She jumped up and down with excitement.

'Not today, Connie; today is Annie and Mike's day. Tell them when I know more about when we are free to go back to America and when I've sorted things with my folks. Besides, I need to apply for permission to marry you from the base and you'll need permission to get into the States, and there's a lot to do before either of us can go back to Montana. But we will do it, gal. We'll get married over there and live with my parents. The house is huge – far too big for just them – you'll love it. My ma will love it.'

Connie caught the excitement in Chuck's eyes – all this time he'd been planning their life together in his head and she had feared he'd gone cold on the idea. Apart from how happy he made her, she would be another step closer to finding her half-brother in the vast, sprawling country of America. But most importantly, it would be a new life for her and Chuck, without the uncertainty and lack of money once the war was ended.

The hallway clock struck eight as Winnie and Molly finally reached home. 'I have never been so tired in my life. What a day!' Winnie slumped down in an easy chair in the front room. 'I thought we were going to be in bother when that ARP warden pulled us up just outside Clitheroe on our way back.'

'Yes, thank heavens he was only asking if we needed directions. You should have seen his face when he saw us lot in the bus in all our wedding attire. And Ivy is half-drunk after drinking sherry with Bernard. She's had a good day, and by the looks of it Connie and Chuck have too. They looked so happy on the way back home.'

'And what about you, miss? Have you had a good day? Seeing Annie getting married must have upset you a little. After all, you are now left on your own with your old mother.'

'I've had a good day,' Molly said, 'except everybody seems to think I should get on with finding myself a fella. I'm just not that bothered, and anyway, I still think of Matt. I can't betray him until I know where he is or what has become of him.'

'I understand. If something has happened to him, his family will know. Have you not got his home address? At least then you would know and perhaps be able to get on with your life.' Winnie suspected that Molly was starting to feel that she was going to be left on the shelf, despite giving part of her heart to Matt and waiting faithfully for him.

'I have, Mam. I keep trying to pluck up the courage to write to his mother. I suppose I just don't want to hear that he's dead somewhere on a battlefield or that he's got a new sweetheart, but something is wrong somehow.' Molly yawned. 'Thank heavens it's Easter Sunday tomorrow – no work!'

'The ideal day to write to his mother and just ask. Then at least you know where you stand. It's no good saving your heart for a ghost, Molly.' Winnie took off the pearl ear clips that had been driving her mad all day, placing them on the side table and rubbing her ears. 'It's no good. I'm going to have to go to bed while I can still make it up those stairs. I'm glad I don't need anybody's help just yet. Unlike poor Ivy – she's getting really bad at walking. Rose has a lot on her plate with Ned away so much.'

'Don't worry about me, Mam, I'm all right. I will write to Matt's mother. I've been fearing the worst for a while now. I just haven't had the courage to confront it.'

'That's my lass. We all want you to be happy. That's all I want for all of my girls. That includes Connie – she'll always be part of the family if she did but know it. The flighty one, she is, not like you three.' Winnie yawned and then kissed Molly on her brow. 'Don't stay up too late. It may be your last week making munitions but Rowntree's will still expect you to work long hours.'

'I won't, Mam, I'll not be far behind you.' Molly sat quietly and breathed in deeply. It had been a wonderful wedding day and Annie had really got everything she had dreamed of: a good-looking man, a farm and freedom to be herself. And Rose had Ned, the perfect job and home. But what had she got? Nothing – a boyfriend missing that she presumed dead and her old job at Rowntree's back. And even that didn't sound as interesting as it used to be. According to Rose, the box manufacturing had been cut right back – no nice decorations, just pre-cut boxes to fill. Perhaps when the war was finally over, it would be time for her to do something new with her life.

19

Molly hesitated beside the post box, letter in hand. It was Easter Monday and the Minster bells were ringing out over York and church goers were passing her by dressed in their finest. She had written to Matt's mother in the early hours of the morning and now she wondered again whether to send it or not. Matt had always said in his letters only to write to his mother if it was an emergency, but surely this *was* an emergency: she didn't know if he was alive or not. She closed her eyes and heard the letter drop into the box. There, it was done now. Hopefully she would know what had become of Matt in a few days, then either way she could get on with her life.

She gave a sigh of relief and looked around her. Barrage balloons still flew in the clear blue skies behind the Minster and all the shop windows were criss-crossed with white tape to stop them from shattering if they were bombed – war was still evident wherever you looked. It had been a long five and a half years, and everybody was weary. However, there was light at the end of the tunnel. The Russians were attacking and making good progress into Nazi-held territories, along with the Allies. Surely war in Europe would be over soon if not elsewhere? Once peace had been declared, life should get easier.

Molly turned up the small paved road of the Shambles to the bakery to knock on Connie's door and offer her a hard-boiled pace egg dyed that morning in onion skins to give it a lovely brown patterned colour. It was an extravagance, thanks to Annie giving her mother two dozen eggs that the hens on the farm had laid. Sometimes you just had to cheer yourself up with things like that, Molly thought, remembering the times when the order books had been filled at Rowntree's for beautifully decorated Easter eggs. Now, with sugar and chocolate sparse, there were no Easter eggs. She knocked hard on the door then stood back and looked up at the blackout blinds which were still pulled, until she heard Connie's voice shouting, 'I'm coming!' She waited on the step and contemplated the unloved bakery – what a waste of a good property.

'You're still in your nightie – it's nearly dinner time!' Molly exclaimed as Connie opened her door and ushered her in quickly before anybody saw her.

'I know I'm late up. I didn't sleep, I had so much to think about. I just tossed and turned all night.' Connie ran up the un-carpeted stairs in her bare feet and stopped at the top. 'What are you doing here anyway? I thought that you'd be sitting down to lunch with your mam.' Connie reached for the kettle and put it onto her small gas stove. 'I hope you like your tea black, I've hardly any milk in. It won't be that strong, either, because I use the tea leaves twice.'

'Mam's gone around to see Rose; she's worried that she's looking tired. I've to go around this afternoon for tea but I thought I'd call here first after posting my letter.' Molly lay across the unmade bed and sighed.

'Letter, what letter? Have you turned down your offer of a job at Rowntree's? I can't blame you if you have; it's not going to be like it used to be. Machines are going to be doing our jobs – no wonder they don't need half of us,' Connie moaned.

'No, not Rowntree's; a job is a job, I'd not be that daft. No, I've sent a letter to Matt's mother to see what has become of him. I just need to know one way or another. Do you think I'm an idiot?' Molly sat up on the edge of the bed to accept the weak cup of tea. 'I don't want to upset her, but I just need to know what's happened to him. Sometimes I think I love him and then at others I think, well, I hardly know him really.'

'You did right. You need to know, but she might not even know herself. He might just be noted as lost in action. You'll not know for sure until this bloody war is over. It can't end fast enough for me. I'm counting the days.' Connie smiled and felt her stomach churn with excitement.

'I thought you were the opposite, because once it's all over Chuck will have to return and then you'll just have to write to one another. Besides, you need a job before anything else, or you'll be out on the street. In fact, you were talking of walking out with Fred Milburn from the shoe shop not so long since because you thought you were going to be in the lurch. It's a good job Kitty at work told you exactly what he was like. She didn't have a good word for him.' Molly took a sip of the very weak tea and then remembered that she had the pace egg in her pocket. 'Here, Happy Easter. I boiled you this, it's patterned by onion skins to celebrate Easter, seeing that I have no chocolate to give you.'

'Oh, that looks lovely. Thank you so much,' Connie said, giving her friend a grateful hug. 'But I could eat a horse, so I'm going to eat it now; it will just do for my breakfast.' Connie knocked the egg on her bedstead and started to peel it and then eat it in almost three mouthfuls. 'I couldn't eat a thing last night, not that I have much in, but my head and stomach were all over the place with what I was thinking about.' She paused, clearly wrestling with something. 'It's no good, I'm going to have to tell somebody and you are my best friend.' Connie grinned and licked a piece of egg from her lips.

'I swear I am going to burst with my news.' She caught her breath and took Molly's hand. 'Chuck proposed to me after the wedding on Saturday, at the farm. We are to get married and I've to join him at his home in Montana. Once he leaves the Air Force, he's going home to the family ranch. Molly, all my dreams have come true!'

'You are getting married and leaving for America! Oh, Connie, congratulations, I'm so happy for you.' Molly felt a moment of sadness; she was being left behind by everybody. 'When are you getting married and where? You'll need a wedding dress; I think I've enough parachute silk just to make one dress if you'd like me to?' Molly gripped Connie's hand and squeezed it tightly.

'I don't know where I'm getting married at yet. It would be lovely if you could, but Chuck says there are various rules and regulations to alien marriages, as the Americans call them. I'm hoping that we're going to get married once we're both over there. I'm to go and live with his parents on their ranch. It sounds idyllic, with horses, open ranges, snow-topped mountains and miles of wide blue sky. And at last, I may be able to track my little brother down and right the wrong that I did to him.' Connie stared across at the blackout window, dreaming of the new life she was going to lead.

'Oh, Lord, Connie, that is one big step. I wouldn't know where to start. You'll need a passport and papers and things like that. Do you love him enough to leave everything you have behind?' Molly felt anxious for Connie, but she didn't want to burst her bubble.

'Of course I do, don't be silly. Chuck is everything to me, and besides, what do I have here? Other than you and your lovely family, of course. Nothing, absolutely nothing, not even a job. But I'll take anything for the next few months just to get some money into my bank ready for my going.'

'Well, I'll miss you,' Molly said quietly.

'And I'll miss you, of course I will. I have you to thank for everything. I can't even think about how hard it's going to be saying goodbye to you and your family. But I've got to go. It's the chance of a lifetime, I'm not going to miss it. Sorry, Molly, I'll feel bad leaving you. Anyway, it won't be for a while yet. The war is being won but it will take ages for everything to come to an end and back to normal. My first task is to find myself a job. I started looking last week but now it will be in earnest. I will need every penny if I'm to sail to America. I walked down Coppergate and noticed that there was a job being advertised in Brown's shoe shop. Only trouble is it's where Fred Milburn works, but I think I can put up with him for a few months. Besides, I'll tell him that I'm engaged and that will put him off.'

'You're asking for trouble, Connie.' Molly looked concerned. 'Fred is used to always getting his way. You should know that after what Kitty told you at work. That's why she stopped courting him. If you've not noticed, they're always advertising for staff there. I bet it's because of him, I heard that he's a bit of a lech.'

'I can look after myself, stop worrying. A job is a job. You need to worry about yourself more than me. Rowntree's is changing, it won't be the same place as we used to know it. You need to make your own luck in this world.' Connie lay back on the bed and turned towards Molly. 'Life is strange. Let's hope that the coming months will bring happiness and peace. That you hear from Matt and I get to Montana. Who would have thought that all of this would happen to us that day we met on our first interview? I saw you and just knew that we would become the very best of friends.'

'Me too, I was petrified.' Molly remembered the days when they had both started at work. 'We've come a long way. We will keep in touch, won't we?'

'Of course we will. Besides, I haven't gone yet. We'll always be the Chocolate Box Girls, me and you.'

Molly came in from her last shift in the munitions factory at the end of the following week and pulled her turban off. 'Well, I can't say I'm going to be sorry to see the back of all this. Do you know, Mam, there are army workers clearing everything now as we sit here, in the middle of the night, just so no one notices what is going on? They say it will be all cleared by next Monday, ready for Rowntree's management to prepare for their new machinery. I've been told to report to the Black Magic department, where I'll be allocated a temporary job until the new equipment is fitted and the area is made clean. Then we'll be moving back into the cardboard box room where I started – but boxing Black Magic chocolates in new boxes. I don't know what they look like yet, but I'm just hoping the glue doesn't smell. I don't even like plain chocolate, so I won't be tempted to eat any.' She sighed. 'I've enjoyed my work at the munitions factory – at least I was given a bit of responsibility.'

'Molly Freeman, you are never satisfied,' Winnie retorted. 'At least you can't blow yourself up making chocolates. I, for one, am very happy that you're going to be in the Black Magic packing department. Things will get back to normal now, no twelve-hour shifts and me having to sneak around the house while you sleep. I tell you another thing, it's nice to be able to pick up a newspaper and not read that there's been anywhere bombed. It's been a good fortnight now since one fell on our country. The headlines this morning showed all these German soldiers with their hands upon their heads surrendering in a place called the Ruhr. Three hundred and seventeen thousand Jerries admitting defeat – what are our lads going to do with all of them? They'll all have to be fed and looked after.' She tutted.

'Hopefully they will be able to go back to their homes,' Molly said quietly. 'They must be feeling deflated.'

'A lot have to stand for their actions when all this ends,' Winnie said robustly. 'I hope some of them are taken to the gallows, especially Hitler and his cronies – Goebbels, Himmler and Hess – they don't deserve to live after all this.' She put a sardine sandwich in front of Molly and watched as she picked at the dry corners of the bread and pulled a face. 'It's all I've got in until tomorrow, it will have to do you. It's better than nothing.'

'I know, Mam, I'm sorry. I should be grateful that we have this. I just don't like sardines, they are full of tiny bones. But I'm grateful.' Molly took a bite and wrinkled her nose; she really did hate sardines.

'Oh, I nearly forgot, with talking about the Jerries. You've a letter, it came this morning. It's got a Sheffield postmark on it – isn't that where Matt's mother comes from? It might be him, he could be home with his mother.' Winnie wiped her hands on her apron and passed it to Molly and watched as she studied the writing. 'But it doesn't look like his handwriting – maybe it's from his mother.'

'I'll open it after when I'm in my room, Mam. You're right, it's not his handwriting. It must be from his mother.' Molly pushed half of her sandwich to one side. She had no appetite for sardines, and now her stomach felt like it had gone into free fall with the worry of what was in the letter.

'Open it here, love, just in case it's bad news and then I'm here for you,' Winnie said quietly.

Tentatively, Molly opened the letter and unfolded it. She began to read:

14 Bank Road
Sheffield
England

Dear Miss Freeman,

I am replying to your letter asking about my husband's health and whereabouts.

Molly gasped. Husband! She'd thought it was his mother that she had written to. She felt her heart racing.

Mathew has unfortunately been detained as a POW in one of the holding camps in Germany. The Red Cross are wonderful at keeping me informed. Hopefully, the way the war is going, he will be returning to me and our two children soon. God willing, he will survive to see this terrible conflict over.

May I ask, how do you know Mathew? He has never mentioned you. Did you perhaps meet him in the York Barracks where he was stationed?

Yours sincerely,
Elizabeth Drummond

Molly's hand shook as she passed the letter to her mother, her eyes filling with tears.

How could he? How could he have spent all that time with her and said all the things that he had and led her on, just for her to find out that he was already married, and a father to boot? It wasn't his friend Danny who had tried to lead Connie astray when they had first met who had been the wild one, but it had been Matt all along. He had led her up the garden path. No wonder he had said not to write to his home address unless it was an emergency. Molly burrowed her head against her mother's shoulder.

'Oh, Mam, how could he? He lied to me and I thought that he did care a little for me,' she sobbed.

'He's a sod, Molly. He had us all fooled. I genuinely thought that he was a nice lad the way you talked about him. Never mind, lass, at least you know where he's at and that he's alive, but perhaps the Jerries are welcome to him.' Winnie re-read the letter. 'A wife and two children. That poor woman – if it wasn't enough that her man was at war and then to get a letter from you. I hope that you didn't say how close you were?' Winnie held Molly tightly and stroked her hair. 'There's plenty more fish in the sea. Throw this one back and catch a good dependable one next time,' Winnie whispered, feeling Molly's grief.

20

'Now, don't you look just dandy! Have you dressed up just for me?' Chuck held Connie tight and kissed her as she checked in the mirror to see if the lines she had drawn up the backs of her legs to look like stockings were straight.

'You, and the fact that I have a job interview at the shoe shop in an hour's time. I need to look my best. I need every penny if we are to marry and go to live in America.'

'Oh, shucks, Connie, I need to talk to you about that. It's not going to be as easy as I thought.' Chuck let go of Connie and stood back. 'I've been asking about and it isn't that straightforward.'

'What do you mean, it isn't that easy? Are you trying to tell me that you've changed your mind? That it was just a spur-of-the-moment thing?' Connie swivelled round to face Chuck.

'Now, doll, don't be silly. Of course I still want to marry you. But I've to seek permission from the Air Force chaplain, we've both to have an interview with him and we have to wait for at least three months before the Air Force will give me permission. Then we would be able to firstly marry at a register office and then if you wish we could have a military ceremony with the Air Force chaplain. I never realized it was going to be so complicated.' Chuck shook his head, 'Even when we've done all that, you will have to apply for a visa to be able to enter America, or else you will end up on Ellis Island as an alien. It's to ensure that we're marrying because we love one another, not because you're pretending to love me to get into the good old US.'

'I *am* marrying you because I love you. I know exactly where I'm going – that is Montana – I'm not interested in Hollywood. Although it would be nice to drive down Hollywood Boulevard and see all the stars,' she added with a grin. 'What a palaver. I thought America welcomed everybody with open arms. If we do all this, are we then clear to go?'

'With the war coming to an end, they would prefer that we waited to see where I'm going to be posted, because you wouldn't be entitled to come overseas with me, other than my home, if I decide to leave the Air Force. Which I am considering, but they don't know that yet. But your passage once we are married will be free – they believe in keeping their armed forces happy when they need to. I'm sorry, doll, I had no idea about all this. It isn't as if you get married every day.' Chuck sighed. 'I've not put you off marrying this useless hunk, have I? I love you too much to lose you.'

'Don't be daft, Chuck, of course it hasn't put me off from marrying you. I love you, not Hollywood or the Air Force. We'll just have to wait. We'll go and see the chaplain and then wait. Three months will hopefully see the war out and give me time to save up. Now, give me a hug.'

'You're going to be late for your interview, I'll walk there with you.' Chuck passed Connie her coat. 'Can we look for an engagement ring next weekend?'

'Of course! I've been looking forward to flashing a ring on my finger when I'm fitting shoes in my new job. I could say I'm engaged to the most handsome man in the American Air Force.' Connie kissed Chuck as he buttoned her coat up for her.

'I'm only ground crew, nothing special. An erk, that's what you Brits call us.' Chuck returned her kiss. 'A grease monkey that keeps planes flying.'

'That's something to be proud of. Besides, nobody needs to know that. I'll tell everyone I'm to marry a top flying ace of a pilot and just watch their faces.' Connie laughed as they made their way down the stairs onto the cobbled street. The bakery shop hadn't opened that morning, and idly she wondered why there was no sign of life inside.

'You'll get found out.'

'Ah, but we'll both be gone by then. Living our lives of complete bliss in Montana.'

Connie was prepared to wait. Three to six months was nothing to wait for certain happiness.

'Good afternoon, Connie, or should I say Miss Whitehead, as you're here for an interview?' Fred Milburn stood at the back of his shoe shop and smiled at the attractive woman in front of him. He just couldn't believe his luck that she wanted to work for him.

'Good afternoon, Mr Milburn. Yes, it is best if we keep things formal, for now anyway.' Connie watched the young girl who already worked for him, and who looked as if she should still be in school as she stood awkwardly with them both.

'You can go now, Gillian,' Fred said sharply. 'The spring stock needs getting out. Hopefully people will feel more like spending when this war comes to an end.' He smiled at Connie. 'Would you like to come this way, Miss Whitehead, and then we can discuss terms, pay and suchlike. I was surprised when I read your letter applying. Are you no longer working at Rowntree's? But then I understand that they've let a lot of folk go – this war has buggered everything up.' Fred opened a frosted glass door that led to his small office, which he nearly filled just by himself: Fred was not the smallest of men.

'No, I'm not. I was surprised myself when I got the push, but I was ready for a change, anyway. It gave me the chance to hopefully come and work for you here, in this wonderful shoe shop. Just smell the leather in the air, it's a lot better than chocolate.' Connie eyed the man who was quite a bit older than her – probably in his early thirties – and knew that she would get the job without even trying. He had often talked to her, even coming out of the shop when she had been gazing through the window at a pair of shoes that she couldn't afford. She didn't fancy him in the least, but she would play a game of flirting if it meant her getting the much needed job.

'Yes, it's a grand smell. We only sell the best shoes and are proud of the service that we give to our customers. I've inherited this shop from my father and I often hear his voice saying to make sure all our customers go out with a well-fitting shoe. You can do anything if your feet are comfortable. Now, to the work that I would expect you to do.' Fred sat back in his chair. 'Hours would be nine a.m. until six p.m., half an hour's break at lunchtime. Customers always come first, no matter what you think they should be wearing on their feet. You need to be polite and courteous at all times. Plus, unlike young Gillian, you must be able to talk to our customers. I know she's only young, but she's not got a way with folk. Best that she is kept busy in the stock room. Do you think you could manage that?' Fred winked at Connie. He knew the hours were easy compared to what she had been working.

'I can do that; the hours are not a problem to me. Can I ask what the pay would be?' Connie asked, trying not to look as desperate as she felt.

'Pay, now, I've budgeted a new worker in at three pounds twelve shillings a week and I think that's a fair pay for the work involved. Of course, there might be a little bit more if I find something else that may need your attention. Now, you are the first one I've interviewed for this job, so what do you think? Are you interested or not?'

Connie crossed her legs and leaned forward. 'Perhaps we could say four pounds, and then I would readily work here. After all, I've been paid nearly double that working in the munitions factory.'

'Mmmm . . . I don't know, that's more than I'd reckoned for. Times are hard, you know.' Fred studied the young woman who had caught his eye more than once. He was still a single man and time was not on his side. Perhaps he would get a chance of finding love or at least sex with Connie Whitehead. 'Go on, but you earn your money and no complaining.'

'You will have no complaints from me, Mr Milburn. Now, when do I start?' Connie smiled and sat back in her seat.

'Tomorrow, nine o'clock sharp, and I think we have known one another long enough for you to call me Fred, but perhaps not in front of Gillian – not yet, anyway.'

'Nine o'clock it is. Do I need to have a uniform or anything?' Connie began to stand up.

'No, just something comfortable on your feet. What you are wearing today is perfect, very fetching.' Fred smiled, imagining Connie climbing the shop's steps to reach for the highest shelf of shoes.

'Really, this old outfit – I've had it ages. Like everyone else, we're wearing clothes that ordinarily we would have given to the rag and bone man. However, I do like to look smart, so you have no worries on that account.' Connie made for the office door but Fred opened it for her.

'Thank you, it has been a pleasure,' Connie said politely.

'I'm sure we are going to work together very well, Connie. I look forward to seeing you in the morning.' Fred smiled as he watched his new employee leave his shop. The pleasure was going to be all his.

Connie sat on the wall outside the Rowntree's factory, lit a cigarette and waited for the factory whistle to blow. She felt that her life was changing for the better, as she watched the dancing daffodils that had been planted in a row to hide one of the Anderson shelters. Her pay might not be a lot, but it covered her rent and would keep her fed. It was only for a few months, after all, and then she would be married to aircraft man Chuck Lawrence. The guard on the Blick machine waved to her and shouted, 'You enjoying not working here?'

'That I am,' she shouted back. 'I'm getting married soon, so I'll not be coming back.'

'Good for you, lass. Is it to that Yank I've seen you with?'

'That it is.' Connie felt all warm and contented inside, as she breathed her smoke out and waited for Molly.

'It's right what they say. They are over here, oversexed and overpaid. But if he makes you happy, lass, I don't blame you. Hey up, here they come, back to being Chocolate Girls instead of yellow canaries and coming out in daylight. I bet they think they're in heaven,' the guard shouted as the factory whistle blew and the workforce started piling out of all the doors in a mass of white aprons and turbans. A lot of the workforce waved and shouted their hellos as they streamed past Connie and she felt a slight pang of nostalgia for the comradeship that had always been there when everyone pulled together.

'What are you doing here? It's good to see you, though.' Molly came up to her and watched Connie climb down from the wall. 'And you're still smoking!'

'Only occasionally, I think it makes a woman look a bit cool. Don't you?' Connie grinned. 'Well, how was the first day? I bet you feel like you've never been away.'

'Nothing's right at the moment,' Molly complained. 'Everyone is learning the new machinery and ways, including management. It's been full of frustration, and I never thought I'd say this, but at least I knew what I was doing making munitions. I could do that job in my sleep.'

'Well, at least you don't change. Every job that you've started in, you've said the same thing and then you end up being star employee. You'll get used to it.' Connie stubbed her cigarette out and kept up with Molly as she headed for home.

'What have you been up to anyway? You look all dressed up. Have you been out walking with Chuck?' Molly quizzed, noticing the bright red lipstick on Connie's lips. It was too brash for her liking.

'I've been for a job interview at Fred Milburn's and I've got it. I start tomorrow. The pay isn't that good, but it's better than nothing. It will keep me in my flat and I'll be able to put a little away for my new life with Chuck.'

Molly gasped, 'Fred Milburn, in his shoe shop? You know he's had his eye on you for a while – you knew damn well he'd take you on. But you wouldn't get me working for him, he's a bit fond. Have you not noticed the lasses that work for him never stay? I thought you weren't serious.'

'Ah, I'll be all right, I'm only going to be there until I sail for America, although seemingly getting married to anyone in the US forces is less easy than we both thought. Chuck says that he will sort it, though, so there will be no problem.' They reached the end of the street to Molly's home.

'Are you coming back home?' Molly asked. 'Mam will make you some supper; she was saying that she thought you'd lost weight since you had left us. Although you've not been gone that long, and I don't think that you have. It's just my mam being a mother hen.' Molly hoped Connie's reply would be a yes. She had missed her at work and she needed to tell her about the letter from Matt's wife.

'It would be rude not to if she's worrying about me.' Connie grinned. 'Besides, I haven't got anything in, and the bakery downstairs was closed today. I don't know what's going on there; I just hope that they keep open and renting me my flat until I go. There are some terrible rows go on in that bakery; I hear them yelling at one another and shouting. I don't think they're very happy.'

'That's a shame, but I think a lot of people are struggling and unhappy at the moment,' Molly replied. She opened the door and yelled, 'Have you enough supper for another one, Mam? Connie is with me.'

'Of course I have, and if I haven't, I'll rustle something up.' Winnie beamed. 'It's nice to see you back with us and I'm sure Molly will appreciate your listening ear after the news that she's had.' Winnie busied herself dividing the supper up into three instead of two and hoped that the amount of corned beef hash would feed them all.

'What news? You haven't said anything!' Connie exclaimed.

'Oh, I didn't want to burden you with my moans, you're so happy at the moment.' Molly felt embarrassed and angry now that she had been taken for a fool by Matt.

'I'll tell you, even if she won't. Matt's been leading her on. He's been married all along and not said a word, would you believe it?' Winnie said as she pushed three plates of supper onto the table. 'I thought he was a right nice lad and then it turns out he has a wife and children.'

'Is that right, Molly? Is he already married?' Connie gasped.

'Yes, he is.' Molly swallowed hard. 'I wrote to the woman who I thought was his mother and it turned out to be his wife. He's being held in a POW camp somewhere in Germany. She wrote back to tell me and ask me how I knew him.' Molly wiped a tear away and gazed at the corned beef hash. She'd always hated this dish, but if she ate it tonight she knew she would be sick as her stomach had churned with upset all day.

'Well, the dirty rat, and there was me thinking Matt was all right, one of the good 'uns. Now, if it had been his mate, the one with the wandering hands, I wouldn't have doubted it. But not Matt!'

'Please, I don't want to talk about it. He hadn't written for so long and I was starting to doubt my love for him anyway. He's best forgotten and I'll get on with my life.' Molly put her head down and pushed her supper around the plate.

'Well, bloody hell, how dare he leave you high and dry! Lying bastard, bloody men!' Connie swore, forgetting that swearing wasn't tolerated in Winnie's house, remembering too late as she looked up at Winnie's stern face.

'Aye, bloody fellas,' Winnie agreed, to her surprise. 'Some of them are not worth the bother or the heartache. I could have told you that if you had both asked me. But you've to love and learn, though it always hurts no matter what. That is, until you find the right one.'

21

Rose sat down and sighed. Since her sister's wedding Ivy had been more and more demanding, and now, with more responsibility at work with the reopening of more of the chocolate factory, she was exhausted. She had been dealing with complaints about the new machinery not working, quality not being as good and the workforce just not happy with the new running of the firm.

They had both sat and had their teas together, and now the pots were waiting to be washed in the sink after Ivy had decided to go to bed early. Ned was back at the airbase not knowing if he would be flying a mission or not that night. She started washing and drying the dirty pots and plates and put what Ivy had left in the slops bucket, ready for the rag and bone man, who was fattening up a pig. He had promised everybody a few sausages or bacon in return for scraps. However, no one would hold their breath: he was a man of words not of deeds. Ivy had hardly eaten anything, Rose noticed, which was not like her mother-in-law, she thought as she sat down in comfort for the first time that day.

'Rose, Rose, I need a drink. Will you bring me one up? A cup of tea and one of those biscuits if we have any left,' Ivy shouted down the stairs, just as Rose had sat down and drawn breath.

'Yes, Ivy, I'll be up in a minute. Is there anything else you need while I'm down here?' Rose got out of her chair and stood at the bottom of the stairs, feeling drained. 'Your glasses, a book?'

'No, I'm just thirsty and now a bit hungry. I didn't fancy my supper, that's all. Once I've had those, I'll go to sleep.'

'I'll be with you in a minute, Ivy. I'll put the kettle on and be with you as fast as I can.' Rose went tiredly into the kitchen, filled the kettle and put it on the gas hob. She couldn't carry on much longer being nurse to Ivy and working full-time. The worry of Ned going on night flights was also weighing on her mind as she stared out at the garden, which was just starting to come to life with spring flowers, giving a piece of colour to her dull day.

The kettle whistled and, like a zombie, Rose automatically filled the teapot and brewed Ivy a cup of precious tea and looked into the near-empty biscuit tin. One left – she would have loved it herself – but she put it on the side of the saucer and poured the tea, carrying it with care upstairs.

'I'm here, Ivy. You've come to bed so early this evening, no wonder you're not sleeping. It's only seven-thirty, it's still light,' Rose said quietly, sitting on the edge of the bed.

'Aye, I am a bit early, but I've felt tired all day. And there's nothing to stay up for, I'm best in my bed. I'm weary of life, lass,' Ivy said. She sipped her tea and took a bite out of the biscuit which she then put to one side.

'Is my lad on a mission tonight? Surely there must not be much left of Germany by now, what with Russia, America and us bombing them? Poor buggers, they're only like us really.' She closed her eyes and rested her cup of tea on her covers.

'He is, Ivy, but not for much longer, I don't think. Ned was saying that the Germans are demoralised and are surrendering on the fields of battle. It's just a matter of time now.' Rose eyed Ivy with concern. She didn't look well and her breathing was laboured. 'Do you want me to get the doctor? You don't look well this evening. He would come straight out to you, I'm sure.'

'No, lass, I'm all right, just tired. I'll finish my cuppa and then if you'll close the curtains I'll lie back down and go to sleep. I don't reckon much to this getting old.' Ivy smiled and took another sip of her tea.

'Do you want me to bring the wireless up to listen to? You could lie in bed and tune into some of your favourite programmes. It's no trouble to me as I'm going to do some ironing this evening.' Rose took hold of Ivy's hand and squeezed it tight.

'No, lass. Here, take my teacup and pull the curtains. It's a shame to close the day out, but I'm ready for some sleep,' Ivy said quietly as she moved her body under the sheets and blankets.

'All right, now you are sure that you don't need anything and that I can't get the doctor? I can ring him on the phone now that we've got it installed.' Rose placed the cup on the bedside table and pulled the top eiderdown over Ivy's shoulders.

'No, I'm all right, I'll shout if I need anything.' Ivy was glad to be in bed; for a few weeks now, she had felt under the weather, but today she had really struggled from the moment Rose had brought her breakfast and made her comfortable before going to work.

Rose drew the bedroom curtains. They were covered with a rose pattern and matched the flowery wallpaper – all the furniture in the room was from when Ivy had first got married and was a mixture of Edwardian and Victorian styles. A little aged now, but it was what Ivy liked. The dressing table was covered with photographs of Ned growing up. She worshipped her only son, Rose thought as she watched the old woman whom she had grown to love close her eyes and try to sleep. She felt guilty now for thinking of how exhausted she herself was. Perhaps she should call for the doctor, just to be safe. Ivy didn't like him, but if she needed him, then they should not hesitate. She picked up the cup and saucer and said softly, 'Good night, Ivy. If you need me, you let me know. Do you want your bedroom door closing?'

'Please, Rose love. Don't worry, love, I feel better already now I'm in my bed. See you in the morning,' Ivy said without moving as she tried to stop worrying about her Ned, flying over Germany and risking his life yet again.

It was six o'clock the next morning and Rose pushed her bed covers back and yawned. She had checked on Ivy a few times before she went to bed, only to find her sleeping peacefully and at one time even snoring. She must just have been tired, Rose thought as she went to the bathroom to do her morning ablutions before checking on Ivy again and making breakfast for them both before going to work.

Once dressed, Rose opened Ivy's bedroom door and quietly walked across to the window to pull back the curtains to let the dim light of morning creep into the bedroom. Ivy was lying underneath her covers, not moving. She often did have to wake her up so, softly, she went and gently touched her shoulder.

'Ivy, sorry, Ivy, it's morning. I'm sorry, but I need to get you up and dressed before breakfast and work.' Rose spoke quietly and shook her gently on the shoulder now. 'Ivy, Ivy!' Rose touched her cold face. 'Ivy, love, please, no!' There was no reaction: Ivy was lying cold and not breathing, curled up under the blankets.

'Oh, no, Ivy, no. Please, Ivy, I knew you needed the doctor.' Rose sat on the edge of the bed and began to weep. 'I should have called him – that's why we had the telephone put in, along with for Ned.' She sobbed for a while before gathering her thoughts and running downstairs to do what she should have done the evening before.

Doctor Lewis sat down in the front room an hour or so later and filled out a death certificate.

'She went quietly in her sleep,' he told Rose kindly. 'Don't worry that you didn't call me earlier, I couldn't have saved her. Ivy's heart has been failing for months now although she would never have wanted you to know that. She promised me to secrecy. You did all you could for her, and I'm sure she knew how well she was looked after.'

'I feel I let her down. I didn't realise just how ill she was because I was so exhausted myself.' Rose bowed her head. 'I feel so selfish.'

'You looked after her so well and managed to keep your demanding job at Rowntree's – it's no wonder that you are feeling under the weather. Do you need anything to help you through the next few days? And has Ned been told about his mother's death? A funeral will need to be arranged and her body laid out.' Doctor Lewis spoke with concern.

'No, I'm all right, just a little tired, I have been of late. I called Ned's base and they were going to give him the news once he had come out of the debriefing that he was attending after his latest flight. He should be back within the next hour and then he will arrange everything,' Rose said quietly and wiped her eyes free of tears.

'You do look a little pale, my dear. I think we had better make an appointment for you to see me at the surgery for a check-up as soon as you can. I expect that you're a little run-down with the care of Ivy and work, but it's best to be sure. Can't have you being ill, or else there will be nobody to keep the chocolate supply running smoothly. Ivy was so proud of you for being management and a woman. She would often tell me that Ned had found the perfect wife and how much she thought of you,' Doctor Lewis said, smiling at her. 'You did your best for her, I know you did, even when she was having a bad day with pain and was testing everybody's patience.' He stood up and left the certificate on the sideboard. 'Now, my dear, will you be all right until Ned arrives back?'

'Yes, I'll be all right, thank you, Doctor Lewis. Thank you for coming out so quickly.' Rose stood up and escorted the doctor to the front door.

'Don't forget to come and see me soon, perhaps after Ivy's funeral – by then you will have had time to get back to a normal routine. Perhaps you have been overdoing it slightly.' Doctor Lewis tipped his trilby hat and went on his way. Rose closed the door behind him and looked up the stairs to where Ivy lay in her bedroom. She crumpled up behind the front door and sobbed until she could hardly cry any more.

Ned sat beside his mother and looked down at her on her death bed.

'Sorry, Mam, I should have been here for you. I hope you knew how much I loved you,' he said quietly and reached for Rose's hand as she stood beside him.

'She did, and she loved you. The doctor says she went quiet in her sleep, and I never heard a thing and you know I'm a light sleeper.' Rose kissed Ned's head and put her arms around him.

'Well, it's the end of an era; there will never be anybody like my Mam. She was a tough old stick but she had a heart of gold.' Ned wiped a tear away. He had seen a lot of death lately, but his mother's hurt so much.

'She's left instructions where she wants to be buried, what hymns she wants and who she wants to be there,' Rose said. 'I found it all in her bedside table earlier this morning after the doctor had gone. She's still in control, even though she's no longer with us.'

'That's my mam. We'll not let you down, mam.' Ned patted his mother's cold, marbled hand, then went to pull the curtains back and saw the undertakers walking up the path. 'Time for you to leave us, Mam, but you'll always be in our hearts, no matter where you are.'

'She will, Ned love, she was a good woman.' Rose bent down and kissed Ivy's brow. 'Night, sleep tight, Ivy.'

Winnie put her arms around Rose. 'She was a good woman, a stubborn old devil when she wanted to be, but a good woman.'

Rose buried her head in her mother's shoulder. 'I should have got the doctor earlier, Mam. I still wonder if he could happen to save her.'

'Now, don't get upset, my love,' Ned urged. 'You know the doctor said that she'd been failing for a while now, there was nothing we could do for her.' They stood together at the graveside and looked down at the coffin holding Ivy.

'Ned's right; we all knew she was failing,' Winnie said. 'It was a blessing that she went in her sleep. She wouldn't have wanted to burden you more than she already had.'

'She wasn't a burden, really, and she always made me so welcome. If only I hadn't been so tired.' Rose wiped away a tear.

'Don't cry, Rose,' Molly said. 'She had a good life and she enjoyed her adventure to see our Annie. She clearly did know how ill she really was.'

She linked her arm through her sister's as they walked out of the churchyard. It didn't seem fair – the day was too beautiful to be such a sad one, and there seemed to be a sense of hope in the air. It was nearly the end of April, the war was coming to an end. On the very morning that Ivy had died, Ned had been told that there would be no further night bombing raids over Germany. The good news had been lost slightly with the death of Ivy. A normal, civilised way of life was just around the corner if Ivy had just hung on that little bit longer. They would have been celebrating.

Ned took her other arm. 'Molly's right, Rose. It was her time to go, and although I will miss her beyond belief, she wouldn't want to see you so upset. She was a one-off, was my mother, tough as old boots, and she never forgot her roots. She was so happy when I met you and got married.'

'I know.' Rose gazed up to the sky as a robin flew just over their heads. 'God bless, Ivy, sleep in peace.'

22. 30 April 1945

Rose tentatively knocked on the doctor's door and waited to be invited into the small surgery that stood on Whitecross Road.

'Come in, Rose. I'm glad that you took my advice and have come to see me. Please, take a seat and tell me how you're feeling. You still look pale.'

'I don't think I'm ill as such, Doctor Lewis. I was sick for the first time this morning and I'm beginning to have an idea why I have been so tired.' Rose blushed. 'I think I could be pregnant. I thought my monthly visitor had stopped because I was exhausted, but it's been three months now, and some smells really turn my stomach.'

'Ah, well, let's have you popping up onto my couch and we'll see if we can confirm it.' Doctor Lewis examined Rose carefully and gently and asked about the exact date of her last period. 'Well, Rose, I'll need a urine sample as well, but I think you're right. I'd say you're around four months pregnant, given the dates you gave me.'

Rose sat up on the edge of the examination couch.

'A new baby, now how happy would that have made Ivy?' Doctor Lewis patted Rose's hand. 'Nature has a funny way of replacing our loved ones, that's the balance. Ned will have to get to grips with the idea of becoming a father. You must be relieved that he has no more missions over Germany.'

'Oh, I hope that we are definitely having a baby! I thought so, but I didn't want to say and raise Ned's hopes and put even more pressure and worry on his shoulders.' Rose touched her stomach. 'If it's a girl, we will have to call her Ivy.'

'I'm nearly ninety percent sure you are. I can't tell you what sex it will be, but I can say she or he should be here at the end of September or early October. Now, let me take a sample of your blood and urine and then we can be more accurate.'

Rose was already prepared. She put her hand in her handbag and pulled out a jam jar with a sample of her pee and passed it to the doctor.

'Ah, excellent. I don't think we need quite as much as that, Rose, but it's brilliant that you thought of bringing some.' Doctor Lewis smiled at the full jar of urine with a Robinson's jam label still attached and a golly smiling at him.

'A baby! Oh, I hope Ned will be happy, if I am pregnant.'

Doctor Lewis took her blood and started to fill in various forms. 'I'm sure he will be. Will he be staying in the RAF after this war is over? Or has he had enough excitement and danger?'

'He is talking of leaving if he can. He's done his duty, and he's more than lucky to be still alive.' Rose felt a warm glow. She couldn't wait to tell Ned and her mother – the first grandchild, how special!

'Well, you can tell him that you are definitely pregnant and that I calculate that your baby is due on the twenty-ninth of September, give or take a day or two. Now, are you going to carry on working? If you are, no lifting, and try to have some time off your feet. You are not ill, but a sensible lifestyle should be followed. Although I'm sure you already have one.'

'The twenty-ninth of September,' Rose echoed. 'That is a long time away – anything could happen by then.' She sighed, then brightened. 'Hopefully it will be a new start for everyone.'

'Indeed, especially for this small one.' The doctor smiled. 'Come back to me in a month and we'll see how you are doing. You are a fit young woman, there should be no complications.' Doctor Lewis stood up to see her out.

'Thank you, doctor, I can't wait to tell my mother and Ned. My mam will be so busy knitting from now on, I just know she will.' Rose left holding her head high and with a huge smile on her face.

She walked through York and gazed in the shop windows. She would need a pram, a cot, and of course a layette for the new baby. She had watched her best friend Mary raising young Jack and knew what to expect, especially if Ned was still in the RAF. It would be hard work, especially if she was on her own much of the time. Work would have to take a back seat for a while. Although Rowntree's had a nursery, she couldn't envisage putting her precious baby into somebody else's care.

The paper seller was yelling the breaking news that Germany was on the brink of collapse and that Berlin had the Russians knocking on its door. As she walked down Coney Street, Rose looked through the newly shatter-proofed windows of Woolworth's. The building had been hit by a stray bomb not long into the war, but it had built the business back up again, determined to keep trading regardless of the damage. That was the spirit that was going to win them the war, she thought. She walked through the revolving doors and went to the baby clothes section. She had always admired their Ladybird range – they were well made and pretty – and now that she knew there was going to be a baby to buy for, she would take a sneak peek. She eyed the cotton dresses, embroidered so delicately, and the rompers for the little boys, smiling to herself as she picked them up and smelt them, dreaming of the baby that soon would be with them. The lovely brand of Ladybird had been originally founded in Germany, but they had fled to Birmingham once the Nazi regime had come to power, and their clothes were soon snapped up for sale by Woolworth's. All the new mothers flocked to Woolworth's to admire them. Rose vowed that once she had got a clothes ration for her baby, it would be dressed in Ladybird clothes. They were quality at an affordable price. However, today she would just look. She had taken a full day off work in anticipation of the news, but it was too early yet and she didn't want to tempt fate.

She wandered the aisles and picked up a knitting

pattern for bootees and gloves and a skein of baby wool in neutral white. At least she could sit and knit those of an evening although, unlike her mother, she hated knitting. It was Molly who had inherited her mother's skills when it came to knitting and dressmaking. No doubt both of them would pass their evenings doing just that, or at least she hoped so as she stood and paid for her goods and lovingly put them into a bag to take home. She checked the time. There was no rush to go home – Ned wouldn't be there until later in the day. She would call in at her mother's and give her the news that she was bursting to tell someone. Ned would understand that she had told her mother first, she knew he would.

'Why don't you get Molly to do that for you?' Rose said as she watched her mother get up from off her knees after scrubbing the front doorstep with her donkey stone in her hand and a head square tied around her head.

'No, she's enough on her plate, and besides, she's in the mood from hell at the moment. She's not enjoying her new job at Rowntree's, and don't I know it. Besides, it just follows that once I've got the washing done on a Monday, I scrub my front step. Always done that since the day your father and I moved in here, and I'm not going to stop now.' Winnie wiped a dewdrop from the end of her nose. 'Why are you not at work?'

'I'll tell you when I've put the kettle on. I'm just on my way back from the doctor. But there's nothing to worry about.' Rose stepped past her mother and entered the family home where she had so many fond memories. She hoped that her child would build the same as they grew up.

'You're sure you're not ill? You have looked a bit peaky for a while now, I've been thinking. Probably the shock of losing poor Ivy and of looking after her, bless her. She was hard work but right enough.' Winnie emptied her bucket of water out down the sink and put her donkey stone and scrubbing brush away under the sink.

By now Rose looked as if she was going to burst; she couldn't wait until the kettle had boiled. She leaned back against the sink and smiled like a cat that had got the cream. 'Mam, I hope that you think this is good news, because I do. I'm so happy . . . Mam, I'm expecting. Ned and I are to have a baby this September if all goes well. He doesn't know yet – I'll have to tell him this afternoon when he comes home.'

'Oh, Rose love, that is wonderful news!' Winnie exclaimed, rushing over to hug her daughter. 'Another bit of cheer in our lives. I bet Ned will be over the moon with the news, but you should have told him first. I'm going to have to get my knitting needles out, and I bet Annie won't be far behind you now that she's married. I can't wait to bounce the little ones on my knee.'

'Twenty-ninth of September, that's the date I've been given. It seems an age away.'

'Now wouldn't Ivy have been proud? It's a pity she's not here to hear this. A grandmother can spoil her grandchildren because she knows she can hand them back to their parents. Aye, I hope that one of you has a little lad. I always wanted a lad and instead, I got you three girls – but of course I loved you all as soon as I saw you.'

Winnie beamed. Now she definitely was going to be a grandmother, but whether Annie would make her another one, she would have to wait and see.

Rose had got out the best china, the set that Ivy had kept in the cabinet for special occasions. Since she had come back from her mother's, she had decided to make Ned's return home that day extra special. Using Ivy's left-over sugar ration, she had made a batch of rock buns, which were now sending out delicious smells from the oven. Her stomach churned with excitement at the thought of telling him the news. They had lost Ivy, but their lives were going to be filled with a new life by Christmas. She sat on the arm of Ivy's favourite chair and looked out down the garden path. Ned would be back any time now, and she wanted to tell him her news as soon as he entered the house.

She held her breath as she saw him draw up in his beloved car and climb out, whistling loudly as he walked up the path and came through the front door, hanging his RAF cap up in the hallway before walking into the front room with a huge smile on his face. He walked straight over to Rose, picked her up in his arms, hugged her tight and kissed her.

'Have you heard? The rumours are rife around the base. Berlin has fallen, the Russians are in control of it. In another few days, the war will be over and life will return to normal. I can't believe it! The Nazis have failed and peace will hopefully return. Oh, Rose, I could nearly cry, it's such a big moment for the country and the rest of the world. Surely Japan will admit defeat now Germany has fallen.' Ned put Rose down, grinning from ear to ear, and yelled, 'It's nearly over! Thank God for that!' He kissed her on the brow. 'It's over – no more night flights, bombing folk who you know are innocent pawns in Hitler's game.'

Ned dropped down into one of the easy chairs and looked up at Rose. She had said nothing as he had exploded with his news. 'You are quiet – are you all right?' Then he noticed the small table laid out with the best china and cakes. Is it our anniversary or your birthday? Don't say I've missed either,' he gasped.

'No, you've missed nothing, my love. That is such fantastic news. I couldn't get a word in edgeways! I'm just as relieved as you are. I walked past the news seller on Coney Street and he was shouting it out. What a day! News of the war coming to an end, and I've had quite a day myself.' Rose went and sat next to Ned. She couldn't keep it to herself any longer despite Ned's marvellous news.

'But we do have some good news of our own. I can't believe it – so much brilliant news in one day.' Rose couldn't contain herself; she breathed in and held his hand tightly. 'You are going to be a father, Ned. We are going to be parents; the doctor confirmed what I suspected this morning when I went to see him. We are to have a baby in September!'

‘A baby! Oh, my Lord, I’m going to be a father? This day just gets better.’ Ned pulled Rose onto his knee and kissed her passionately. ‘The war is nearly at an end and we are to be parents.’ He squeezed Rose tight and gazed out of the window. ‘If only my mother was still with us. If she could just have hung on a little longer, she would have been so full of it.’

‘She would. I was thinking we could call our baby Ivy if it’s a girl and Peter if it’s a boy. A way to remember them,’ Rose said.

‘Peter, yes, but even my mother wouldn’t want us to call our precious girl Ivy – she hated it herself, never mind saddling her granddaughter with it. We will think of a nice modern name if it’s a girl. Something to greet the new age in style.’ Ned held Rose tight. ‘A baby! Well, I’ll be blowed, I’m going to be a father. How proud I am of you, my love. We’re going to be parents – now that is something to celebrate.’

23. 1 May 1945

The voice of the excited Rowntree's radio newsreader was being listened to by all the staff at Rowntree's as they heard the latest from Germany.

> 'The body of Germany's leader Adolf Hitler was found alongside that of his new wife Eva (née Braun) early yesterday morning. He is believed to have shot himself with his own pistol, while Eva Braun is believed to have committed suicide by taking cyanide capsules that had been first tested on Hitler's dog Blondi. It is only a matter of time now until Berlin will surrender to the Russian army and indeed until the whole of the German Seventh Army surrenders to Russia and the Allies. This follows the public hanging of the tyrant Mussolini and his mistress by loyal Italian partisans. Their bodies have been made examples of in the city of Milan, where people have shown their anger at the ruthless dictator. Let us all hope that the war in Europe will soon be over.'

Molly could nearly have cried as she stood and listened to the news being broadcast from the newly installed Tannoy. The war was coming to an end, life would return to normal – no more blackouts and air raid sirens, and eventually no rations. She had nearly forgotten what ordinary life was like. Hitler was dead and a roar of celebration could be heard all through the factory. Seebohm Rowntree and all the directors who were present came out of their offices and smiled down at their staff and shouted 'Hip, hip, hooray!' They were met with the biggest cheer, it was a wonder the roof of the Rowntree's building did not come off.

'It's over, it's truly over! I can't believe it!' Kitty Sugden yelled and hugged Molly as she stood looking up to the heavens thanking God. 'Life will soon be back to normal and better times are just around the corner.'

'I can't believe it. It's been so long!' Molly wiped a tear from her cheek. The war was coming to an end, Rose was going to be a mother, and hopefully, her own life would improve. Matt would soon be coming home to find that the truth had been found out about him – at least by her if not by his wife, as she had never replied to his wife's letter.

Still, she couldn't help feeling less enthusiastic about the future stretching out for her at Rowntree's. Nowadays, the chocolate boxes were ready-printed and didn't need much love to assemble. Her work was not like it used to be. When she'd worked in munitions, she had proved to be competent and able to give advice to the workers there. Even when she used to make chocolate boxes in the days before the war, there was more involvement in her work. She could take pride in the box that she had made from scratch, covered and lined with beautiful coloured papers and then finished with individual decorations. Now it was mind-numbing.

Fold the card here, secure it there, and put the frilly cases in ready for the chocolates to be added. There was nothing to the job, although she was grateful to still be employed and paid. Perhaps she should be like Connie and move on to somewhere else. But just where she didn't know. Her life and that of her family revolved around chocolate; it was all she had ever known.

'Bloody brilliant news, Molly!' Madge, who worked across the opposite side of the workbench, broke into her thoughts. 'That bloody bastard the coward, shot himself – that is typical, sent all them lads and boys to their death and then when it was his downfall he couldn't face the world. Do you fancy going for a drink to celebrate tonight? I thought I might just go and have a half of stout in the Golden Fleece. Come along with us and we can have a laugh – I bet everybody will be out tonight.'

Molly smiled. 'Oh, I don't know, I'm not a big pub goer. My mam doesn't like us drinking and standing at a bar like a man.'

'Do you always listen to your mam? Heavens, Molly, you're old enough not to bother what your mam tells you to do. Go on, everybody will be in right good spirits, it's something to rejoice about. Our menfolk will be coming home soon, now that's something to celebrate if nothing else.' Madge nudged Molly and grinned. 'Go on, Molly Freeman, join us for a drink – just the one if you want, what's the harm in that? Kitty, are you joining us or will that new fella of yours be taking you out?'

'Too right, Madge, I'll get him to take me on the

razzle. He's timed it well being on leave from the navy. Molly, get yourself out with Madge, you've got to celebrate. You could even take your mam.'

'Oh, I don't know. My mam very rarely drinks and I don't want her to be on her own. And perhaps I should go and see Connie; I haven't seen her for a day or two.' Molly tried to make her excuses; she knew everywhere would be heaving.

'Well, if we go to the Golden Fleece it's only at the bottom of the Shambles, a few doors down from where Connie is living. You could ask her along.' Madge was determined to drag Molly out since she had heard about Matt being already married. She could see that Molly's confidence had plummeted and she also knew she wasn't happy in her new position. 'Go on, Hitler's dead, let's celebrate his demise.'

'I'll see. What time will you be there? I'm not walking in on my own, I'll meet you outside if I do go,' Molly said hesitantly.

'Seven-thirty. We might go on to Ye Olde Starre on Stonegate, but there's a right good-looking barman at the Fleece that I can't take my eyes off, so we might stay there a while.' Madge was footloose and fancy-free, and she hoped that tonight would be her lucky night.

'Well, when you go on to Ye Olde Starre, I'll walk home, but I will go to the Fleece with you.' Molly decided. 'I like it there despite its reputation.'

'Ah-hah, me hearties, One-Eyed-Jack in his scarlet coat and pistols will be there to haunt you along with his ghostly friends,' Madge declared. It was well known that the Fleece was one of the most haunted pubs in York, with One-Eyed-Jack making regular appearances, according to its drinkers.

'It will be the other sort of spirits I'll be seeing,' Molly replied, 'not those of dead and long-gone pirates, so he won't be scaring me. I'll be there – just for one though, nothing more.'

Molly looked up towards the window of Connie's flat as she knocked on the door. The blackout blinds were down and she couldn't see if Connie was in or not.

'She's not in, she's not been back all day since she went to work,' Wilf Atkinson yelled, sticking his head out from the door of his bakery. 'She's hardly ever in, and when she is, she usually has that Yank with her, making their noise.'

'Oh, thank you, Mr Atkinson, I didn't know if she was home or not. You are working late,' Molly replied.

'I'm just getting my yeast to work overnight, makes all the difference – not that folk appreciate the hours I put in to keep them fed.' With that, he closed the door, leaving Molly standing in the narrow lane down the Shambles. It wasn't quite dark yet, but people were making no attempt to pull down their blackout blinds now that the war was nearly at an end. Connie's must have been left down from the previous night, Molly thought. She made her way down towards the fifteenth-century pub with a large golden sheep hanging over the entrance. For once the small street was filled with people laughing and chatting, and there was a buzz of optimism.

Molly spotted Madge waiting for her.

'Just listen to the chattering and laughter,' Madge exclaimed. 'Everyone's so happy that Hitler is dead. I walked up from home and passed some bomb-damaged land where there was a bonfire with an effigy of Hitler on the top of it, and a load of young lads were dancing around it. The ARP warden just shook his head at them and then yelled, "Aye, that's it, lads, he'll be burning in hell now, that's for sure."' Madge put her arm through Molly's as they entered the pub.

The narrow entrance opened out into long, large rooms, all packed with people celebrating the news and having a drink. In one corner men were singing patriotic songs and sipping from their beer glasses, while others gathered around the bar, talking politics and slapping one another on the back as they celebrated the demise of the Third Reich and Hitler.

'Come on, we will go in the snug, it will be quieter there. Your mam is right – a respectable woman doesn't sit at the bar, but it's all right to sit quietly in a corner. Besides, if we take our seats over there, I can still see that good-looking barman. I think he's Italian; he speaks with an accent and when he looks at you he has such smouldering dark eyes.' Madge put her handbag down on a decorative cast-iron table in a quiet corner and got her purse out. 'Right, what are we having? I'm fair dying for a half of the stout; I've been thinking about it all day.'

'Do you think I could have a port? I don't like beer of any kind,' Molly said and then quickly added, 'I'll get the next ones', as she saw Madge pull a face at her expensive taste.

'Port it is, and then we'll just have another one here before we go to the Starre.' Madge seemed to have forgotten that Molly wasn't going on to the next pub. 'It doesn't look like there's anybody I know in here tonight,' she added, gazing through to the busier room.

Molly watched Madge as she went and stood at the bar, thinking how at home she looked there, just as good as any man, and tried not to worry that she would have to buy the next round. It wasn't ladylike, as her mother had been so quick to remind her when she'd said she was going for a drink with Madge.

'Oh, isn't he lovely? I'm sure he's Italian but I daren't ask him.' Madge returned and glanced again at the dark-haired barman as she placed her half-pint and Molly's port down on the table. 'I could stop here all night and just watch him. What do you think, Mol, or is he not for you?'

'He's all right, I suppose, but you don't know the first thing about him. I'm going to be wary of any men I don't really know. I thought I had a good one until his wife wrote to me and told me he was married with two children. Trust nobody, that's going to be my motto from now on,' Molly said. She took a long sip of her drink, looking across at the good-looking figure of a man. Madge was right, he was handsome.

'Oh, Molly, put that sod behind you. Not all men are like him else nobody would ever get married or love one another. Although saying that, I seem to have had more bad 'uns than good 'uns – that's why I'm still on the hunt for one.' Madge got her compact out and powdered her face, looking at her reflection in the mirror. 'I think this ginger is finally going from my hair and the blonde is returning. Thank heavens for that – I thought I was always going to look like a canary. My skin is improving as well.'

'Yes, mine is too – that is one good thing about going back to work for Rowntree's.' Molly sipped back her port; she needed a drink to brighten her mood. Even if the war was coming to an end, there were so many things wrong with the world – and her world. She took a long sip and decided to get in the mood. Nobody liked a misery, especially on a night like this.

Two hours later, Molly's mood had changed. 'Thank the Lord that you've cheered up,' Madge said. 'It's taken four ports, though. I thought we were only going to have two in the Fleece, but that got blown away in the wind when you got a taste for them.' They were walking down Stonegate towards their next drinking place at Ye Olde Starre. Laughter and conversation spilt out onto the street as they opened the door. All inhibitions had gone after a drink or two, and Molly led the way towards the bar, partly leaning upon it to ask for a port and a half for Madge. She had never drunk as much and she quite liked the feeling as she concentrated on her order and finding the money from her purse.

'Do you know, Madge, I should do this more often. I'm having a right good night,' Molly said, grinning, as she sat down with the next round of drinks.

'Your port is a lot stronger than my stout – you don't drink it like pop, you know,' Madge said. 'You're going to regret this in the morning when you get up for work and have the hangover from hell. Don't drink so fast.'

'But it makes me feel so much better. This is just what I needed, thank you, Madge. Bloody Hitler is dead and I've got to look to the future, despite everything else in my life. I think I did deserve a drink,' Molly said, slurring her words.

'I think this will be our last one. We had better get you home, if I can in the state you are in,' Madge said. Molly's character seemed to have undergone a transformation with the aid of the port.

'I'll get home, don't worry. Don't worry about anything – the war is nearly over and everyone is going to be happy.' Molly sat back in her seat, looking across to the far side of the room. There, in the darkest, quietest corner, sat Connie and Fred Milburn. Connie was nearly sitting on his knee and they were lost in one another's arms. Molly shook her head. One minute Connie was planning to marry Chuck and the next she was in that creep's arms. She was taking after her mother. If I weren't feeling sick already, I am now, Molly thought. She felt let down by her best friend. She had done her best for her, but now Connie's true colours were showing. Molly felt her stomach churning and rushed out into the street to be sick.

'I told you not to drink it like pop. I should have made you slow down,' Madge said as she took Molly's arm and helped her along the street in the direction of her home. 'Now, I need to go down here to get home – will you be all right on your own or should I see you to your door?'

'I'll be all right, I'll be all right, I just need my bed,' Molly replied, feeling stupid as she tried to walk in a straight line.

'Well, I don't think you'll be worth anything at work in the morning. I'll tell them that you're not well, gone down with sickness, and then they won't dock your pay,' Madge said. They stopped at Monkgate and Molly tried to come to her senses.

'Thanks, Madge, you're a good friend.' Molly tried to focus as she stood underneath the ancient archway to the centre of York.

'Come on now, let's get home.' Madge turned suddenly, hearing a male voice from behind her.

'Evening, ladies, it looks like you two have had a good evening. Molly especially!' William Allen walked up to them and shook his head at the state Molly was in.

Molly tried to focus and then smiled at William. 'It's you. Mam says you keep asking about me. How are you?'

'Oh, William, thank God it's only you. She's had a good evening. I was just asking her if she could get herself home because I live down here, nowhere near where she lives.' Madge sighed.

'William, my old friend William, it's so good to see you.' Molly smiled at her old school friend. He had altered – how come she had never noticed how handsome he was before? He no longer looked like she remembered him, with spots and carrot-coloured hair.

'It's good to see you, Molly. Now have I to walk you

home and then we can let Madge get home?' William gave Madge a wink.

'Thank you, else neither of us will ever get home,' Madge whispered. 'Mol, William is going to walk you home, all right? I'll see you when I see you.'

'Night, Madge, love you!' Molly shouted as Madge left the pair of them and William put his arm around Molly and steadied her.

'Now, Molly Freeman, let's get you home safe and sound and face your mother's wrath if I know your mother. It's a good job that it was me walking back this way and not some lech.' William took her arm and started to walk in the direction of Molly's home.

'My best friend from school, that's what you are, William. You used to always look after me,' Molly said, trying to keep up with his brisk walking.

'Yes, Molly, I've always been there for you, but now let's just get you home. You always were headstrong, that's why we were friends. We used to get into some scrapes, didn't we? Can you remember when the lad behind us got the cane for making rude noises? When it was really me and you.' William put his arm around her and tried to keep his face straight as Molly struggled to stop herself from falling over.

'Yes, I remember. It was George Coates – he was a bully anyway, so I never felt guilty about it.'

'Nor me, but we should have owned up to it really.' William grinned. 'We were a right pair. I've missed your antics.'

'And I've missed you, William, I just had to be reminded.'

24

'What a state you were in last night, and look at you this morning. I've never known you do anything like that before.' Winnie chastised her daughter as she sat across the breakfast table from her.

'Mam, I know, I don't know what got into me. The more I drank the better I felt, and then I was sick and I felt such a fool. I'm sorry, you know I never, ever do anything like that.' Molly stirred her porridge and made a note of the time. Her mother had made her get up and told her to get to work once she had something solid in her stomach, but the porridge didn't seem appetising as she felt quite bilious and her head still felt light. She had hoped to do as Madge had advised, but her mother had other ideas.

'How embarrassing it will be for me to go into the butcher's this week,' Winnie continued. 'William Allen was a perfect gentleman walking you home. You are lucky – anybody could have taken advantage of you in the state you were in.' Winnie shook her head. 'I doubt that he'll want to walk out with you now. He will think of you as nothing more than a drunk soak.'

'Mother, please stop lecturing me! I'm not a child. Last night was the first time that I had too much to drink, and I only did that because I was celebrating that

Hitler was dead. Now I'm going back to bed. I don't feel like going to work. I hate my new job at the best of times, even when I don't feel like this.' Molly got up from the table.

'You will do no such thing. You will take a glass of water and an Alka Seltzer and you will get yourself to work. You have only yourself to blame for the state that you are in. You're lucky to still have a job at Rowntree's; poor Connie wasn't as lucky as you, poor lass.' Winnie placed a glass of water in front of her daughter, added two spoonfuls of Alka Seltzer and stirred until it had dissolved. 'Now drink this up and then get dressed for work and get on your way.'

Molly winced at the glass of hangover relief and gathered the courage to drink it back in one. She screwed her face up as the gritty concoction trickled down her throat and nearly made her feel sick again.

'You think you have problems with me. You should have seen Connie! It was a good job that Chuck wasn't in the Olde Starre last night, the way Connie was acting with her new boss, Fred Milburn. She was showing herself up something terrible. At least I didn't sit on any fellow's knee and look like a common hussy,' she said.

'The silly lass, she's got the chance to make a new life for herself in America, what does she think she's doing? This is why women shouldn't go into pubs. They can't drink like men and they usually end up getting talked about. Now, come on. Get a move on and get to work – the walk there will freshen you up, and an early night might be in order. Get your turban and overall on and get gone.' Winnie cleared the table and watched as Molly went upstairs, coming back down prepared for work. 'Let's wait and see what today brings. I don't suppose you will be the only one at work with a hangover this morning. Everyone will have celebrated Hitler's downfall; even I had a tipple of sherry when you were out.' Winnie watched as Molly pulled her coat on and made for the door, looking a bit more herself. 'Things will get better soon, Molly love. I told you that William Allen was a good lad. Happen you'll see a bit more of him now.'

'We'll see, Mam. Sorry I showed you up, I bet I came out with all sorts of rubbish. I'll not be getting drunk again in a hurry.' Molly opened the door and made her escape into the early morning air which awakened her senses. As she walked through the main gates, saying 'Morning' as usual to the Blick machine checker, she breathed in and got ready to face Madge. She knew that she would have plenty to say once she realized that she had made it to work.

'Well, you've made me look a right fool,' Madge told her over the workbench, speaking in a low voice. 'I told them upstairs that you weren't well, that you had sent me a message asking me to say you were sick. They'll know that I was lying.'

'I couldn't stop at home,' Molly said. 'My mam was nagging and said she was ashamed of me coming home in such a state. I'll never hear the last of it.' She started folding the cut-out boxes and putting them together.

'Well, by the looks of it there are a few not in work today, probably because they were in the same state as you. At least you got walked home by William Allen. I knew that you would be all right with him, he's a nice steady lad, else I wouldn't have left him with you. Not a real looker, but a good lad.'

'I can't remember what I said to him,' Molly admitted. 'I hope I didn't make a fool of myself. I can't even remember climbing the stairs to bed. I know one thing, the next time I see him I'll go as red as a tomato.'

'Well, I'm sure whatever you did you wouldn't be as bad as your friend Connie. Did you see her in that corner with Fred Milburn? She was sat on his knee and he'll nearly be old enough to be her father. That's no way to carry on with your employer, and I thought she was going steady with that Yank. I know she's your friend, but she always has had an edge to her.' Madge busied herself folding boxes and filling them ready for the chocolates to be added.

'I didn't think you saw her,' Molly said. 'I tried to ignore her else I would have said something, the state I was in. I don't know what she's playing at. I was surprised she took the job in his shoe shop. I think she was desperate and worried that she had no money coming in. She knew he liked her but always dismissed him as a dirty old man.' She sighed. 'Sometimes I think she doesn't know what she wants.'

'Well, them two left nobody doubting what they were wanting from one another last night. They were outright blatant with it.' Madge shook her head and then smiled as the Tannoy announced it was time for their fifteen-minute tea break. 'Thank heavens for that.

I don't know how I worked in munitions without my drink of tea.'

'No, I don't either, back to a civilized way of life for some of us.' Molly was glad that it was the morning break; her head was still thumping.

Connie lay in her bed and stretched out. It was ten o'clock in the morning but there was no need to rush to work, if she showed her face at all. Fred had told her that she could have the day off as an extra thank you for the evening they had shared. She closed her eyes, rolled over in her bed and thought of Chuck. She wasn't proud of what she had got up to with Fred Milburn, and Chuck must never find out. It was an extra piece of money to get her what she wanted, she told herself. Less worry about the rent payment and a way to save money for her voyage and new life in America. She tried to shut out the thoughts of Fred's podgy hands on her body and his whisky breath as he kissed her. She had put up with his pathetic lovemaking and hoped that it would not take him long, trying to think of Chuck's passionate lovemaking instead. It was just to pay the rent, she whispered to herself and felt a tear running down her face as she remembered hearing her mother and Bill in the bedroom next to hers when she'd been a child. Bill had been a means to an end in her mother's eyes, and look where it had got her.

She would never be like that, she thought to herself. Last night was just the once. She picked up the pounds left on the bedside table by Fred. It was only because she was desperate and needed the money to be with her beloved Chuck when the war was over. It would not become a habit, she told herself.

The end of the working day couldn't come fast enough. It had been a long day for Molly, and she was relieved when the home time whistle blew and the production line stopped, and she and Madge could clear their workbench.

'No pub tonight, an early night,' Madge grinned as they walked out of the factory together and clocked off.

'No, I've learnt my lesson. Today has been one of the longest days I've ever had. I'm going to go home, fill the boiler, have a bath in front of the fire and go to bed early. I feel half dead.' Molly pulled her turban off her head and let her brown hair fall onto her shoulders as they walked out of the factory gates.

'I don't think you are. Look who's sitting over there on top of the wall.' Madge grinned and nodded at William Allen, casually smoking a cigarette as he waited for Molly to come out of work.

'Oh, Lord, he's not waiting of me, is he? I don't know what to say to him. I feel such a fool for last night.' Molly put her head down, feeling her cheeks turning red.

'Well, he's coming this way,' Madge told her as William stubbed his cigarette out and waved. 'Hey up, here he comes, I'll get myself home.' Madge grinned. 'Evening, William, have you come to see if she survived?' she asked cheekily. 'See you tomorrow, Molly.'

William nodded. 'That I have. I thought her mother

was going to have a heart attack when she saw the state she was in.' He looked at Molly. 'Are you all right, Molly? I bet you've had a rough day today. But you're not on your own – there's been a lot worse for wear today. Two of our lads didn't turn into work this morning.'

'You're right, it's been a long, long day but I have only myself to blame.' Molly took a deep breath. 'I'm sorry I was an idiot last night. Thanks for walking me home. It was a matter of one step forward and two back – I'd never have got home under my own steam.'

'Aye, you were struggling a bit. It was funny watching you.' William put his hands in his jacket pocket and grinned.

'I don't know what got into me. Hitler dying was no excuse; I just decided to enjoy myself a little too much.'

'Well, you did that all right. It's a good job I came along when I did. Anyway, it's been nice to see you again. I often ask your mother about you when she comes into the shop. I always remember you from school, but I never get to see you nowadays.' William looked bashful.

'Yes, Mam says she talks to you often. This morning she told me she won't ever be able to look at you again when she comes into the shop, knowing what state I was in last night. I'm never going to hear the last of it.' Molly hesitated for a moment. 'Do you want to walk home with me and say hello to her? Then she won't feel such a Charlie when she walks into the shop.'

'Aye, I can do that, it would be grand and I'd hate for her to feel embarrassed – there's no problem. I'd never say anything about it in the shop. I'm just glad that it's got us back talking to one another – it's been a long time since we were at school together. I still remember you getting the blackboard cleaner thrown at you on our last day. She was an old stickler, that Mrs Stanley. She's still teaching. She walks past the shop every day, never comes in though.'

'She was all right. I deserved all I got, I was always daydreaming. I did enjoy school, though, far more than being back at Rowntree's. It's not as challenging as it used to be. The box production has altered and I get bored.' Molly had forgotten how close their friendship was when they were young. Her mother was right: he had altered. In fact, he had turned into quite a handsome man.

'Well, let's get back to your mother so I can assure her she has nothing at all to be embarrassed about. I think half of York were in a similar situation with the news of Hitler's death. The news continues to be good today; it's only a matter of time before Germany surrenders.'

'When this war is over I'm going to change my life,' Molly announced.

'Oh, are you now? And what do you plan to do?' William asked as they turned the corner to Molly's street.

'I don't know, but I'm not going to be working for Rowntree's all my life. They're a good, caring firm, but I just think I'd rather work for myself. I got a feel for it when I was supervisor at the munitions. Now I'm back packing chocolates, I need more. Watching boxes come down the production line, folding them and then filling them is not taxing enough. I get so bored.' Molly had been thinking about it for a while, but had not dared say anything to anyone else.

'Sounds like a businesswoman talking. Don't you become a rival to me and my father,' William joked.

'No, it will be anything but meat; I'd be sick at the first butchering. Ugh, no, you're safe there.' Molly opened the front door of her home and shouted as she stepped over the threshold. 'Mam, I'm home, and we have a visitor.'

'A visitor at this hour? Let me guess. It will be Connie, she'll have come for her supper,' Winnie shouted from the kitchen.

'No, it's not Connie, but he might like to stay for supper if I ask him.' Molly smiled at William and whispered, 'Do you want to stay? It'll probably be corned beef or Spam.'

'That would be lovely,' William said and followed Molly into the kitchen.

Winnie turned quickly from her frying pan. 'I thought I heard your voice. Oh my Lord, William, has she dragged you back again? I hope she's apologized. I was so embarrassed last night – what a state to get in, I tell you! And here I am now with batter spilled down my pinny, from making Spam fritters. You'll think what a family.'

'Not at all, Mrs Freeman. We've been making light of what happened, and I just thought I'd see if Molly had survived her day.' William stood next to the kitchen table. 'Them Spam fritters smell really good. I'd love to stay and join you for supper, if I may.'

'Of course you can, lad. Molly, set another place and I'll finish off the tin of Spam. It's only Spam fritters and warmed-up potatoes, William. Nothing flash – will that do you?' Winnie carved the remaining Spam into two thin slices, dipped it into her homemade batter and smiled to herself. Perhaps Molly getting drunk was the best thing she had ever done – it had got William Allen sitting at their dinner table.

'It will indeed, nothing wrong with Spam in these hard times. But hopefully things will soon be back to normal, the way the war is going. My father is talking of expanding once it's all over. He hopes to open another butcher's shop on Micklegate on the far side of the river. He says I can run it for him.' William pulled the chair out from under the table and made himself comfortable. He was used to the Freemans, since he had often come home with Molly when they were young.

'He must be doing well, that's good,' Winnie replied.

'Molly says she fancies going into business. So happen we will have competition,' William said flippantly and then took in the horror on Molly's face.

'I only said I thought it would be good to own a business and work for yourself,' Molly said, giving an anxious glance at her mother.

'There are worse things I've heard her say, but she's all right working at Rowntree's for now, until perhaps something or someone comes along.' Leaning forward with a full plate, Winnie patted William's shoulder. 'There now, William, Spam fritters and warmed-up potatoes and cabbage. Help yourself to bread and HP sauce. It is nice to see you back around this table. Kettle's on, I hope, Molly?' She was like a spider with an extra juicy fly in her web that was just right for her youngest, and she wasn't going to let him go.

Later that night Winnie sat with Molly listening to the radio.

'He's a nice lad, is William, you could do worse for yourself.'

'He's all right Mam. I forgot how close we were at school, he's easy to talk to,' Molly replied.

'He's got brass, too, and you'd never go hungry,' Winnie commented, looking down at her knitting.

'Mam, stop it!' Molly said. She noticed what her mother was knitting. 'Is that for Rose's baby? It looks pretty.'

Winnie smoothed the partly knitted matinee coat on her knee. 'Either Rose or Annie. I forgot to tell you, she's coming to see us shortly, probably on Monday the seventh. She says she has some news to tell us.'

'Annie's coming home, that will be lovely,' Molly said, then took in her mam's last comment. 'What do you mean, Annie, she's not . . . is she?'

'I might be wrong, we'll see.' Winnie smiled. She was right, or else Annie wouldn't be coming home. She would want to share her news with her family if she knew her lass.

25

The weeks had flown since Connie had started working at the shoe shop and she was finding money came easy if she pacified her new boss.

'You can take your lunch break now, Gillian, we are quiet. Miss Freeman and I will check the stock on the top shelf and then you can sort out the lower shelves on your return. We need to put some of the old stock of men's shoes in the window; there will be fellas coming back from the war wanting a new pair of shoes. Now's the time to be getting rid of them.' Fred Milburn stood and watched his youngest assistant and wished that she would take her time over lunch. 'If I give you some change, would you get me a newspaper? The news is altering by the minute at the moment.'

'Yes, Mr Milburn, I'd be happy to do that. Your usual, the *Mirror*?' Gillian asked and watched as he put some change from the till in her hand.

'Yes, it's as good as any. You take your time and enjoy the sunshine, it's a bonny day out there.' Fred opened the shop door for her and watched as she walked down the street until she was out of sight and then bolted the shop door and turned the sign to closed. 'There, that will give us half an hour to ourselves, Connie, just enough time for a quick fondle and a bit of how's your father in the back office.' Fred ran his hand the length of Connie's leg and pulled at the hem of her knickers as she stood at the top of the steps that she had just climbed to arrange a new display.

'Fred Milburn, do you never stop? I'm sure there's something wrong with you, all you think about is sex. You could do with some bromide in your tea like our soldiers.' Connie tried to ignore him as he stepped on the two bottom steps of the ladder and caressed her leg.

'Come on, Connie, a quick one on the desk. Nobody will see us, and think of the brass. You'd never make money as easy as this, not even when you worked for Rowntree's. Come on, you know you want to.' Fred's hands wandered and Connie had to turn and tell him to stop it else she would fall off the ladder.

'You are impossible. I'm nearly an engaged woman – what if my Chuck was to find out? He'd break our relationship off straight away.' Connie climbed down and stood with her body squeezed between the ladder and Fred.

'He's not going to find out, now is he? An extra quid in your pay, and did you say you liked that ring that you saw in the pawnshop? It would look good on this finger of yours.' Fred took her hand and kissed her ring finger. 'It would look better than any engagement ring from a Yank.'

'Fred Milburn, you know just what words to say to a girl. Now you are sure that the door is locked? I don't want Miss Prissy Pants walking in and catching us.' Connie smiled and led Fred into the office.

'It's locked, I know it is, and I won't take long. Just a quick one.' Fred sniggered and patted Connie's bottom.

'Just a quick one, Fred, and then you leave me alone tonight, because Chuck is visiting and I don't want you anywhere near my place.' Connie closed the door behind them and started to roll down the stockings that Chuck had bought her, hoping that it really would only be a quick one. It usually was with Fred – the quicker the better, she thought as he fumbled with his trouser zip, and hoped that she would soon have enough in the bank to stop her unhealthy relationship with her over-sexed employer.

Later that evening Connie tried to forget the advances of her boss and concentrate on the man she really loved. 'I've been looking forward to seeing you all day, Chuck. I've really missed you, it's been nearly a week since the last time I saw you.'

'I'm sorry, doll, work has been like nothing I've ever known. I've managed to see the pastor, though. He wants to meet you and talk to us together.' Chuck ravished her with kisses and she let his hands run over her body.

'When? I'll have to make it right with Fred in the shoe shop, but that shouldn't be a problem.' Connie kissed him back and held him tight. 'The war's coming to an end – will that make any difference? You'll still be here for a while yet – long enough for us to get married?'

'Yes, doll, don't worry. Even if I have to go back to the States, I'll send for you. Anyway, it won't be for a while yet. We can't just pull out of a place, it isn't that simple. Get a day off work and then we can meet the pastor and fix a date to get married. I've written home and told them that I've met an English gal and that we're going to get married. Come on, Connie, loosen up, everything will be all right. Don't worry, we'll be married before they ship me home, even if I have to bribe the pastor. We will be married, I promise you.'

'All right, I just worry. I don't want to lose you and be left here on my own.'

Chuck pulled her to the bed and kissed her passionately, but she lay worrying, wondering if she would ever be married to the man she truly loved. The end of the war was more than welcome, but it came with a new set of worries.

The following day Molly decided to visit Connie. She had left it a while, so as not to offend when she said what she had to say about what she had seen her up to with Fred Milburn. Besides, she was in no place to criticize the state that she had been in that night, but she needed to talk to her best friend and also tell her about William and how Rowntree's had changed.

It was a lovely late spring evening as Molly walked through the streets to where Connie lived. She admired the magnificent spires of the Minster rising above the medieval buildings of the Shambles as she stood on the doorstep and waited for Connie to answer. There was a feeling of expectancy, of joy that the war was coming to an end now Berlin had surrendered to the Russian army, and it was only a matter of days before Germany admitted defeat. Already there were meetings between the housewives down her street, planning a celebratory street party once victory had been declared.

Molly heard the door open and turned to face Connie, who looked tired. 'I thought I'd come and visit. I haven't seen you for a while and so much is happening, and we're both so busy with our jobs.'

'Yes, sorry, I should have come around to see you, but as you say, we're both busy. Come on up and we'll have a natter. I'm glad that you've come, I could really do with a friend.' Connie smiled wanly, truly grateful to have Molly as a visitor.

'What's up? Surely things aren't that bad? You've got work and you're soon to be engaged – if you aren't already for all I know. And the war is nearly over.' To her alarm, Molly could see that Connie was near to tears.

'Come on up and we'll have a right chinwag,' Connie said. 'There's only you I can talk to, and believe me, I need a friend, because I'm being an idiot at the moment.' She hugged Molly and then led the way up the stairs to her flat.

'Oh, Connie, for someone who has a bright future to look forward to, you look miserable,' Molly said quietly as they sat close together around her small table.

'Oh, Mol, I'm an absolute idiot. I don't know how I get myself into such situations.'

'Is this to do with Fred Milburn? I knew you'd regret working for him. I did see you and him in Ye Olde Starre being rather friendly, so nothing that you're going to tell me will shock me,' Molly confessed.

'You did! I never saw you. Oh Lord, and there was me thinking we were being discreet in that small dark corner.' Connie shook her head.

'You can't be discreet in any part of that pub, but I'm sure not many other people noticed you; I only glanced at you as I got up from my seat. It's a good job you didn't see me. I've never been so drunk in my life and don't plan to be again.'

'You never hardly drink; it would go straight to your head. Oh, Mol, I'm ashamed of myself; I should never have gone and worked for Fred Milburn. The trouble is I knew exactly what I was doing, and now I'm regretting everything. I knew he was a lech, but then I went on to see what I could get out of him for *favours*, as he calls them.' Connie bowed her head. 'I get myself deeper in with him every day, and he expects more every day, and all the while I have Chuck promising to marry me. He's seen the pastor, so that is something, but the war is coming to an end and he'll be moving on if we don't get married soon.'

'Oh, Connie, how could you? Fred Milburn – we both know what he's like, he's always been after you. But to take money? I presume you mean money, well, that's nothing but being a . . .' Molly stopped herself.

'Yes, go on, say it, I'm nothing more than a prostitute. But it pays the rent, and look, he bought me this ring the other day, not that I can wear it as Chuck would notice.' Connie reached for the ring that she had hidden in a trinket box on the kitchen shelf.

'Heavens, he must think something of you, or be desperate.' Shocked, Molly looked at the sparkling ring that Fred had bought Connie from the pawnshop. He was well off, and to him a pound here or there to keep himself happy would mean nothing, while it meant a lot to Connie.

'I'd leave, Connie,' she said eventually. 'You don't want to be his plaything, no matter how desperate you are for money. Come back and live with us, Mam will feed you until you find another job. Anything is better than being a scarlet woman.'

'A scarlet woman. Now I never thought I'd be called that. The stupid thing is, I know exactly what I'm doing – I'm following in my mother's footsteps when my dad died. There were men coming and going at all times of the day and night when I was growing up, but I didn't know why.' Connie bowed her head.

Molly's face softened; she felt for her friend. 'You don't have to follow your mam's path, I'll help you. I'll tell Mam you're coming back to stay, and you can look for a different job. Fred Milburn is just a mucky old man and we both know that, just don't go back. Leave! Before Chuck finds out about it all,' Molly said forcefully.

'Are you sure? I think I'm going to have to. I mustn't be like my mother. I can't carry on like this and I'm so frightened that I will lose Chuck, either because of Fred or with the war ending.'

'Then come back. There's less shame in admitting you can't afford this flat than bedding Fred Milburn in order to be able to.' Molly's face said it all as she thought of the plump, middle-aged shopkeeper who might have money but certainly did not have looks, integrity or morals.

'I will, at least I think I will, but I can't just leave like that. I'll give him a week's notice and this ring back; I do need a good reference from him if I'm to get a new job. Don't look like that, Molly. I will leave, believe me. I'll hopefully be going to America soon. Chuck will send for me, I'm sure, if he gets sent home before we can marry, and I'll go and see the pastor once I've left Fred's.'

'Well, please do before you get in too deep with that awful man. I'll tell Mam you're coming back. Honestly, she'll be glad to have you; she hoped it was you coming to supper the other day when William came back with me.' Molly smiled and tried not to show how she felt.

'William, not William Allen? Have you finally given in to your mother's matchmaking? Molly Freeman, and there's you telling me what to do!'

'It just happened by accident,' Molly admitted. 'He came across me on the night you were in the Starre, the night I was drunk. Madge was attempting to walk me back home and then William came out of nowhere and walked me back instead. It's a good job he did, because I couldn't walk straight, I was in a right state.'

'Oh, Molly, we are both idiots.'

'Perhaps, but my mam made me go to work the following morning, not showing a bit of sympathy for my headache and churning stomach. He was waiting for me as I walked out of work. I could have died, I felt so ashamed of the state I'd been in the previous night.'

'He wasn't, was he? Oh heavens, you hadn't gone and done anything daft when you were drunk, had you?' Connie gasped.

'No, you know I'm not like that. He had come to see if I was all right. Anyway, the long and short of it is that I invited him home and he had supper with us.'

'Oh, your mam would be happy; she's been trying to pair you two off for months now.'

'Well, to be honest, perhaps she could have been right, because we got on like a house on fire. I'd forgotten what good friends we were, and he is quite good-looking. We found we had a lot in common.'

'What, you and William Allen?'

'It's better than you and Fred Milburn, Connie Whitehead! Anybody's better than that dirty old devil!'

26. Friday, 4 May

'I hope Connie isn't thinking of moving back in this week, I've just made the spare room up for Annie. I am looking forward to having her back here, albeit for just a day or two. All my girls together and the war close to an end, I couldn't wish for anything more.' Winnie passed Molly her turban. 'I'm going to meet her down at the station on Monday. It's a pity you can't come, but work comes first.

'Anyway,' Winnie added, 'I'm glad that you suggested Connie came back here to stay. I could tell that she wouldn't be all right living above that bakery. I'm surprised she hasn't got cockroaches climbing the walls, the bakery is that mucky.'

'I'm glad that you'll have her back,' Molly said. 'She's been hopeless at looking after herself and she'll be a lot better if she leaves working for Fred Milburn. I don't know why she ever went to work for him; she knew she didn't like him.' She pulled her coat on.

'Ah, well, a job is a job when you're desperate, but she's not that – she should know she could come back to us anytime. That Fred Milburn is a devil anyway. He keeps a woman and his illegitimate child over in Filey; I'm surprised he's never married her. Not that anybody with any sense would want him.'

'I bet Connie doesn't know that, I'll have to tell her.' Molly kissed her mother on the cheek. 'I'll see you tonight, Mam.'

'Yes. Will William be walking you home from work again?' Winnie smiled. She had been right all along if Molly had only listened to her.

'No, Mam, just because he walked me home the other day doesn't mean he's going to be doing it every day. Now, I'm going, I'll see you tonight.'

Winnie cleared the breakfast things away and then sat in the kitchen chair and thought about her family. They were everything to her and soon there would be another generation for her to love. Burt would have been proud of his family; all of them had turned out to make their own way in the world. A world that had been turbulent for nearly six years, but on the whole they had come out of it unscathed. Her thoughts moved on to Connie. She was a good lass but headstrong, and Winnie would have her back until her Yank boyfriend took her home with him. She hoped that she would be happy with him. She deserved a bit of happiness.

'Winnie, Winnie, are you in, have you heard the news? Isn't it just grand? I could just about cry!' Winnie heard the front door open and slam as her next-door neighbour Jean ran into the kitchen with a huge beam on her face, her hair in rollers under her headscarf. 'It's over, Winnie, the German army has surrendered! It's on the wireless, put it on and listen.'

'Never! I know they were struggling but I didn't think we were that near victory. I can't believe it!'

'Go on, switch your set on, they keep repeating the news.' Jean tugged on Winnie's arm. 'Come on, listen!' Jean pulled a disbelieving Winnie into the front room where the wireless had pride of place and waited for the jubilant sound of the BBC commentator.

Winnie struggled to take it in. According to the newsreader, High Commander General Alfred Jodl, Chief of Staff to the German Armed Forces, had that morning agreed to an unconditional surrender. All forces under German control were to cease operations at 23.01 hours. Subject to that, the newly placed German President, Admiral Karl Doenitz, would authorize the official surrender of all the armed forces of Nazi Germany on Monday the 7th of May.

'Oh, Jean, it's over, the war is over, thank heavens for that!' Winnie pulled her handkerchief out of her pocket and wiped her eyes. 'That's the best news I've ever heard.'

'It is that. My lad will be coming home, your Rose's husband will be safe for the birth of his baby and hopefully things will get back to normal. Whatever that is, I've forgotten. But I can't wait to taste a banana or an orange again and have something more than Spam and corned beef in my cupboards.'

'My Annie is returning home to visit on Monday, I hope she's still coming after this news. It will be busy on the trains, but troops won't be returning back home yet.' Winnie smiled at Jean. 'I know it's only early in the morning, but let's have a tipple to celebrate.'

'It's not quite over yet, Winnie. There's our lads still fighting the Japs and they aren't bothered if they send one of their own on a suicide mission. Kamikaze – fancy knowing you're going to kill yourself on purpose for the honour of your country. They are fanatical, nothing will stop them.'

'They'll be stopped,' Winnie said confidently, 'I know they will. Without Germany next to them, surely they will surrender. Italy has seen sense.' She poured out her sherry and took a sip. 'Cheers, Jean. Here's to a more peaceful life.'

The news had been heard by the staff in Rowntree's, and they were hugging one another and crying. Molly hugged Madge and exclaimed, 'It's over, I can't believe it! It's over.'

'It is, now we might get a bit of freedom,' Madge said jubilantly as production came to a halt and an announcement was made for everyone to gather in the main dining hall.

Seebohm Rowntree looked around at all his staff and smiled. He cleared his throat and his voice rang out around the hushed room.

'What a wonderful day, there is light at the end of the tunnel. This country is great, just as it proclaims itself by name. Germany is defeated and it is because of people like you and your family. Now, today we will work as usual; there will be plenty of time to celebrate with your families tonight. However, on Tuesday the eighth, I understand the country as a whole is to celebrate and it will be a National Holiday, VE Day, Victory in Europe. Now, before we go back to work, let us raise our voices by singing the National Anthem and thank the King and his government for leading us through this abominable war. And thank you for standing by this firm and your country in their hour of need.'

Seebohm's strong voice started the anthem and soon the hall was filled with voices ringing with patriotic pride. Madge nudged Molly and whispered, 'The tight old devil! He could have given us today off, because not a lot is going to get done.'

'Never mind, we have Tuesday off. I bet there will be parties all over the place. I know my mam will be organizing one down our street with the neighbours,' Molly whispered back. 'Not that there's a lot of food to celebrate with, but they will manage somehow.'

She looked up at her sister Rose standing with the directors and management and felt a glow of pride that her sister was the only woman among a line-up of men. She also knew that the announcement of Germany's surrender would mean the end of her sister's worries, just what she needed with a baby on the way.

'Now, that's what I call bloody good news,' Fred Milburn said after hearing the news from a customer who had just called in. 'Gillian, consider this afternoon a holiday, I'll pay you. I'm off to celebrate in my usual style. Miss Whitehead, would you like to join me in a quick gill? I think we deserve it.' Fred turned the shop sign and winked at Connie. 'Nobody's going to be buying shoes today, so let's not waste our time in here.'

'If you insist, Mr Milburn,' Gillian said, beaming. She couldn't wait to get home and made for the door onto the street which was filled with people celebrating to the sound of the Minster bells.

'Now then, Connie, stop what you're doing and let's go for a drink or two, and then who knows what,' Fred grinned. 'It's a grand day and we should do something to remember it by. A few pints at Ye Olde Starre and then we can go back to yours for a change.'

'Oh, I don't mind the few drinks, but perhaps not to go back to my humble abode, you'll not like it there,' Connie replied. She didn't want Fred to see where she lived or, even worse, have Chuck arrive.

'If you're ashamed of where you're living it makes no difference to me. I know you're above the bakery on the Shambles and that it'll be not the most salubrious of dwellings. It isn't your home I'm going to see. Now come on, lass. Let's celebrate!'

Connie walked out of the shop and Fred locked the door and felt for his wallet in his pocket. 'Here, lass, treat yourself to something to celebrate the good news. Call it money in advance for services rendered this afternoon.' He watched as Connie put the money in her handbag which also, unknown to him, contained a note saying that she no longer wished to work for him. 'That's it now, a drink or two and then back to yours.'

Connie put her head down as they entered a crowded Starre. She had vowed never again, but five pounds was a huge sum and it was worth one more last time with Fred, even if it was to be in her flat, the place she had never wanted to take him to. She accepted her first drink and sat next to her employer in their usual dark corner. Tomorrow she would tell him that she was leaving both him and the shop, move back into the Freemans' home and look for employment elsewhere. It was just a means to an end, she thought as Fred put his chubby hand on her leg and winked. Just one more time.

Chuck couldn't drive fast enough in his jeep to tell Connie that he was to be shipped back to the States in the next few weeks. The pastor could see them both at the end of the following week, and his parents had written back to him, overjoyed with the news that he had found a British girl and that he was to marry. He couldn't wait to see her face as he parked his jeep in the Minster Square and pushed his way through the joyous crowds, everyone patting him on the back and cheering him for being an Ally and helping to win the war. He ran to the shoe shop only to find that it was closed, so he turned and headed for the flat above the bakery, thinking that Connie would be home. Perhaps they should delay the wedding until both of them were safe on the ranch in Montana. He'd had enough of the Air Force; he'd leave and join his father on the ranch to have a real American wedding with his British bride on his arm. He'd even take her to the jeweller's that very day so they could choose a ring, a day they would never forget. He stood outside the door to Connie's and checked if it was open. He'd surprise her, celebrate with a dinner and a drink. Chuck's face was all smiles as he quietly crept up the stairs. He expected to find her looking out over the crowded Shambles, but as he reached the top of the stairs he heard a man's voice and the familiar sound of Connie's mattress springs. Chuck stood stock-still, utterly shocked. Surely he couldn't be hearing what he thought he was? He entered the room, and reality hit him like a punch in the stomach. There he saw Fred and Connie, engrossed, too busy to have heard him or noticed him.

He felt that his heart was going to break as he stood for what seemed like an age watching the woman he loved being unfaithful to him. She was in bed with her boss, how could she? He breathed in, feeling a rage inside but also feeling a fool. He said nothing and turned to go just as Connie spotted him standing there, looking angry and hurt. She sat up in utter horror and panic. How had she let this happen?

'Chuck, Chuck,' she cried desperately. 'He means nothing to me, I'm so sorry.' She pushed the half-drunken Fred off her and grabbed the bedsheet, clutching it to her as she ran down the stairs after him.

'I don't care.' Chuck stood at the bottom of the stairs. 'You can go to hell, and to think I was going to marry you. They warned us all about girls like you, out for what you can get. Well, you're not catching this one, no sir, you are nothing but a whore!' He slammed the door and left Connie clutching the sheet while the odious Fred called for her to come back to bed with him.

She picked up Fred's clothes and shoes and threw them down the stairs. 'Out, get out!' she yelled at the top of her voice. 'I never want to see you or your shoe shop ever again. You're a drunken old lech and I've always known that.' She manhandled him out of the bed and pushed him down the stairs, tears welling up in her eyes. She felt sick. 'You've ruined my life, I've lost everything because of you.'

'You weren't complaining a minute ago when I was spending money on you and making you happy,' Fred said as he stumbled downstairs and started to dress. 'The lad's right, you're nothing but a whore, that's why I paid you.'

'Out, get out!'

Fred slammed the door with his jacket still in his hand and his braces hanging down around his waist.

Connie had lost everything: her future, her job and, most of all, her Chuck. How could she have been so stupid? She sat on the edge of her bed and cried her heart out.

27

Annie sat on the train wedged between two elderly gentlemen, and opposite a vicar and a young girl with a very curious fox terrier that was showing a great deal of interest in the basket on her lap, filled with a few treats from the farm. She had placed a small suitcase on the luggage rack over her head, containing just enough clothes to see her through her two-night stay at her mother's.

The girl pulled the terrier back as it sniffed up at Annie's basket.

'Sorry, he knows that there's food in there, he's a devil for begging.' The girl smiled at Annie.

'That's no problem, he's right,' Annie told her, 'it's filled with food from home. I'm taking it to my mam's at York. I know now she'll be organizing a street party for Tuesday – she won't be able to help herself. Are you going to one? I'm sure you are!'

'I think so,' the girl replied. 'Nobody has said anything yet, but I keep seeing my mam raiding our pantry and taking it to our next-door neighbour's, so they are planning something.'

'It's a wonderful celebration, ridding the world of tyranny. I have prayed for peace for so long,' the vicar commented. He bent down and patted the dog's head.

'Your baby will be born into a peaceful world, thanks be to God,' he said, looking at Annie's only just noticeable growing stomach which she was hiding under the basket.

'I hope so. I'm going home to tell my mother the good news that she's about to be a grandmother; it couldn't be better timing. My sister is also expecting her first, so the next generation should grow up without the threat of war over their heads.' Annie smiled at the vicar. He was an observant soul, she would give him that. She looked out of the carriage window, seeing the outskirts of York as they started to draw in to the magnificent Victorian station. She had missed her home town. Clitheroe was a bustling market town with its own castle, but York stood serenely in its own vale, filled with beautiful architecture, Roman walls and medieval streets. There was nowhere quite like home. The train jerked as it crossed the points into the station and everybody stood up, getting ready to leave their cramped seats.

'Allow me,' the vicar said, reaching for Annie's case.

She put her basket down on her seat. 'Thank you, that's kind of you.'

'Not at all. Now you enjoy your visit, I'm sure your mother will welcome the news of a new child in the family. Oh, I say! The dog has stolen a sausage from your basket, a very good-looking sausage as well, if I may say so.' The vicar and all the coach gazed at the dog and the girl blushed bright red and whispered sorry as the sausage disappeared in one frantic gulp.

'That was more than my ration of meat for a week, wasted on a dog,' the vicar growled.

Annie wanted to say 'All God's creatures, vicar', but she thought better of it as she saw her mam standing on the platform waiting for her. The girl and the dog made a quick exit.

'Oh, Annie, I can't believe you're here and on such a day as this. The war is over and my lass is back at home visiting us all.' Winnie wrapped her arms around her daughter as she emerged from the train. 'Come on, give me your suitcase, you look weighed down with stuff.'

'I thought I'd bring you a few bits, Mam. I knew you'd be planning something down our street if I know you.' Annie smiled and looked around the station. 'Do you think they have enough flags up? Anybody would think we had won a war,' she joked as she walked out of the station with her mother. It felt good to be back in York as they walked past the city walls and made their way across town. Everywhere flags and bunting were being put up and for once everyone sounded happy as they enjoyed a Monday without fear of Jerry putting a stop to it.

'There we are, nearly home. It won't be long before Molly's back. She wanted to come and meet you, but Rowntree's are still working today. At least they have a day off tomorrow.' Winnie put the key in the lock and opened the door to let Annie into her old home.

'Oh, I've missed this smell! It's home. The smell of lavender polish and baking and the homeliness of it all. Nothing is better than home and seeing you, Mam.'

Annie put her basket on the table and looked around. 'How many jellies have you made? There must be a hundred of them in their little paper dishes.'

'They're for tomorrow. The men of the street are going to put chairs and tables the length of the street, and us women have begged, borrowed and nearly stolen to get what we can to eat, especially for the children.'

Annie removed the newspaper from the top of her basket, revealing the contents which included just short of two pounds of best pork sausage.

'I'm afraid a dog on the train helped himself to one of the sausages when my back was turned,' she apologized. 'The temptation for the poor creature was too great as he'd sat and smelt them all the way from Whalley. But there is some sliced ham and some brawn for sandwiches that he never got his mouth around. I always make sure I come with things I know I take for granted but which I know are in short supply here.' Annie emptied her basket onto the table and watched her mother gratefully put it all away in the coolness of the pantry.

'There's a lot to be said for having a farmer's wife in the family! How is that man of yours and his relations?' Winnie asked as she put the kettle on.

'Frantic, we have pigs farrowing and I'm here leaving him to it, so I can't stop longer than Wednesday morning. He needs me back. As for Bernard and Lizzie, they are happily settled in Clitheroe. I don't know if their neighbours appreciate them, but no matter how they moan, they are not going to change their ways.'

'I must say, when we came down for your wedding, the house was looking a lot tidier, it was like a different place. You must have put some time in, both of you, to have got it that straight so fast.' Winnie passed Annie her cup of tea and gave her a quick glance – she was right. Annie had come home to tell her some more good news.

'Mike's going to get the old end of the house fixed; the roof is more like a sieve so this is our biggest job this summer. We want to get it done before . . .' Annie hesitated.

'Let me guess, before the baby comes.' Winnie smiled. 'Annie, I'm so happy for you both. A baby is a baby, perhaps a little too soon after the wedding, but I'm over the moon for you both.' She took her daughter's hand across the dinner table. 'My Annie to be a mother, my headstrong Annie. You haven't sailed the high seas like you once wished, but you have made your own path in life.'

'I should have guessed that you would know before I even told you,' Annie exclaimed. 'I saw you looking at me on our wedding day; I should have told you then but I didn't want to spoil the celebrations.'

'I guessed, that's true. I'm already knitting for you and Rose. I've nearly completed one white layette and then I'll start on the next one. Both of you will get the same until I know what sex the good Lord blesses us with.'

'They won't ever have a better grandmother, that I am sure.' Annie got up from her chair and hugged her mother. She hadn't appreciated her all the time when she was at home, but now she loved every inch of her. There was nobody quite like her mam; she was special.

'Oh, it's good to see you, Annie. I never thought I'd say this, but I don't half miss you,' Molly pulled her turban off her head and gave her sister a big hug before sitting on the settee in the front room next to her.

'Oh, that brings back memories, the smell of chocolate,' Annie said. 'I must admit it's considerably better than the smell of pig muck. However, I'll not swap you. At least I'm my own boss.' She grinned.

'I'd swap,' Molly confessed. 'I hate my job at the moment. It isn't Rowntree's fault, it's just the times we are in, but it is so boring. I'm thinking of leaving if I can find something else.'

'It's good money, Mol, and you have our Rose working with you. I'd think twice,' Annie advised. 'I know what work is now.'

'So do I after working in munitions for these past years; at least it gave me a chance to put away some savings. I've got quite a nice healthy bank account at the moment, unlike Connie, who spent it as fast as she made it.' Molly sat back and closed her eyes, wishing her mother would tell them their supper was ready.

'How is Connie?' Annie asked with genuine concern. 'Mam said she's going to marry the hunk of a Yank who brought you all down. She'll have fallen on her feet if she does and may even be able to find her baby brother if she goes over there when she's married.'

'She's supposed to be moving back in here next week,' Molly said. 'The flat costs her too much and she works for Fred Milburn in his shoe shop now. Rowntree's didn't take her back on, they don't need as many staff.'

'Oh Lord, she's always going from one disaster to another. I'm not keen on her, but she is a good friend to you, that I do know.' Annie patted her sister's hand.

'She is, but even I have lost a bit of patience with her,' Molly admitted. 'There's more to it than her just working for Fred Milburn; I think they have an understanding. Wink, wink, say no more.' Molly smiled at her sister. 'So, is our mam right, am I to be an aunty again?'

'I don't know how she spotted it,' Annie said. 'I was hardly showing on my wedding day and I'm not much now, I don't think, but people seem to know that I'm expecting.' She put her hands proudly on her stomach. 'It will be a lovely childhood growing up on a farm in Bowland, better than breathing in chocolate every day.'

'Oh, I don't know. We had a good childhood here, I wouldn't swap it. Mam and Dad were always there for us and we never really went hungry,' Molly said. 'I'll get knitting like Mam, then. It's a pity you're a long way from home – I'd have loved babysitting.'

'You'll have to help Rose out instead. Is she going to carry on with work at Rowntree's or has she not said? I bet Ned goes back to work there now the war is over.' Annie picked up her mother's knitting from down the side of the chair and smiled. 'She's at it already, preparing.'

'Yes, for Rose or for you, she told me last week. She can't wait to be a grandmother.' Molly grinned.

Winnie shouted through to her girls, 'Come on, you two, supper's out. A real treat – spring cabbage, potatoes and some boiled ham.'

'It isn't for me,' Annie chuckled. 'I live on this at least twice a week, but it will be lovely that someone else has made it for me, especially Mam.'

'Believe me, it is a treat for me. If I see another plate with Spam or corned beef on it, I'm going to cry,' Molly said as they walked into the kitchen and sat down to start their supper.

'Hello, hello, I'm sorry, I know it's supper time and that Annie is here, but I had to come. I've cried all weekend and I need someone to talk to.' Connie slammed the Freemans' front door and walked into the kitchen looking white as a ghost and wretched. 'I've been an absolute fool and now I've ruined any hope of a decent life. Chuck has finished with me, I've told Fred Milburn where to go with himself and his job and now I have absolutely nothing in my life.' She broke down and burst into tears.

'Oh, Connie, come here.' Molly got up from her chair and put her arms around her best friend. 'Come on, come upstairs and tell me everything. Have you had something to eat?' Molly looked round at her sister and mother as she put her arm around Connie and guided her to the bottom of the stairs, leaving her partly eaten meal. 'I'm sure Annie and my mam don't want to hear all about it. Come and tell me all about it upstairs and then you can have a proper cry.'

'No, I've not eaten a thing, I haven't anything in the flat,' Connie sobbed. 'But I'm not hungry, I just want to talk.' She trudged miserably up the well-known stairs to Molly's room where she sat on the bed and told her what had happened and how stupid she had been. Winnie sighed and shrugged her shoulders. 'That lass goes from tragedy to tragedy; she attracts trouble like bees are attracted to honey. I'll make her a sandwich and a cuppa and keep Molly's dinner warm.'

'Nothing alters here, does it, Mam? You feed everybody and the house is always open for everybody's woes to be listened to. I hope my home will just be the same,' Annie said warmly.

Winnie quickly put a ham sandwich together and poured a cup of tea before leaving both on the stairs for Molly to give Connie.

'It will be, love, because that is what good mothers do, no matter what age your family are, and sometimes those that aren't even yours. Everybody needs somebody in this world.'

28. 8 May, VE Day

'Are you all right?' Molly turned over and looked at her best friend as she lay next to her in her bed.

'I'll have to be, won't I? After all, I have only myself to blame. I had the perfect life in front of me and I had to go and spoil it. I always think I'm doing my best at the time and then when I look back and think what I've done, I realize how stupid I was.' Connie's eyes were red with crying and her face was pale, but she felt a lot better for being able to talk to her best friend Molly.

'Well, at least the war has ended. Anything can happen now and our menfolk will be returning before long; there will be a lot more fish in the sea shortly.' Molly tried to sound positive, but she knew Connie had made the mistake of her life. She put her feet down on the cold linoleum floor and went to open the bedroom curtains. 'It's a lovely day out there. It's only seven o'clock, but the men of the street are putting trestle tables up already and the flags are flying.'

'I don't feel like showing my face today,' Connie said. 'Just leave me here and let me sulk.'

There was a knock on the door and Winnie called out, 'Is everybody decent?'

'Yes, we're not dressed but we are awake. Are you

up already? You could have had a lie-in,' Molly said, accepting two cups of tea from her mam.

'A lie-in, don't talk so daft!' Winnie scoffed. 'We have quite a few mouths to feed today if this row is going to celebrate. Lord knows how we're going to feed them, but we will manage. Now, get dressed, you two. I've a job for you seeing you're both good at folding and shaping card. I need you to make paper hats from old newspapers for all the children down our row.'

'Mrs Freeman, I can't face the world. Everyone will be talking about me,' Connie said and hid back under the bedclothes.

'Believe me, love, today they will not give a damn. Besides, who knows what's gone on inside your home? Here, nobody does, and that's how it will stay. That man of yours might go back to America and decide to give you another chance once he has calmed down.' Winnie stood with her hands on her hips. 'As for Fred Milburn, he's just a dirty old man who took advantage of you, just like he did with the other woman he's got over in Filey. Although she got lumbered with a baby to him. Dirty devil. Now, come on, Annie's up and she's just toasting some bread for breakfast. There's only Bovril to put on it, but that's better than nothing. All my butter and margarine ration has been used for the party. Now, see you downstairs in five minutes; it's all hands to the pump today.'

She hurried off and Molly began to get dressed. 'If I'd told you everything that I'd heard about Fred, perhaps you'd not have made the decisions you did,' she told Connie. 'If I had done, this might not have happened.' She pulled her skirt up and fastened it before buttoning up a baby-blue knitted cardigan and looking at herself in the wardrobe mirror. 'Mam's right. Perhaps when Chuck goes back home or has had time to have a rethink, he might come back to you. He'll just need to calm down.'

'Do you think so? I don't, but I suppose it is something to hang onto, and I have his parents' home address; I could write to him there when he does go back home.' Connie threw back the covers and sat on the edge of the bed.

'Oh, there is life in you, then?' Molly smiled.

'No, not really. I need a pee and I need to beat you to the lavvy, so I'll have to get up and get dressed.' Connie quickly slipped the dress she had worn the previous day over her head and made for the door. 'Thanks, Molly, for listening to me blubbering and crying. I don't know what I'd do without you.'

'Hey, that's what friends are for,' Molly replied. She listened to Connie's heavy footsteps running downstairs to the outside toilet and hoped that she wouldn't take too long as she sipped her tea.

'Are you all right this morning, Connie?' Annie asked, pulling a chair up to the kitchen table as Connie came back from the outside toilet. 'You were in a bit of a state last night.'

'No, not really, but I have only myself to blame. I'm not terribly proud of myself at the moment. I deserve all that Chuck said to me in honesty.' Connie went and took her cup of tea from Molly as she came downstairs with both hands full.

'She's going to write to him and sort it out. I've told her if he loves her he might forgive her,' Molly said, eyeing the pile of old newspapers on the table waiting to be made into paper hats.

'That's an idea. He might listen if you explain; you can but try.' Annie placed a plate of toast in front of them and sat down while their mother put a dozen eggs that Annie had brought with her on the stove to boil before sitting down and joining them.

'Rose will be here soon. She's on bread-spreading duty, but she'll not have to stand on her feet too long. It's bad for you when you are expecting. You'll have to take care as well, Annie.'

'Congratulations, Annie, Molly told me last night.' Connie didn't ask the due date as Molly had made it obvious that the wedding had come just in the nick of time. She was only hoping that she would not have been left in the same situation by either Fred or Chuck, which would make her life unbearable.

'Right, come on, misery drawers, let's get these party hats folded. Do you want them put on the tables when we've finished, Mam?' Molly put a pile of newspapers in front of Connie, hoping that it would distract her from her worries.

'If you would, love; the tables are getting covered with tablecloths now. The party is due to start at twelve. Nearly every street is holding one – it's amazing what us women have found and been able to make out of nothing. Jean from across the road has put her gramophone outside her house so that we can have music all day, just as long as somebody is there to wind it up. Thank heavens it's a beautiful bright day, else it would have been a washout. God must have been on our side,' Winnie said as she busied herself with the many jobs that she had to do.

'I'll do the washing-up, Mam. There's always a shortage of washers-up. I wish Mike was here – he would have loved to take part, but he couldn't leave the farm.' Annie sighed and thought about what Mike would be doing without her. He had mentioned that he might go into Clitheroe to have a drink with Bernard and Lizzie to celebrate, but then return home, and she hoped that he would be doing that.

They all turned when they heard Rose's voice as she walked through the open front door.

'It's like a production line in here and out there,' she exclaimed. 'Ned is outside; he's brought some chairs from the Rowntree's boardroom and they've sent over a hundred little parcels of chocolate misfits. I'll put them in the pantry to keep cool, Mam, until after the children have had their dinner.' She stepped forward and hugged Annie. 'It's good to see you, sis. Are you keeping well?'

'Yes, I am, and I know Mam will have told you my news, I never could keep a secret from her. How are you keeping? We can compare notes.' Annie smiled.

'I'm fine, just tired. I'll be a lot better now I know Ned is going to be at home. He's saying he thinks he will leave the RAF if he can. Hopefully, he will get back onto the Rowntree's board again and then I will resign and stay at home when the baby comes, although I haven't quite made my mind up yet. It would be good to still keep my hand in at work, but we will see. Thank heaven this war has come to an end. I just wish Ivy was still alive to see all this.'

'I'm sorry I never got to the funeral.' Annie squeezed Rose's hand.

'Thank you. Now, this isn't a day for being miserable; it's a day of celebrations.' Rose glanced at Connie. 'You are here early – are you back staying here?'

Winnie quickly intervened, 'Don't ask, our Rose. Now come on, let's get on with buttering the bread and I'll mash these eggs that are boiling. Annie has saved the day with her supply of eggs and brawn – at least everybody is going to be fed.'

'I've had words with Chuck, that's all. I needed to talk to Molly,' Connie replied, trying to look cheerful.

'Ned said that the Yanks at the base have all got the freedom of York today, so he might come and say sorry. Will he know where you are?' Rose could tell Connie had been crying.

'Yes, he will have a good idea. If he finds me he finds me,' Connie sniffed.

'Plenty more fish in the sea like Mam says,' Molly said.

'Ah, well, they will be leaving a few broken hearts when they all return,' Rose went on, 'and not all of them are what they seem to be. Some thought they could win any girl they wanted with their lipstick, stockings and gum. Perhaps you'll be better without him, Connie. After all, you know absolutely nothing about him really.'

'I knew I loved him. And that I was looking forward to life with him on his ranch in Montana,' Connie said, trying to hold the tears back as Winnie guided Rose into the pantry to keep her quiet.

Rose looked up, surprised, clearly about to say something else. 'Will you shut up?' Winnie whispered.

'Montana? Is that true?' Rose asked, her voice low. 'Ned always thought he was from the Bronx, but then again he might be wrong. Ned might see him daily but he doesn't mix that much with the ground crew.'

'Oh Lord, it gets worse. The poor lass. If Ned's right, she does know how to pick 'em. Let's not tell her that just yet, or even mention it. Hopefully Ned is wrong.'

'Happen the next one will be a good one, fingers crossed.' Rose smiled. 'Now come on, egg sandwiches.'

It was eleven thirty and the street was full of its residents. Women and men in their Sunday best, with children running up and down the street, flying toy aeroplanes, playing hopscotch and skipping. The whole street was celebrating with pints of homemade beer, followed by a lot of laughter. Jean's gramophone was playing 'The White Cliffs of Dover' sung by the adored Vera Lynn.

'This couldn't be more perfect,' Winnie said as she and her helpers started laying out the food. 'What a party! Just look at the flags flying, and the lilac is in full bloom in a lot of the gardens. It's early this year.'

'Yes, it's a grand day,' Jean said and then looked up as Winnie was tapped on the shoulder by William Allen, who was carrying a large wooden tray.

'My father has sent these – a batch or two of sausage rolls. They're only small, a mouthful, but they're better than nowt.' William smiled as he put them on the table and everyone rushed to sit down in order not to miss out on the feast. It was the most food anyone had seen for years.

'Oh, William, that is kind. Thank him from me, won't you? Are you staying to join us?' Winnie saw Molly's cheeks go pink as she saw William talking to her.

'I will, if you will have me?' William looked around for Molly.

'Of course we will. Go and join Molly over there, she's standing with her sisters and Connie.' Winnie watched as William walked towards her youngest daughter and kissed her on the cheek. She had been right all along: William was right for Molly, just as Ned was right for Rose and Mike right for Annie. Connie would find somebody, she was bound to – after all, she was a bonny lass.

The main thing was that they had survived the war. Winnie looked at her family with pride. Somebody had been looking after them all despite the dark days, and what's more, they had all found love. Now it was time to party and look to the future.

If you loved *The Chocolate Box Girls Find Love*
then discover where it first began in
The Chocolate Box Girls,
the first book in the Rowntree's series.

I

York, 1935

'Molly Freeman, this may be your last day in school but I am still your teacher.' Mrs Stanley yelled loud enough for all the pupils at Haxby Road School to hear, let alone the day-dreaming Molly.

Molly quickly brought herself back to the world of the schoolroom as she heard Mrs Stanley shout at her to concentrate on the job at hand, just as a blackboard rubber whizzed past her ear and landed on the varnished wooden floorboards of her classroom, leaving a cloud of white chalk dust floating in the summer's air like a host of tiny fairies.

'Sorry, Mrs Stanley, I was just looking out of the window, it is such a nice day and I've only another hour before I leave school for good anyway,' Molly said quietly, hoping that her teacher of the last year would understand.

'There is another hour for you to learn and put some common sense into your head, Molly Freeman. You will need every ounce of knowledge when you join the real world because, believe me, you will look back and realise just how happy your days here at school were.' Mrs Stanley looked over the top of her glasses and glared at the girl she had tried to prepare for the rest of her life, just like she had prepared countless pupils before her. However, in Molly Freeman's case, she pitied her future bosses; she was by no means the brightest button in the box and if her siblings had not already been working for York's main employer, Rowntree's, she would have struggled to get herself an interview even.

'I'm sorry, I'll try to concentrate.' Molly put her head down and looked at her arithmetic book, but could not see the need for any of the elaborate fractions and equations that she was supposed to be able to work out. What would she need these for? She was going to make chocolate like the rest of the family and would have no need for such knowledge. Her mam had always said, 'Do your best and that's all you can do,' and that's what she had always done, regardless of what Mrs Stanley said to her. She glanced over at William Allen as she put her head down and tried to concentrate on her sums, but he stuck his tongue out at Mrs Stanley and then grinned cheekily at Molly as she sniggered.

'You might think that I cannot see you, Molly Freeman and William Allen, but believe me I do have eyes in the back of my head. Any more disrespect from either of you and it will be a caning that you will be receiving on your last day in school.' Mrs Stanley turned and stared at both of them as she finished writing on the blackboard.

'Sorry, Mrs Stanley,' William and Molly said together, not daring to look at one another.

'Just get on with it, and then you can leave with your heads held high,' Mrs Stanley said and sat down in her chair. This was one of many classes that she had seen through the last year of schooling. Most of them were following in their parents' footsteps in family businesses, some were leaving to work in the local shops and some of them, like Molly, were hopefully going to work at the sprawling chocolate and pastille firm that had spread over the outskirts of York. The unshowy, philanthropic Rowntree family were to be praised for bringing much-needed work to the ancient city; not only had they helped people afford their own homes and take pride in themselves, but with their strong Quaker values they had put York onto the map. They had also made her own life easier, especially when it came to the likes of Molly, who she knew would be nurtured by them once at work. Elizabeth Stanley put her head down and started to check the papers that she would have to take home with her that evening, but for now, at least, the classroom was quiet and that was just how she liked it.

Molly concentrated on her arithmetic, but her mind was focused on going home and leaving the school that she had attended since the age of five. It wouldn't matter what she put in her book, she thought, nobody would be bothered once she had walked out of the doors. So, instead of figuring out the set sums, she sketched pictures of her classmates in the margin, cartoon-like and funny, just like she thought of them. Finally, just before the bell rang for the end of the lesson and the end of the summer term, she sketched Mrs Stanley as a long, tall skinny woman with extended arms and huge glasses and whiskers – every pupil laughed about the whiskers on the end of her chin, which she obviously didn't know were there. She sat back and grinned and added a caption, 'Mary Hairy Stanley, the worst teacher ever!' Then she closed the book and watched as the minute hand finally reached half past three and a child in a lower year rang the home time bell.

That was that, then: school was done for good and at long last she could hope to make some money to help the family. She stood up and pushed her school chair under the oak desk which so many past pupils had scratched their names into when bored with their lessons, and placed her book under the desk lid. School was over and now it was out into the wide world, whether she was ready or not.

'Well, that's it and it's about bloody time – my father has been wanting me to help him in the shop for weeks now. I can learn far more working with him than I can in this place,' William Allen said as he walked out of the school with Molly, not giving it a backward glance.

Unlike Molly, who lingered at the doorway and wondered if Mrs Stanley's words were right about school days being the best. She had struggled at school sometimes, but she had always known that it was for her benefit that she attended. Unlike William who was often absent, only to be found working in his father's butcher's shop on Haxby Road – for he had a future working in the family business. She, however, did not have secure employment yet and even though her siblings already worked for Rowntree's, and she was to attend an interview on Monday, she was dreading entering the sprawling works of the chocolate factory. She had heard her two sisters gossiping and talking about their work life and coming home each evening smelling of the chocolates that they made and packaged, and it sounded a completely different world to the safety of the school. They both came home exhausted and full of moans most days, having to think for themselves but at the same time sharing the comradeship of working together and gossiping around the kitchen table.

'I'll see you then, Molly, I'll probably be serving you or your mam in the shop next time you see me,' William said, pushing his hands into the pockets of his tight-fitting trousers. He was a big lad, well fed at home, unlike most of the rest of her class, whose families struggled to feed them.

'Yes, I'll see you, William. You take care,' Molly said, watching as he walked down the road towards home as a pang of panic overcame her: she was about to enter into the world of work and she was scared.

'Is that you, our Mol? Well, that will be that then.' Winnie Freeman had just finished making a pie crust and was wiping flour from her hands onto her cross-over apron. She looked up towards the kitchen doorway as she heard the front door slam on the small terraced house that she and her three daughters lived in.

'Yes, Mam, I'm home. Is there anything to eat, I'm starving,' Molly said as she entered the kitchen and slumped into one of the rickety wooden chairs set around the kitchen table.

'You can make yourself a sugar sandwich, but only one, mind. I only got that loaf of bread this morning and already it's half gone because your two sisters insisted on taking their own dinners to work with them. You would all eat me out of house and home if I let you.' Winnie sighed as she ran a knife around the edge of the enamel pie tin, tidying up the crust before placing it into the oven of the Yorkshire Range. 'I don't know why either of them can't have their dinners in the dining block with the rest of the workers instead of taking what they can get from under my nose.' Winnie watched as Molly sliced a doorstep from the loaf and buttered it liberally before sprinkling a good spoonful of sugar on it and biting into it. 'Don't make another, you have meat and potato pie for your supper. Although there's not much meat in it . . . I'm sure that Thomas Allen's scales are wrong; I don't seem to have got much for my money.'

'William is starting work for him full-time now, he says,' Molly said, licking the sugar crystals away from the side of her mouth.

'He might as well have been this last month or two; he never seems to be at school, from what I hear. The truancy officer is always knocking on the door, according to Lizzie Mason, but they'll not get any sense from that family, no matter how many times he knocks on their door.'

'Well, he's no need of school, he's known all along that he is going to work for his father,' Molly said, looking at the loaf and hoping that her mother would allow her another slice.

'No, you don't, miss, you'll thank me in another year or two when the boys are showing interest in you. Nobody wants to be walking out with the plump one; a slim waist and a petite figure are what's wanted. Especially if you are to attract somebody with a bit of money in the bank,' Winnie said, smacking Molly's hand as she reached for the carving knife. 'And as for William working in his father's shop, he still needs to be able to weigh things correctly and to charge properly. Although perhaps that's what is wrong with his father, perhaps he makes it up as he goes along,' she continued, as she started to peel four potatoes to boil in a pan to accompany the pie.

Molly retracted her hand sharply and watched her mother as she filled a pan with cold water for the potatoes.

'Mam, I don't want to go to work for Rowntree's, I've been thinking I'd rather go and work in a shop or happen to learn to type and be in an office,' Molly burst out, looking worried as she saw her mother's face cloud over. Nobody ever questioned her mother's decisions, she was the matriarch of the family, and she had held her family together since the death of her husband from a particularly bad bout of influenza nearly ten years ago. Her word was set in stone.

'Don't be daft, our Molly! You, work in an office? You can barely spell; you even say to yourself that the words don't make any sense to you, no matter how much you look at them. You should be thankful that Rose got you the interview on Monday; she's put her neck on the line for you. It was either Rowntree's or Terry's on the other side of town and you wouldn't want to trail there every morning. Besides, you haven't even been taken on yet, but you should be all right, as long as you don't say you struggle with reading.' Winnie looked at her youngest – she knew she had problems, but at the same time she was not daft, she just couldn't make sense of letters like she should.

'I won't, Mam, but they may ask me to take a test, our Annie says they will, so they'll soon find out. That's what I'm worried about.' Molly sighed. Annie had tried to get into an office job, and she was a lot brighter than Molly, but she had frightened Molly with her talk of the test that she had been put through. Even though Molly knew that she would not be given a second look at an office job, she was worried about any tests that she would have to do for even the most menial of jobs.

'They are a good, understanding firm, they'll find you a place. They know your sisters are good workers and you've come from the same stable, so they'll take you on,' Winnie said as she added salt to the handful of potatoes and hoped that she would be proved right.

But Molly hoped that her mother was wrong for once; the smell of chocolate filled the house and the surrounding streets all the time and she had wanted to break the trend in the Freeman household.

'Hey up, the other eggs have chipped,' Winnie said, meaning her other two daughters had arrived home from their shift, as she heard them entering the house chattering excitedly. 'They'll just have to wait for their teas for a minute, I must be running late.'

Rose, the tallest and oldest of the sisters, entered the kitchen first, pulling off the white turban that protected her blonde hair that was immaculately held in place by hairgrips. Her make-up was like that of a movie star too. Rose loved to look just right and she had taken the eye of many a fella as she walked the two streets to and from the factory. She had also impressed the management and been told that she was going to be put in charge as a Grade A overlooker once the new product that they were developing was in place. This was good news for Rose as she was walking out with Larry Battersby and everyone knew that wedding bells would soon be ringing – every penny would be needed for them both to set up home together.

'Now then, our Mol, how was the last day at school then? Are you ready to join us Chocolate Girls come Monday?' Rose said cheerfully, leaning against the pot sink as her other sister Annie lit a longed-for cigarette and sat down across from Molly with her legs crossed and her turban still covering her head of tight dark curls.

'I don't know. Annie, do you think I'll be all right? I'm beginning to worry about working there,' Molly said, looking at her other sister who, unlike Rose, didn't care about how she looked, or what folk thought of her; she was the tomboy out of the trio.

'Of course you'll be all right; we'll be there to look after you. Just try not to be put into the Card Box Mill, the stink of glue really gets on your chest,' Annie said, taking a long drag on a Craven A cigarette, which made her cough.

'Not as much as those things do, our Annie, I wish you would stop smoking, it is most un-ladylike,' Rose complained and then turned to look at Molly kindly. 'You'll be fine, love, wherever they decide to put you. The Rowntree family might be strict but they are fair and care about their staff, they have to, or else they wouldn't be honouring their religion. Quakers are known for their caring ways.' Rose put her arms around her youngest sister briefly to reassure her.

'Listen to her! No wonder she is getting a promotion, creeping and sticking up for the management. They are like any other business; if you don't make them money then they will get rid of you. Just like they sacked Brenda Crosby the other week,' Annie said, shaking her head as she remembered that one of her friends had been given instant dismissal without listening to a word in her defence.

'That's because she had been helping herself to the chocolate bars and selling them on to her friends. What else were they supposed to do?' Rose said, glaring at Annie.

'She swore to me that she didn't, that that old bag Agnes Moore, her overlooker, just held a grudge against her. I believe her as well,' Annie said, flicking her butt end into the fireplace and hoping that her sister would not argue back.

'You need better friends, our Annie, everyone knew what she was doing and it was just a matter of time before she was caught. She's lucky that she didn't get the police knocking on her door.'

'Girls, please, no arguing, just for once let us have our supper in peace,' Winnie said and smiled at Molly. 'You will be just grand, love. Just do your best, keep yourself tidy and mind your own business, that is all that they will want. Now, Annie, put the kettle on and change that look on your face, it's as black as the chimney back and it will stay that way if the wind changes.'

'Well . . .' Annie moaned.

'Well, nothing, kettle filled, please, and stop your whinging. We will have a game of rummy after supper, that will pass the night,' Winnie said as she prodded the potatoes with a fork to check if they were ready.

'Count me out, Mam, I'm meeting Larry, we are going to the pictures. There's *Shall We Dance* on at the Odeon and I love Fred Astaire and Larry loves Ginger Rogers.'

'Fred Astaire, Ginger Rogers, listen to you, what's wrong with Laurel and Hardy, now they give you a good laugh,' Annie said as she filled the kettle and placed it on the range.

'Annie, you would argue with your own shadow if you could. Now all of you, let's have some peace and enjoy our supper together in a civilised manner.' Winnie sighed, her girls had all had the same upbringing but none of them were alike in their ways and it often led to many an argument. However, all her girls had spirit and knew right from wrong so she couldn't have done too badly, even though sometimes it had been hard bringing up three girls on her own for the best part of ten years. With Molly finally going out to work and Rose heading for marriage, life should finally become a little less hard.

2

Monday morning had come around all too soon for Molly's liking. She lay in bed listening to her two sisters who shared a bedroom getting ready for work and could hear her mother in the back yard filling the boiler in the outhouse for the Monday wash. She pulled her bedcovers over her head, blocking out the sunshine that was coming through the skylight window of her attic bedroom. She felt sick as she thought about what she had to do that day: it would be the start of her new life as a Rowntree's employee if things went well, and if they didn't she had no idea what to do. There wasn't much employment in York except the chocolate and confectionery factories of Rowntree's, Terry's and Craven's, and out of the three, Rowntree's was the nearest, being only a couple of streets away from where she lived. So it went without saying that she should hope to get taken on there.

'Molly, move your shanks, its seven fifteen and your interview is at nine,' her mother shouted from the bottom of the stairs, and then her bedroom window shook as her sisters slammed the front door in their hurry to get to work and to clock in on time, running down the street arguing with one another as ever.

'I'm coming,' Molly replied and felt a wave of nausea

overcome her yet again as she climbed out of bed and looked at herself in the wardrobe mirror. She analysed every inch of herself as she pulled her nightdress over her head, did up her skirt and buttoned the ditsy patterned blouse that her mother had ironed especially for her interview. She studied her reflection as she pulled her knickers and socks on and realised that she was still a schoolgirl in looks, unlike her sisters, who were grown women and beautiful. She had bobbed, short, mousy-coloured hair that she held back with a hair clip, and freckles over her nose. She was gangly and not yet fully grown where it mattered, unlike Rose, who had the best figure anyone could ask for. Nevertheless, it was what God had blessed her with. There was no way she could change it now, she thought, as she washed her face in the bowl that stood on the washing stand and hoped that she looked the part.

She ran down the stairs and outside to the back yard to spend a penny on the wooden-seated lavvy next to the outhouse. Steam was coming out of the outhouse where her mother was preparing the weekly wash and she could hear her putting the tin lid on the huge pot that she washed the whites in and smell the carbolic soap and Dolly Blue that her mother used religiously every washday. She sat on the lavvy seat and wished she could disappear and not have to face the day, but her mother was not going to let her, and sure enough here she was knocking on the lavvy door.

'Tea's on the table and there's some porridge in the pot. We can't have you fainting at your interview. I'm about to scrub the front doorstep, so move yourself,' Winnie called as Molly reached for a sheet of last week's cut-up newspaper to wipe herself clean.

Monday was her mother's busiest day; it was washday, step-scrubbing day and it was the day the rag 'n' bone man came. Shouting his usual call of 'Rag 'n' bone!' and exchanging a new supply of Dolly Blue bags, or donkey stones that her mother scrubbed the front doorstep with until it was almost white, for leftover bones. The bones went to be sold to the glue factory, and any outgrown clothes or rags traded were to be sold on as shoddy to the nearby mills. The rows of terraced houses might not be the wealthiest ones in York but there was pride within the women who lived there, and if a standard was not kept then it would be worse for the woman who let the row down. Windows were cleaned, steps scrubbed and the nets kept pristine just to prove that you were a good housewife.

Molly looked at the porridge that had been left for her in the pot. It had skinned over and congealed and she didn't fancy it, even though she was hungry and her stomach was churning, so she poured a cup of tea and looked at the clock. Another half hour and she would have to be out of the house and walking the few streets to the Rowntree's works. She looked at the washing-up that had been left behind and decided to do that to distract herself and help her mother. Pouring hot water from the kettle into the sink she washed everybody's breakfast pots and left the porridge pan to soak. Another ten minutes and she would go, she thought, it was always better to be early than late, so her mother had told her.

'Oh, Molly, look at your skirt, it's soaked from you washing up, and you can't go to an interview with that big wet patch on you,' Winnie exclaimed, looking across at her daughter as she made her way back through the kitchen. 'Go and get changed, you'll have to go in your other skirt, the one you had on yesterday, although it's not as good or as pretty, but at least it's not covered with washing-up water. But hurry up, it is nearly eight thirty and your interview is at nine.' Winnie sighed, noticing the panic on her daughter's face as she ran up the uncarpeted wooden stairs as fast as she could. Poor Molly, she was the kindest out of her three daughters, but nothing ever went right for her, no matter how she tried.

'That's better, not as posh as the one you were supposed to go in but at least it is clean,' Winnie said as Molly pelted back down the stairs and stood in front of her. 'Hands, nails, are they clean? They always look at your hands,' Winnie told her and held her hands out for Molly to place them in hers for inspection. 'Yes, you'll do, now remember your manners and no matter what they ask of you, you do it. You need this job and it's good of our Rose to get you this interview. Now, get gone and don't dally.' Winnie wondered whether to give her youngest a hug for good luck, but hugs were few and far between on her busiest day of the week and Molly would only cling to her and cry by the look on her face.

'Mam, I don't know if I want to go,' Molly said, looking

pitiful as her mother walked her up the oil-clothed hallway to the front door.

'You go, and you come back and tell me that you start working at Rowntree's tomorrow. We need the money; you need the money now that you've left school. You are not a little girl any more, Molly, now go.' Winnie virtually pushed her out of the front door and over her newly cleaned step and watched as she walked down the street, giving a final backward glance at her as she turned the corner. 'Please let them take her on, I know that she will be looked after at Rowntree's,' Winnie whispered under her breath, before going to find the bones that she had kept for the rag 'n' bone man who she could hear yelling at the end of Rose Street.

With each step, Molly felt more butterflies in her stomach and more fear as she neared the sprawling complex of the Rowntree's factory. It was a huge complex, covering most of the north side of York, with its own railway sidings and a small station called Rowntree's Halt and its own wharf on the Foss Lock. Along with the huge factories that filled the air with the smell of chocolate, there were tennis courts, a library, a swimming pool, dining rooms, a cinema and even garden allotments to keep their employees happy and fit. There was everything an employee wanted and needed as long as they were willing to work hard and be proud of the job they did.

Rose and Annie had told her everything about the place and she had often met them outside the blue fence and gates that surrounded the factory after work, but as she reached one of the main gates, she could easily have fled, the terror inside was so bad. She looked up at a large clock positioned just inside the fence, reminding the employees to hurry if they did not want their pay for the day docked. Ten minutes to go, she was in good time, she thought as she passed the red-stoned arts and crafts building that was the library, and the flower beds which contained a memorial to the founder Joseph Rowntree, as she made her way to the sprawling dining block where Rose had told her the interviews were taking place. She tried to compose herself and smiled as one of the workers passed by her with a smile and a reassuring word.

'They don't bite, you'll be fine, love,' said the woman with the same white turban on her head that her sisters wore.

Molly smiled back and breathed in. 'I will be all right; I will get this job and make my mam proud of me,' she whispered to herself as she pushed the heavy oak doors open.

'Here for the job, are you?' an efficient-looking young woman asked her, showing little interest beyond that.

Molly nodded.

'Wait over there then, somebody will be with you shortly,' the woman said, pointing to a wooden desk where another young girl was sitting.

Molly tried to say thank you but only a squeak came out and the secretary looked at her as if she was an inconvenience to her day.

'She's a flarchy one, as my mam would say, couldn't work all day in those heels,' the lass sat next to her said and grinned. 'You here for the job and all? I didn't want to come but my mam said I had to and besides there is a train that brings me straight here, which is not something you can knock when you live out at the end of the world in Selby.' The lass grinned again. 'Besides, I need some money, I don't want to live at home for ever, it's hell there at the moment. My mam lives with this fella and my baby brother Billy is always bawling. I need to get out before it drives me crackers.' She pulled a face behind the secretary's back as she turned and gave her a black look. 'I only live two roads down, it'll be easy for me to come back and forward to work,' Molly replied, trying not to look at the lass whom her mother would have called a bit common.

'Well, that's all right for you then, I don't suppose you've got a spare room at yours, I could leave home then and have no travelling.' She looked at Molly with a twinkle in her eye.

'No, I live with my mam and my sisters; I sleep in the attic bedroom as it is,' Molly said quietly.

'Bedroom to yourself, eh! Luxury, I share with two of my sisters when they are at home, I dread when they come home from tattie picking. Mucky back-breaking job, you wouldn't get me doing that,' the lass said. 'Anyway, what's your name, I never heard you give it when you came in?'

'It's Molly, Molly Freeman. Should I have given my name when I came in, she never asked for it?' Molly looked worried and thought of walking over to the secretary who was now sitting behind her formidable oak desk.

'Nah, there's only me and you waiting, they'll know who we are. I'm Connie, Connie Whitehead. Whitehead by name and whitehead by nature. My mam says she doesn't know why I'm so blonde when all the rest of us are quite dark. I think I must have been the milkman's.' Connie laughed and then went silent as the secretary put her finger to her lips.

'I'm just a little nervous, I babble too much when I'm nervous,' Connie whispered and then went silent as she could hear footsteps coming down the winding stairs towards them both. Looking up they saw a young girl not much older than themselves but dressed for office work, and with an air of superiority about her.

'Interview? Are you two here for the interview? If you are then follow me,' she said, turning back up the stairs expecting both girls to follow, walking with confidence and not even bothering to wait for their answers.

Connie shrugged her shoulders and stood up, followed by Molly, and they both followed the untalkative girl to the top of the stairs where she motioned for them to take a seat on a long leather bench next to glass cabinets filled with commemorative chocolate boxes for special occasions like Easter and Christmas. Both girls gazed at them and knew to be quiet.

Molly felt her stomach churn as a door along the corridor opened and a woman dressed in a smart plain suit stepped out and looked at them over the top of her spectacles. Her hair was tied back in a neat bun and her facial expression did not change as she looked at both the girls.

'I'm Mrs Spencer, now come this way with me, we need you to fill in a form or two and take some tests to see which part of Rowntree's you will fit into the best.'

Mrs Spencer led both girls to individual desks not too dissimilar from school ones and gave them a form to fill in giving details of themselves.

Molly looked at hers and felt a panic come over her; could she fill it in correctly and without making a mess and blotting the ink? She picked up the ink pen and started to complete her personal details. She was aware of how quickly Connie had completed hers and looked up at Mrs Spencer as she finally finished her form, a look of worry on her face.

'Now we want both of you girls to take some tests to see what part of Rowntree's you would excel in,' Mrs Spencer said, and noticed both girls look at one another with worry on their faces.

'It's nothing to be anxious about and won't take long, and then we will need you to visit the doctor and dentist.'

Molly felt sick; she had never been to a dentist, and what if she couldn't manage the tests? Her sisters were always making fun of her for sometimes not being as sharp as them. She said nothing as Connie was sent through one door and she through another across the way where two women were waiting to assess her skills.

'Hello, Molly, don't worry, it's not like an exam,' said the younger of the women, and it was then that Molly noticed a man in the corner taking notes, which made her even more worried.

'Here you will find different shapes to go into these

holes in the board, but not all the shapes will have a matching hole. It is up to you to decide what goes where and how fast you can do it. Do you understand?'

Molly nodded and felt her stomach churn as she waited until she was told to start. All she could think was, why hadn't her sisters told her there were so many tests, and then at least she'd have known what she was in for. Next it was about putting coloured cards into matching boxes, and then came a set of puzzles to solve. After this, somebody took her temperature and felt how cold her hands were. This, she was told, was to see if she would be able to use a chocolate piping bag, as if her hands were too warm the chocolate would go white once cooled. Molly's head was spinning when at last she was asked to pack shapes into a box. The shapes were made of plaster of Paris and the tester smiled as Molly's face fell when she realised that they weren't edible.

'Pack them in exactly the same way as you see in the completed box just there and make sure each one is contained in a frilly paper cup. When I say go, the gentleman over there will time you,' the instructor said, and watched as Molly stood at the table and waited, a determined expression on her face.

'GO.'

Molly felt her hands sweating and her brain tried to calculate where each chocolate should go. Could she do it quickly and correctly enough to get into the chocolate packing department along with her sister Annie? She had told her how fast they all worked in there, so she knew her hands had to be nimble and her mind sharp.

Suddenly she dropped one of the pieces and it landed on the floor, causing her to lose precious seconds. She did not dare to look at the inspector's face as she hurried to finish the task and at last heard the man click on the stop-watch as the last shape was given its allotted place. She sighed and stepped back; surely that was all the tests over.

'Thank you, Miss Freeman, if you could go and take a seat out in the corridor we will come to a decision and let you know.'

Molly's legs felt like jelly as she walked back into the corridor and sat down with relief on one of the leather seats. There was no sign of Connie, she was either still taking part in the tests or she had already left, Molly thought as she clenched the palms of her hands together and just hoped that she would not be going home with disappointing news. Had she put the coloured cards in the right boxes, and would dropping a pretend chocolate count against her? It was too late now, the instructors would have made their decision and there was nothing she could do. Her heart beat wildly as the door opened and the instructor stepped out and smiled.

'Providing that you pass your medical, I'm pleased to say that we would like to welcome you to employment with Rowntree's, to work in the Card Box Mill, making and printing the various chocolate boxes that we have for our products. Well done, Miss Freeman.'

Molly sighed. She had passed the test, and that was the bit that she had been most worried about, but she had really wanted to be a part of the chocolate icing team. 'Thank you,' she said, trying to smile. Perhaps she would eventually get there if she proved herself. She would try and ignore what her sister Annie had said about the Card Box Mill, she always did exaggerate slightly.

'Don't thank me yet, let's get you through the medical and then you can. Follow me,' the instructor said, and walked a little further down the hallway, stopping to open a door with an 'Occupational Health Department' sign on it.

Molly walked into the room. It was large and airy and smelt of carbolic soap, and she was greeted by a man in a white coat.

'Ah, you must be Miss Freeman, please take a seat and I will then examine your eyes and ask you to read from the board over there as far as you can, then my colleague Nurse Jenkins will ask you a few questions and will ask you to undress for a full-body examination.'

Molly sat down in the chair and looked up towards the light that the doctor shone into her eyes, and then once he had made notes she was asked to read a series of letters that got smaller line by line.

'Excellent! Now you just have the nurse to see and then on to the dentist.'

Dentist – she had seen a doctor before but never a dentist, and she didn't want to undress in front of somebody she didn't know. She was acutely aware that her knickers were patched and worn and was embarrassed by the state of them as she stood in front of the nurse and answered question after question about her health before being asked to strip off to her underwear.

'Hold out your hands. Now turn them over so that I

can see both sides.' Molly held her hands out and noticed them shaking as the nurse ran her hands down her spine and legs and then parted the hair on her head. 'Just looking for nits,' she said, 'and then we will measure your height and weight.'

Standing under the wooden measuring stick and then being weighed, Molly felt thankful that her ordeal was nearly over.

'You are a bit thin for your height but it's something and nothing. Tell your mam to give you a slightly bigger portion at dinnertime,' the nurse said, and smiled as she wrote her notes down.

'I don't think she'll do that, there's not that much to go around anyway,' Molly said, and wondered why her weight was so important.

'There will happen to be a bit more, once you have started working for us, every penny counts,' the nurse said, and then walked her to the door once Molly had pulled her clothes back on. 'Next door down, just knock and enter, the dentist is waiting for you.'

'Thank you,' Molly said, and felt a tingle of excitement and fear as she left the nurse and walked into the dentist's surgery.

'Ah, Miss Freeman, welcome, come and sit in my chair and let me examine your teeth.' The dentist, dressed in white, ushered her into his chair and pressed a pedal to make it recline as he hovered over her with a dental mirror in one hand and a steel thing that Molly had never seen before in the other. 'Now this should not hurt, but if it does, then let me know.'

The smell of the surgery and the all-new experience frightened her and if she could have got up and run away she would have done, but Molly knew that she needed the job too much to show how scared she was and to leave. So she closed her eyes tight, blocking out the dentist's face as he prodded and poked about in her mouth.

'Ow!' Molly yelped as the steel probe hit a nerve in a decaying back tooth and then wished that she had said nothing as the dentist pushed the pedal to bring the chair upright again.

'I'm afraid, Miss Freeman, that back tooth is very badly decayed and will have to come out immediately. We will do that right here and now and have you home in no time.'

Molly felt the blood drain from her face. 'I've never had a tooth out before, will it hurt?'

'No, you'll not feel a thing, I'll give you some anaesthetic and some gas, and it will put you to sleep for a short while, just until I extract the tooth. Now when did you last eat?'

'I didn't have any breakfast this morning, I was too nervous,' Molly said and felt like crying, but if a tooth was stopping her from making money for the family then she would have to put her faith in the dentist.

'Excellent. I'll get my nurse just to place you in a white gown, we don't want you walking home with blood on your clothes now, do we?'

Molly felt like crying as the nurse prepared her for the tooth extraction. She watched as clinical devices were put into an enamel tray next to her chair and finally, a stand with two bottles of gas and gauges was wheeled up, to which a mesh mask was attached. The nurse checked that the white gown was tight around her neck and then the dentist loomed over her.

'You won't feel a thing, my dear, you will only be asleep for a short while and when you wake up we will take you next door into the nurse's room where you can recover.'

Molly looked at the dentist and noticed every vein and blemish on his face as he placed the mask over her nose. It smelt of rubber and something stranger that she had never smelt before and she wanted to run as she heard a hissing sound and her mouth went dry and her head went dizzy and she felt slightly sick as the gas did its work and she slipped off into sleep.

Molly had no idea how long she had been asleep when she heard the nurse speaking. 'Molly, Miss Freeman, are you back with us?' She felt a gentle hand on her shoulder and then tasted the horrible irony taste of her blood in her mouth as she tried to sit up and leave the chair. 'Not so fast, you will be dizzy and disorientated for a while. Take your time,' the nurse said as the dentist came back over and asked her to open her mouth for a final check.

'Everything looks fine, now don't wiggle your tongue in the cavity, else it will start to bleed, don't eat anything until teatime, and remember to brush your teeth twice a day and then you won't have to return to me in a hurry, hopefully.' The dentist indicated that the nurse should help Molly back into her room.

'Oh, and no toffees or chocolate,' the dentist added as

Molly found her legs with the aid of the nurse and made her way to a chair to wait in until her full senses returned.

Molly felt groggy as she took the nurse's arm. Toffees or chocolate, she never had either except at Christmas, and was he supposed to say that to someone when after all he worked for a chocolate factory? She'd never go back and sit in his chair ever again if she could help it, she thought, as she spat a mouthful of blood into the clean white hanky that her mother had made her bring.

After a short while the nurse looked across at her and smiled. 'Feeling better now? Do you think you can stand and walk all right?'

Molly nodded, she had to get away from the smell that she now knew to be the anaesthetic. She never wanted to smell it again.

'Right then, I'll walk you back to the main office where you took your aptitude test. There are a few things that you will need before you start work in the morning.' The nurse opened the door for Molly and waited for her to slowly gain her ability to walk and for her head to clear from the fumes of the gas.

Work in the morning, she was to start work in the morning, she thought as she sat across from Mrs Spencer, who nodded to the nurse, taking Molly's new dental records for her files.

'Right, Miss Freeman, you start with us tomorrow morning at seven thirty sharp in the Card Box Mill. You will work a forty-four-hour week and will be paid eleven shillings a week. This is a copy of the Works Rules and Regulations: make sure you read them before you start in the morning.' Mrs Spencer hesitated and looked at Molly for acknowledgement.

'Yes, Mrs Spencer, that sounds fine,' Molly said and then realised that school hours had been a doddle compared to the hours she was about to work.

'You need two white turbans and two white aprons that you can buy from various stores in town. I advise that you wear stockings and flat shoes, no high heels, no sandals and no jewellery, other than a wedding ring. You need money for whatever you eat, dinner can be bought and eaten here in the dining block, the food is good and is cheap.' Mrs Spencer must have said the same thing over and over again and had got the patter off to a fine art as she looked across at Molly's pale face. 'Are you all right with all that, Molly, have you heard all that I've said?'

'Yes, thank you. I already know most of that; I have two sisters that already work here, one in the boxing room and one I don't know where at the moment, she isn't allowed to say.' Molly looked across at Mrs Spencer who looked quizzingly at her.

'Oh, you should have told the dentist that you had sisters that already work here; they would have been allowed to stay with you when you had your tooth removed. Would you like me to fetch one from their work to make sure that you are all right?' Mrs Spencer asked, leaning over and looking at Molly closely.

'No, I'm all right now; it was just when I woke up that I felt a little light-headed and queasy,' Molly replied, saying nothing more.

'Now, let me see. When you say you don't know where your sister is presently working in the factory, that must make you Rose Freeman's sister, she is helping us with an exciting new product that is about to be released. She is sworn to secrecy so it is good to hear that she has not discussed her present work. So, that also makes you Annie in the packing department's sister. We like to give employment to full families, so I'm glad to welcome you into our family, Molly,' Mrs Spencer smiled.

'Thank you, yes, I'm the youngest and my sisters have told me how good it is to work here.' Molly wasn't entirely telling the truth: Rose spoke nothing but well of the Quaker chocolate factory, but to Annie, it was just a job to be endured. She would soon be finding out which she agreed with.

'You'll know then to report to the timekeeper each morning and not to be late else you will lose your morning's pay and will be locked out?'

Molly nodded. Annie had been late a morning or two and had come back home to get a good dressing-down by her mother, and she wasn't going to let that happen.

'Right then, seven thirty sharp, report to the timekeeper's office and someone will meet you and take you over to the Card Box Mill, where you will be taught your job.'

Molly made her way home past the larger houses of Hambleton Terrace and the terraced houses of Rose Street, turning onto her home street of Belgrave. She could see her mother standing outside talking to their next-door neighbour, her brush in hand from sweeping the small front path.

'Been sweeping the muck up from the rag 'n' bone man's horse. I've just put it around the rose that's flowering at the back door; waste not want not,' Winnie said.

'Well, how have you done Molly? Do you start work in the morning?' Jenny Campbell asked, showing more interest in her neighbour's daughter than her own mother did.

'I start in the Card Box Mill in the morning,' Molly said. 'But Mam, they had to take one of my back teeth out, they said it was rotten.'

'Only one? You won't remember, but our Rose had three out when she started. We never warned you because we thought you wouldn't go.' Winnie ignored the fact that she had just got a job until she saw the upset on her youngest daughter's face.

'Well done, lass, it will be work in the morning with the other two. You'd better do what you want this afternoon as it will be the last time you will have some time to yourself for a while. I've already bought you new turbans and aprons, I knew you'd get a job there.'

'Thanks, Mam, I might have a walk into town while I've got the chance,' Molly said and thought that she would make the most of having some time away from school and home.

'There's threepence on the kitchen table, you get what you want, my lass, but perhaps not toffees, not until that gum heals over. My treat.'

'Thanks, Mam, that's a real treat.'

On a station platform, with nothing to read, and a four-hour train journey stretching ahead of him...

That's where the story began for Penguin founder Allen Lane. With only 'shabby reprints of shoddy novels' on offer, he resolved to make better books for readers everywhere.

By the time his train pulled into London, the idea was formed. He would bring the best writing, in stylish and affordable formats, to everyone. His books would be sold in bookstores, stationers and tobacconists, for no more than the price of a ten-pack of cigarettes.

And on every book would be a Penguin, a bird with a certain 'dignified flippancy', and a friendly invitation to anyone who wished to spend their time reading.

In 1935, the first ten Penguin paperbacks were published. Just a year later, three million Penguins had made their way onto our shelves.

Reading was changed forever.

—

A lot has changed since 1935, including Penguin, but in the most important ways we're still the same. We still believe that books and reading are for everyone. And we still believe that whether you're seeking an afternoon's escape, a vigorous debate or a soothing bedtime story, all possibilities open with a book.

Whoever you are, whatever you're looking for, you can find it with Penguin.